GILDED CURSES

THE SHADOW REALMS
BOOK 9

BRENDA K DAVIES

BRENDA K. DAVIES

CHAPTER ONE

As THEY CREPT through the town, Sahira's eyes flitted from one building to another. Every part of her tensed for an attack. Her muscles ached, her heart galloped, and she didn't realize she'd clenched her teeth until her jaw started hurting.

Her hand remained entwined with Orin's. His warmth helped bolster her confidence even as she prepared to face down whatever new monster came for them next.

And she didn't doubt something was coming soon. There were no other options. She'd spent enough time in the Cursed Realm and Barren Lands to know *nothing* was ever simple or easy.

She glanced at Orin's profile as his crow-black eyes searched the town. His hair was the same color as his eyes and had grown since she first met him. It now curled against the collar of his black, fae tunic. The tips of his pointed ears, a feature of all fae, dark and light alike, poked through his hair.

His slightly pointed chin jutted out as his anger crackled against her skin. She almost felt bad for whatever awaited them in this strange town... *almost.* Because, at this point, she'd gladly gut, behead, or choke to death anything or anyone who came at them.

She'd had *way* more than enough of all this bullshit.

Sitting on Orin's shoulder, Pip hefted her spear and held it at the ready as what remained of her burnt tail stood in the air. The brownie's face showed no fear as she glowered at the buildings.

Like all brownies, she wore some form of brown clothes. Instead of a dress like some of the other females in the town they'd left far behind wore, Pip dressed in pants and a baggy shirt.

She was about six inches tall when standing, which was average for her kind. She had the mouselike face of a brownie, with a pointy nose, big front teeth, a tail, and whiskers. But despite their cute appearance, the tiny immortals were ferocious when necessary.

Pip's friend Fath sat on Sahira's shoulder. Normally, he was far quieter than his more talkative companions, but Loth and Pip were both taciturn now. This wasn't the place where one sang songs as Pip loved to do or talked about the scenery as Loth did.

Loth perched on Elsa's shoulder. They'd started this journey with four of the small creatures but lost Gior on the geyser field. Sahira hoped they could get the three remaining brownies out of here and back home, where they belonged.

She hoped she could get *herself* out of this too.

Maybe, once free, they could find a way to help all those they'd left behind. But first, they had to survive this awful place and whatever it still had to throw at them.

When the shadowy figures inside the homes slid simultaneously into all the windows again, Sahira jumped a little as her fingers tightened on Orin's. She knew those things were there, she'd seen them before, but wasn't prepared to have them all emerge in that same creepy way again.

Whatever they were, they hadn't attacked yet, but she *hated* them more than the spiders. At least they'd known what to expect from the spiders; she had no idea what was happening here.

Orin's thumb stroked her hand as he sought to soothe her. She wasn't sure how long she'd been trapped in the Cursed Realm anymore; the days had all blurred into one, especially once they entered the Barren Lands. But two or three months ago, if anyone had told her she'd willingly hold hands with *Orin*, she'd have laughed in their face.

Now, not only was she *willingly* holding hands with the exasperating man, but she'd also had sex with him and sort of grown to like him... when he wasn't being a complete, obtuse asshole.

That wasn't very often.

And he'd only reinforced his complete idiocy when he confessed to her, in a bathroom, that *she* was the only woman he'd had sex with since she entered the Cursed Realm. All the other women he'd paraded in front of her, after they first had sex, were only another way to mess with her head, upset her, and keep her on her toes while playing his *games*.

During this confession, she realized how *fucked* in the head Orin was. Afterward, she vowed to never let him in again, but she couldn't release his hand despite still being livid with him. No matter how messed up he was—and it was *so much*—she needed him.

The weird thing was, she believed he needed her too.

They could sort through the convoluted mess of their relationship later—or not, if something ate them first—but for now, they had to concentrate on escaping this place and the horrors it harbored.

They had to be closer to finding answers and getting free. They just had to be.

And if they weren't, she might finally spiral out of control and lose her mind.

Maybe that's why they were here. The Cursed Realm was meant to break them and make them die a drawn-out, miserable death full of despair and loneliness.

There you go, always looking at the bright side.

But it was hard to be optimistic about anything when everything was an endless maze of nightmares.

CHAPTER TWO

As soundlessly as they materialized, the shadow figures vanished again.

"What *are* those things?" Elsa whispered.

No one answered her. Whatever they were, they didn't appear dangerous, as they hadn't rushed out to attack. But they were in those homes, working as one strange unit and keeping an eye on *them*.

A shiver ran down Sahira's back as they edged past the second set of buildings and moved deeper into the town. Around the bend, the road was still hardpacked dirt, and the buildings remained turned, so the front doors and windows all angled toward the street, allowing for more windows to look down on them.

In every building, *all* the curtains were open, and a dim glow filled the windows, but no lamps or light fixtures showed through them. Most buildings were wood and painted different shades of pale yellow, blue, red, and green—a few brick buildings mixed with the others, but not many.

In this section of town, side roads branched off from the

main one. They led through more houses angled so she could see the front doors and into their windows.

Although they didn't discuss it, no one ventured down any of those side roads. They stayed on the main street but would traverse those roads when they finished here... if they didn't discover anything.

It was only a matter of time before they entered one of the homes to discover what the shadowy figures were, but no one suggested doing so... yet.

When they slid into the windows again, Sahira couldn't stop herself from jumping *again*. She cursed herself for being an idiot. She'd faced far worse in the Barren Lands and Belda's town; she should be used to those awful things by now, but these still surprised her.

Probably because there was no rhyme or reason to their movements, they were there and gone. This time, she counted the seconds until they vanished again; fifteen passed.

From the time they disappeared, she counted again. She was up to ninety when the entities reemerged; they stuck around for thirty seconds before retreating.

"I didn't think it was possible to hate anything more than those spiders, but this place is starting to vie for first," Zeth growled.

Sahira didn't look at the demon as she counted while searching the windows. She was up to over two minutes when they reemerged. No, there wasn't any rhyme or reason to these... other than making life miserable.

When they vanished again, Orin's fingers squeezed hers before releasing her hand. "Fuck this. Stay here."

Before she knew what he intended, he stormed away. Sahira lurched forward to stop him, but he was already too far gone, and her hands encountered only air while he stalked toward one of the homes.

Elsa grasped her arm, holding her in place as Pip readied her spear while Orin grabbed the knob and twisted. When the door swung open with a creak, it didn't astonish Sahira to learn it wasn't locked.

"Orin, wait!" Sahira called.

But Orin pulled his sword from his sheath and charged inside.

CHAPTER THREE

DETERMINED to stop Orin from killing himself, Sahira started after him, but Zeth's large, claw-tipped hand encircled her forearm. She tipped her head back to take in the man who, at seven feet tall, was over a foot and a half taller than her five-foot-five frame.

"I'll go," Zeth said.

Sahira started to protest, but the demon squeezed her arm as his yellow eyes held hers. Handsome, with a broad nose, deep black skin, strong cheekbones, and a solid jaw, Zeth had two red horns protruding from each side of his skull; they curved toward the middle of his bald head. Two sharp, bony hooks jutted from the tops of his shoulders.

"The four of you should stay out here to let us know if something changes or comes our way. But let me do this. I owe him for saving me from the spiders."

When Sahira nodded and relaxed in his grasp, Zeth released her arm and stomped toward the house with his spear at the ready. Heart hammering and throat dry, Sahira stepped closer to Elsa as she waited for something to explode out of the house, someone to scream, or the whole thing to collapse.

She was certain something bad was coming as she searched the outside of the house, but it remained calm. Which only made it worse.

Elsa's fingers brushed her arm, and Sahira looked away long enough to return her friend's fleeting smile before focusing on the home again. She'd give anything to see past the pale yellow wall.

A second later, movement from within caused her to jump as the figures emerged in the windows again. They didn't look any different from before, but she couldn't help feeling like an air of menace now radiated from them.

This time, when those things vanished again, she was certain it was because they were finally coming for them.

~

WITH HIS SWORD at the ready, Orin stalked into the living room as he prepared for an attack. He was desperate to destroy something and looked forward to them coming at him.

It had already been an extremely shitty day, and these unknown creatures only made it worse. They would pay for that.

At this point, he'd kill anything that came at him. He didn't care if it was a six-inch-tall brownie or a rat; he'd stomp whatever it was into the ground and dance on their obliterated bodies.

However, nothing charged at him, and the living room was nothing more than white walls. No furniture cluttered the wooden floor. He'd assumed this was the living room but couldn't be sure.

He had no idea where the dim light reflecting off the pristine walls came from, as no lamps or fixtures hung from the ceiling. The same magic fueling the lights in the towns throughout the Cursed Realm probably did the same here, but somehow, that magic was more ominous in this place.

He hadn't believed it was possible, but he hated this realm

more with every passing minute. Scanning the room, his eyes settled on a shadow near the wall, except it wasn't a real shadow.

He was a dark fae; he knew shadows, controlled them, and used them to help him survive. This wasn't a real shadow. It was something more.

CHAPTER FOUR

WITH HIS SWORD at the ready, he prowled toward the humanoid shape and prepared to strike it down. The closer he got, the more he realized there was nothing to strike down.

Lowering his sword, he stopped before the shadow that was nothing more than a cutout. Lips curling into a sneer, he seized what should be its shoulder.

The thing was solid beneath his hand and an inch thick, but it wasn't living or breathing. The figure was cool beneath his palm, and it took a second to realize he was holding on to wood.

"What the hell?" he muttered.

Pip shifted uneasily, and when she spoke, like all brownies, her accent held a hint of the human's Scottish brogue. "What is going on?"

By now, he should have been used to all the games and endless bullshit of the Cursed Realm, but this was a literal in-your-face mindfuck unlike anything else they'd endured. This was tangible proof someone was screwing with them.

When he discovered who that someone was, he'd tear their guts out with his bare hands.

A step in the doorway alerted him to Zeth's presence. He

glanced at the demon before shifting his attention to the window and where Sahira and Elsa stood in the street.

Elsa turned in a circle, searching for a threat; Sahira's attention remained on the house. He didn't like leaving her alone but had to see what else was in this house.

When the wood vibrated beneath his hand, he ripped it from its motorized track and threw it across the room. It hit the wall with a bang.

A few seconds later, the rattling of the track drew his attention back to the floor and the small piece of wood. It slid forward to stop in the middle of the window.

"What is this?" Zeth asked.

Orin turned to find the demon inspecting the wooden cutout. He twisted it in his hands before lifting his head to meet Orin's eyes.

"What *is* this?" the demon demanded.

"One more game."

Normally, Orin loved games… when *he* was the one playing them. He thrilled in being the cat on the hunt but *despised* being the mouse.

What these things here didn't know—and he was sure there was something here—was that he was more than a mouse. They may think they had him trapped in a maze, roaming endlessly, but this mouse would claw his way out.

"Do you think all those shadowy figures are like this?" Zeth inquired. "Or are some of them a decoy, and there's really something deadly in this town?"

"There might be something deadly in this house."

Zeth's scowl deepened as he tossed the wooden figure down. When Orin threw it, he'd created a hole and left a streak of black on the pristine white wall.

"You should go back outside with them," Orin said. "I'll go through the rest of the house."

On his shoulder, Pip shifted but didn't protest his words as she kept her spear at the ready.

Zeth rose and wiped his hands on his pants. "They can take care of themselves and watch out for each other. We're not too far away from them, and someone has to have your back too."

"I have it," Pip said.

"Then I'll have both of your backs."

Orin glanced back out the window to Sahira. His chest constricted at leaving her out there, even with the witch and brownies.

Something, or someone, had set the town up like this, which meant it was probably a trap, but they had to explore this house. It would go faster with the demon's help.

Besides, he wasn't that far from her. If necessary, he could jump out the window to get to her. He'd have to keep to this side of the house, so he could see her while the demon explored the other side.

And the faster we get it done, the better.

With a resigned sigh, Orin turned and followed the demon from the room.

CHAPTER FIVE

SAHIRA KEPT her attention on the house as, once again, the figures slid into view. This time, the one in the bottom left-hand window didn't appear.

What is happening in there?

Her hands clenched on the shaft of her spear as sweat beaded her palms. She had no idea what was happening in this place, but the hair on her nape rose as the uneasy feeling in her stomach grew.

Then, the laughter came.

Sweet, childish laughter drifted from the street near her. The sound was so beautiful but out of place that she was certain it couldn't be real. When more of it came, her uneasiness turned into a knot of anxiety that threatened to empty the meager contents of her stomach.

When she searched the houses and street, all she saw was the dim glow radiating from the buildings. On her shoulder, Fath pointed his spear toward the laughter.

She exchanged a look with Elsa when her friend edged closer until their arms touched. The witch's chestnut brown eyes were wide as her mouth parted and her pretty face paled. The crown she'd created from a braid of her chocolate brown hair had come loose to dangle against her nape.

Elsa was probably still a little mad at her for not telling her about the trapdoors in the pubs they'd traveled through, but Sahira didn't doubt they'd fight whatever this was together....

But can we fight children even if they turn out to be monsters?

Sahira gulped at the possibility that, after everything they'd been through, they might soon face their worst encounter. Another giggle came from somewhere to her right.

Without a word, she and Elsa shifted so their backs were to each other. The thud of tiny feet followed the next round of laughter; their steps reverberated off the buildings they ran between.

"I don't like this," Loth growled.

As far as she was concerned, the brownie was stating the obvious, but she didn't say so. What was there to like about any of this?

More laughter came from her right; when she turned her head in that direction, she caught a flash of movement as something ducked away. Her heart beat so forcefully against her ribs she was sure it was about to explode.

A trill of laughter came from her left. The sound of tiny feet dashing across hardpacked dirt followed it, but when she looked, she didn't see anything.

"Shit," Loth said from Elsa's shoulder.

"Has anyone seen anything?" Elsa whispered.

"No," Sahira breathed.

Neither of the brownies responded, but Sahira guessed their answers as a giggle came from nearby. This time, she couldn't tell the direction.

Adjusting her grip on her spear, Sahira twisted it as she debated what to do if monstrous children descended on them.

~

THE SMALL BATHROOM consisted of a sink, toilet, and shower. No shower curtain hung alongside the tub, and when Orin twisted the knobs on the sink, no water emerged.

It was as if this whole town was nothing more than a prop for those things in the windows... or for something more... something worse.

The small window over the toilet only offered a view of the house behind this one. He couldn't see Sahira from here and didn't like it.

Leaving the room, he strode down the small hall, past the bedroom he'd already explored, and on toward the room facing the street. He'd intended not to stray so far from the windows facing the road, but the demon had gone into the attic, and they had to explore this floor.

He'd vowed only to take a few minutes away from the windows, and it had probably been less time than that. It was still too long.

Through the doorway, he saw Zeth, having returned from the attic, approaching the window. The demon's shoulders stiffened when he gazed down at the road.

As Orin stepped into the doorway, the demon spoke. "Something's not right."

Forgetting all about keeping his calm, Orin rushed over to the window. Sahira stood with her back to Elsa, her spear before her and Fath on her shoulder.

Nothing looked wrong, but they were all tensed as their eyes darted around the street. They hadn't been this on edge earlier.

With a sick feeling settling in his stomach, he sprinted out of the room. Pip's tiny hands entangled with his tunic as he took the stairs two and three at a time on the way down before leaping the last five feet down.

His bare foot didn't make a sound against the wooden floor

while his one remaining boot thudded against it. Orin had always prided himself on remaining calm in any situation.

Still, Sahira had completely rattled all his restraint and turned him into one of those more emotional immortals he'd always disdained. He should hate her effect on him; all he could think about was getting to her and ensuring she was safe.

Without caring about any noise it created, or what it might draw to them, he flung the front door open and descended the steps. As his gaze searched the night, he held his sword at the ready.

He'd gladly kill anything that came at them, but when Sahira's eyes flicked to his, the uneasiness in them slowed his steps. He didn't understand it when he saw no sign of a threat.

"What is it?" he demanded.

Before she could reply, girlish laughter came from his left. Orin's head turned in that direction as his brow furrowed.

It sounded like a child, but he didn't care what it was. In this realm, everything was the enemy until proven otherwise, and he'd carve it to pieces if it attacked them.

A flash of movement caught his attention; someone poked their head around the corner of a nearby house as Zeth's boots thudded against the steps. When more laughter sounded behind them, Zeth froze; his eyebrows drew together over the bridge of his broad nose.

The demon had a wife and son waiting for him at home... or so he hoped. Because of this, he might have a soft spot for children. And Sahira, with her too-big heart, would hesitate to kill them, and so would Elsa.

That might leave only him to fend off these things. While he didn't relish the idea of destroying a kid, he suspected these ankle biters were far deadlier than their childish laughter and playful hide-and-seek indicated.

With his eyes scanning the road, Orin closed the distance between him and Sahira. "Have you seen them?"

"No," she whispered. "We've only heard them."

"There's been a couple of flashes," Fath said.

As soon as the brownie spoke, something small dashed across the road. It moved so fast it was nearly a blur, but a banner of gold hair followed the small creature.

He gripped Sahira's arm as he held her gaze; she had to understand this was a battle for her life. One he wouldn't let her lose. "It might look and sound like a child, but that doesn't mean it is."

Sahira gulped before wiping away the sweat beading across her forehead. Unable to stop himself, his hand squeezed her arm as he sought to comfort her.

Comforting someone had always been a waste of time to him and a sign of weakness from those who needed their hands held. But Sahira was far from weak, and it didn't feel like such a waste of time with her.

What had the Cursed Realm and Barren Lands turned him into? He barely recognized himself anymore.

He'd always tried to protect his family, even while on opposite sides of the war, but he'd never been like this with them. If something happened to her….

No. Nothing is going to happen to her.

And he'd make sure of it, even if he had to fight these new monsters alone.

CHAPTER SIX

THE DETERMINED GLEAM in Orin's eyes told Sahira he wouldn't hesitate to kill whatever was out there. But what if they were murderous *children*?

When she glanced at his hand on her arm, she realized he was seeking to comfort her. He would destroy any enemy to keep *her* safe.

She didn't know how to feel about that, but her fingers found his, and she squeezed before another giggle drew her attention away from him. A small head popped around a home fifty feet away before pulling back from view.

It was the most she'd seen of the children, but it was enough to reveal a sweet, cherubic face framed by hair the color of midnight. Unlike the spiders and sand monsters they'd encountered in the Barren Lands, that face didn't look like it belonged to someone who wanted to rip her head off.

She might be projecting what she believed a child should be like onto these creatures. *And they might be trying to figure out how to best eat your kidneys.*

Sahira shuddered at the possibility as her mouth went dry.

"Come on." Orin squeezed her arm again before releasing it. "Let's keep moving."

Sahira dreaded going further into this town, but they didn't have many options, as turning back would only put them back in the Barren Lands. They knew what awaited them there... starvation and death.

No matter how much she hated it here, they could be heading toward freedom. Despite that possibility, their steps were much slower as they progressed further down the main road.

"What did you find in the house?" she asked when the shadowy figures slid into the windows again.

A muscle ticked in Orin's cheek. "Wooden cutouts. They were set up on a metal track to move them in and out of the windows."

Sahira's breath rushed out as she tried to process his words. "Are you kidding me?"

"No."

With a renewed feeling of unease, she glanced around the town. The laughter had stopped, but eyes bored into her back, and the occasional pitter-patter of little feet thudded against the dirt road.

Those feet weren't nearly as sweet as when Lexi was a little girl and Sahira could hear her running down the hall before she arrived to fling open Sahira's door. She'd jump into bed with her and bounce up and down while excitedly squealing, "Get up! Get up! Get up! It's morning and time to play!"

Sahira would always groan on those mornings, pull the blankets over her head, and grumble at the exuberant, beautiful child to go back to sleep. Secretly, she'd loved the tiny hands that peeled away the blanket before a little finger poked Sahira's nose.

"You can't hide from me!" Lexi would call before throwing her arms around Sahira and snuggling in.

They'd cuddle for a few minutes before boredom set in, and

Lexi would tear out of the room. She'd always yell over her shoulder, "Come on, sleepyhead, it's time to play!"

Unable to resist her niece, Sahira would smile as she climbed out of bed.

She wasn't smiling now.

"Do you think these kids set up the cutouts in the windows?" Elsa asked.

"I think someone with a sick sense of humor and a death wish did it," Orin snarled.

This time, the shiver making its way down Sahira's spine had nothing to do with the children and everything to do with the fact he was so irate; she worried he wasn't thinking clearly. They were all sick of whatever was happening here but had to be careful.

As they neared the end of the street, the houses tapered off as a large rock wall came into view. At first, Sahira assumed the wall was the end of it all, that they'd come this far only to encounter a dead end, a trap, or *nothing*.

But when they made a right turn around the last house, a small archway came into view. At first, hope leapt in her chest at the possibility of something more… maybe *freedom*.

She was so excited about getting out of there that it took nearly a minute to process what surrounded the archway… skulls. Lots and *lots* of skulls.

CHAPTER SEVEN

"THAT CAN'T BE GOOD," Loth muttered.

They halted ten feet away from the tunnel with a dim glow at the end of it. All those skulls looked down from empty sockets that seemed to scream at them to turn back; who was she to argue with a head?

"It's the literal light at the end of the tunnel," Fath said.

"Are we going in there?" Elsa inquired.

"Do you have any other suggestions?" Orin asked.

When Elsa glanced over her shoulder, Sahira could tell she was contemplating returning, but there was nothing there for them. In *all* the other towns they traveled through, the trapdoor in the pub had emerged into the lot behind the building.

In Belda's town, that pub and the surrounding land were enough to keep them alive. In the pub that led them here, there was nothing to help them survive.

They were nearly out of food and barely had enough water for another day. While they were immortal and wouldn't die from it, their starvation, dehydration, and resulting weakness would make them easy prey in a realm full of nightmare creatures.

They couldn't go back but couldn't stay here, and she'd prefer not to go forward. A tunnel of skulls leading straight into a bright light was exactly the sort of thing *everyone* should avoid walking into.

"Do you think we're already dead?" she whispered.

She had no idea where the idea came from, but once it took root, it festered like a splinter that went too deep.

"What do you mean?" Pip asked.

"Maybe we didn't survive the geyser field, spiders, or sand monsters. Maybe we didn't survive opening a portal into this realm. Maybe, the second we stepped into the Cursed Realm, we died, and everything that's followed has been some sick, twisted Purgatory. Maybe, if we walk into that light, we'll finally be free."

No one said anything for a minute, and then, as she knew he would, Orin gave a derisive snort. "I'm still very much alive. This realm hasn't taken me out, and it isn't going to. Besides, we'd recall if one of us died."

"Would we remember if we died when we stepped out of the portal that brought us here and into Purgatory?" Elsa asked.

"Can you fuck in Purgatory?" Orin demanded.

Elsa blinked at him. "I… I have no idea."

"Well, I don't think you can, and I've done a lot of fucking here."

He shot a pointed look at Sahira, who scowled at him.

"I don't think you can get drunk either, bleed, or be battered against rocks by giant spiders," he continued. "We're not in Purgatory. We're in Hell, and it's time to get out."

"If this is Purgatory," Zeth said, "then we're already dead, and it doesn't matter. Walking into the light is our way out. So, we can stay and keep running in circles or move forward and see what awaits us."

"Let's go then," Sahira said.

She wasn't ready for an end to any existence, Purgatory or

not, but if that light was an escape from this realm, she'd take it. Without looking back, she entered the tunnel with the others.

Once inside, she realized the jagged rocks protruding from the walls weren't all stone. They were more skulls.

She couldn't tell if someone had carved them into the walls or if they were actual heads, and she refused to examine them more closely. When a giggle sounded behind them, she glanced back and spotted a handful of children at the entrance.

When the kids crept into the tunnel behind them, Orin muttered a curse under his breath. Adrenaline coursed through Sahira's body, but the children didn't attack as they remained at least fifty feet behind them.

The endless skulls with their mouths slightly parted in what could be laughter or a scream surrounded them. They were most likely shrieking, but maniacal laughter sounded in her head as those empty eye sockets followed them through the tunnel.

As they progressed, the glow at the end grew brighter. Nothing good could come from the end of a tunnel of skulls, but none of them stopped.

When they emerged from the shadows and into the brilliant radiance of the world beyond, unable to see, Sahira shaded her eyes against the glow.

Sahira blinked as she tried to take in their new surroundings, but her blindness made her feel incredibly vulnerable as she kept her spear thrust out in preparation for an attack she'd never see coming. While waiting for her eyes to adjust, cheers and applause erupted from some unseen entity.

CHAPTER EIGHT

ORIN BLINKED RAPIDLY as he tried to bring all the noise into focus. He didn't know what to make of the cheers and applause; they didn't lead him to believe they were in imminent danger, but not being able to see was pissing him off.

Whatever this was, it was done to further mess with their heads and disorient them. Pip gripped the collar of his shirt as a small hiss issued from her.

Where is Sahira? Closing his eyes, he opened them again in the hopes that would help, but he still struggled to see her.

She'd been standing beside him in the tunnel, but he couldn't tell if she was still there. He shifted his sword into one hand and reached for her.

Instead of finding her, someone grasped his hand and started shaking it profusely. He immediately knew it wasn't her, as coldness instead of warmth seeped into him.

Instinctively, Orin spun with his sword and swung it at whoever dared to touch him. They released him, and his blade clashed against rock, as it missed its target and bounced off the ground. Baring his teeth, Orin snarled at whatever was out there.

"Whoa!" someone yelled in an accent that sounded French as

they grasped his wrist and jerked it down when he tried to lift his sword. "There will be none of that here. We're a peaceful race."

"There's nothing peaceful about anything in this realm," Orin grated through his teeth.

"Relax, dark fae. We mean you no harm. You're safe here."

The deep voice was meant to reassure, but Orin wasn't soothed by it as he yanked his wrist free and swung out with his sword again. He felt the soft give of flesh before the blade encountered more rocks.

A scuffle from his right side alerted him something was happening there too. The cheers and applause died off as the fight continued.

"Sahira!" he shouted.

"We've got the demon," someone called out with the same accented tones. "I'm not sure for how long."

"Sahira!"

"I'm okay," Sahira gasped.

Hands grasped at Orin, pulling on his clothes and yanking at his weapon as something heavy pounced on his back. He staggered forward and nearly went down but remained on his feet.

He could draw the shadows around him and vanish, but he had to find Sahira and the others first. Besides, though he was still having trouble seeing, he sensed a lot of bodies around him and might not be able to slip away. He had to see before he could make that decision.

"Give them a chance to adjust!" the voice that greeted them called out. "They can't see, and they've been through so much. Once they can see, they'll know they're safe."

The dozens of hands suddenly released Orin, and feet scuffled away. The weight on his back eased, and he started to spin with his sword to lash out at whatever was there but stopped himself.

He didn't know where Sahira was and couldn't take the

chance of cutting her by accident. Orin edged toward where he last heard her voice but didn't connect with her.

Finally, his vision cleared enough that the tunnel came into view. Standing at the end of the tunnel, the children stood with their lower lips trembling. They stared at the seven of them as if *they* were the monsters and not whatever had been screwing with them for far too long.

Specks of blood spotted the rocks in front of him, and a man, dressed all in white, slumped near the tunnel entrance. Two women bent over him, examining the vivid red stain spreading across his back.

Turning, he discovered Sahira standing beside him. Her eyes must have adjusted too, as she looked completely shell-shocked while her attention remained riveted on whatever lay on the other side of him.

Next to her, Elsa was just as captivated. More immortals in white were moving away from Zeth as the demon rose from where he knelt on the ground.

Satisfied that, for now, nothing behind him could become a threat, Orin turned to take in his surroundings. Since Sahira arrived in this Cursed Realm, he'd been changing into a more emotional, less callous dark fae like he preferred to be.

However, even that once distant, dark fae version of himself couldn't have hidden his amazement over the land sprawling before him. He'd never seen anything like it.

CHAPTER NINE

A COBBLESTONE ROAD rose and fell in waves before them as it wound up and down hills surrounded by countless wildflowers. Those flowers were every possible color of the rainbow, and then some as they glistened beneath the sun's rays.

Specks of gold covered those flowers and sparkled in the light. The white cobblestone also glistened with the same golden glitter.

And the flowers and cobblestones weren't the only things with flecks of gold in them. The few thousand immortals surrounding them also glistened with specks of gold.

The sun shining on their faces emphasized their different colored complexions, from the palest of ivory to the deepest of blacks. Their skin tone varied greatly, but they all looked like someone had ground up a gold bar and tossed handfuls of the remains over them.

Those remains had settled to cling to their hair and skin. When he glanced back at the children, golden flecks also speckled them.

Most of those immortals wore all white clothing, but a few dozen or more wore more elaborate clothes of vibrant colors.

Many were also dressed in dark blue as they stood toward the front of the crowd, and despite the proclamation of being a peaceful race, the men and women in blue all held weapons.

What are these things?

He didn't know, but now that things were calmer, the man standing before him started clapping again. The others all followed suit as they beamed, cheered, and some stomped their feet.

As they continued to clap, Orin shifted his grip on his sword. They didn't act like a threat, and he didn't know if they were the ones who'd kept them in the Cursed Realm, but they were here, and he was eager to kill something.

Unfortunately, there were far too many for him to take on. Peaceful or not, their sheer numbers would overwhelm him after a while.

He was irate enough to hack through a few dozen of them before then, but he couldn't take them all on, not even with Zeth and the witches at his side. Plus, he didn't know if these things were the enemy or the freedom they'd been seeking.

If they were the key to freedom, killing some of them probably wouldn't ingratiate him into getting their help to escape this place.

"Welcome! Welcome!" a tall, platinum-haired blond man said as he strode toward them and stopped a few feet away. His voice held that semblance of a French accent. "Rest easy, my friends. My name is Desmond, and you are safe with us. We're so happy to have you here. *Finally*, someone has succeeded!"

The man's eyes were so pale a shade of blue, they were nearly as white as his hair, but specks of gold sparkled within them. He was handsome in a way that would make some women fall at his feet, but the gleam in his eyes would make others feel like they were facing a ravenous dragon.

Those wiser women would back away from his too-dazzling

smile with his too-white teeth and the too-perfect alignment of those teeth. It was the smile of a wolf in sheep's clothing.

Orin didn't want Sahira anywhere near this man. He'd far prefer to face the spiders again and the sticky web they'd weaved than the trap he was certain they'd just walked into.

"Succeeded in what?" Sahira demanded.

Desmond's smile never faltered as his head turned toward her. "In escaping the Cursed Realm, as you call it."

"Of winning the game," a beautiful, dark-haired woman with brown skin added.

Orin somehow managed to keep his face impassive while inwardly his blood boiled. *A game! This was only a game!*

"And we know how much you love games, Orin," Desmond said.

Orin showed no response to this man knowing his name or anything about him. Instead, he forced a smile. It grew bigger and more natural when he imagined pummeling Desmond's too-perfect countenance into a bloody mess not even his mother would recognize.

"I *do* enjoy a good game," he agreed.

Orin's blithe reply didn't fool Desmond, but that stupid smile never left his face. Oh yes, once he got the chance, Desmond was as good as dead.

"Have you been watching us?" Elsa demanded.

Desmond clapped his hands before turning away from them. The immortals gathered around him fell back to give him space to walk.

"It's time to return home. Come along now, so you can reap the benefits of your glory," Desmond called over his shoulder.

Orin glanced at Sahira as all the rest of the immortals encircled them, making it clear they had no choice but to follow.

CHAPTER TEN

It wasn't until they came over the top of one of the many hills that a gold-flecked city appeared below them. A castle sat in the city's center, surrounded by walls stretching for hundreds of acres around small, cabin-style homes.

There were hundreds of those cabins inside the walls but not a single one outside them. Sahira didn't understand the intense security; from what she'd seen so far, it was a peaceful land, and the big bonus was that nothing had tried to eat them yet.

If these immortals were concerned about giant monsters or sand creatures eating them, they didn't show it. And if scarogs were about to descend, they wouldn't have walked the few miles it had taken to greet her and the others.

Even with the weapons carried by those in blue, some of the monsters they'd faced throughout this would have eaten a good chunk of them. And if these immortals were worried about enemies, why did they build their castle in a valley?

Every other realm, and every immortal and mortal with a brain, built their fortress high so they could see an attack approaching. Not these immortals.

The hair on her nape refused to settle as the wooden gates of the bailey swung open. She almost planted her feet and refused to continue, but there were so many of them, and they'd never let her remain outside. She didn't have to fight them to know that.

She couldn't embarrass herself by being carried inside. These immortals proclaimed peace, but like a rabid dog, it was only a matter of time before they turned. Until then, she would have to play along and learn as much as she could about them in the hopes of ferreting out some weaknesses.

Like the immortals, the entire town, walls, and especially the castle glittered with gold. She knew what these immortals were, or at least what others had called them.

Everyone had heard tales of the Golden Ones, also known as the dagadon, throughout the years. They were a fairy tale told to children before bed, make believe... but they weren't.

She had no idea how they'd gotten here or why they'd hidden themselves away so well that they'd become nothing more than a tale. They had to be dealing with the dagadon, and she had no idea what to make of this place or them.

Though, she did *not* trust Desmond. He creeped her out.

As she walked through the gates, she tried to recall everything she'd heard about the Golden Ones, but despite the many stories of the lost golden immortals, none of the tales revealed much about them.

As soon as the gates closed, the children laughed as they ran forward to race excitedly around them. Their eager chatter filled the air while also sending a shiver down Sahira's spine.

Many continued to smile, but others strolled with looks that said they'd prefer to be elsewhere. *She'd* prefer to be anywhere else too, but she doubted she'd get any better options anytime soon.

While they walked, she'd surreptitiously tried to open a portal and failed. They were as trapped in this golden city, with that smiling freak Desmond, as they were in Belda's town.

She yearned to run screaming from this place; they'd only

swarm her and bring her back if she tried. Tensed beside her, she knew Orin was waiting for an opportunity to carve through them all, but they were far outnumbered, and he was far from a fool.

Infuriating, stubborn, and completely afraid of commitment? Yes.

An idiot with a death wish? Not so much.

Zeth's fingers kept opening and closing, one at a time. When they did, his claws clicked together as his yellow eyes glistened with murderous intent.

But like Orin, he wasn't an idiot and wanted to return to his family. Trying to attack these immortals wouldn't help with that. It might not only result in his death but *all* of theirs.

For the most part, other than the occasional murmur from a Golden One and the click of Zeth's claws, everyone was hushed. Sahira was pretty sure these golden immortals were the enemy but couldn't be certain.

So far, they'd done nothing wrong and might be as trapped as the seven of them were. She could only watch, wait, and hope they weren't killed.

When no one emerged from the doors of the small cabins, and she didn't see any pedestrians on the streets, Sahira realized the entire town had come out to greet them when they emerged from the tunnel. It had truly been an event for these immortals. And she didn't understand any of it.

This place was beautiful, and its residents literally shone in the sun, but she'd rather be running from another scarog beetle than standing in this golden city. There was a reason why no one lived beyond these walls; whether that was because of an outside enemy, or an inside one, she didn't know.

She suspected it was the latter.

CHAPTER ELEVEN

THEY MADE their way up a hill and toward the golden castle. As far as castles went, it was on the smaller side but still towered above the humble cabins surrounding them.

Its highest tower was five stories, but most of the main building was only two floors. A single section at the front consisted of three floors.

One of the Golden Ones, who wore a white, floor-length dress, hurried forward to get in front of Desmond. She grasped the golden handle, shaped like a lion's head, and pulled the door open.

It glided soundlessly outward as Desmond swept into the castle with many followers close on his heels. Most of the Golden Ones hung back to stand outside the doorway as they watched Sahira and the others enter the castle.

Sahira glanced back and realized the numbers with them had been cut to almost a third of the original ones. Still, at least four hundred or so of the immortals remained, and while they were all strong, they couldn't take down those numbers.

She wasn't sure Orin and Zeth felt the same way, especially

as the speed of Zeth's clicking increased, but neither did anything foolish.

"Welcome to Epoch," Desmond said as he gave a sweeping gesture with his left arm to encompass the grand entryway.

An open layout spread out before them. A floating staircase twisted its way up to three floors above their head. A golden dome with a glass ceiling allowed the sun's rays to spill onto the white marble floor beneath her.

The stairs on the second floor branched off to a balcony leading into the separate wings of the castle. From there, the steps wound up to the third floor, where they once again split off into separate wings.

Flickering lights, that resembled flames, sat inside golden sconces. They weren't real flames, but the magic illuminating this place made them dance like they were.

Nothing adorned the pristine white walls, and despite the sheer number of immortals crammed into the space, not so much as a smudge marred them. The place was beautiful and sterile, and she hated it.

When she finished taking in this section of the castle, Sahira shifted her attention to Desmond. "Is Epoch the castle's name or the realm's?"

Desmond turned his patently false smile on her. Beside her, Orin stiffened as a rumble made its way up his chest. When Sahira rested her hand on his arm, his vibrating muscles revealed how close he was to snapping.

He relaxed a little beneath her touch. She realized she'd made a mistake when Desmond's white-blue eyes fell to her hand and his smile widened.

She shouldn't have touched him; it had given away too much to this freak. But these things might have already known there was... *something* between them and had planned to use it against them.

They'd known Orin's name, after all. Between his coloring,

ears, and ciphers, the fact he was a dark fae was obvious, so they would have known that, but *how* had they known his name?

These immortals had been watching them somehow or listening. By doing so, they would have learned there was something between her and Orin.

It was complicated, slightly twisted, and possibly broken, but powerful too.

"You are in the realm of Epoch," Desmond said. "We call our castle Epoch too. Maybe it's not the most original name, but it's who we are."

His self-deprecation was blatant and more than a little annoying, but Sahira chose to ignore it. "Epoch has to do with time."

The gold specks in Desmond's eyes twinkled. "So it does, my friend. So it does."

Sahira refrained from telling him they'd *never* be friends. She was sure he already knew.

"And what are *we* doing here?" Zeth growled.

Throughout all the time she'd known him, Zeth had always been different than the demons she encountered in the past. Those demons had the volatile tempers their species were renowned for, but Zeth had always kept his restraint.

It was because he had a wife and son to get home to and was determined to do so. But being here, surrounded and outnumbered by the things that most likely trapped them in the Cursed Realm, was getting to him.

She could only hope he didn't do something foolish enough to get them all killed after they'd made it this far. However, the Golden Ones were probably already plotting their demise.

Without the ability to open a portal, she didn't know what good making it this far had done them. They'd traversed nightmare after nightmare only to end up encased in this gilded city.

Her hand tightened on Orin's arm, not because she was seeking to give comfort, but because she needed it.

"You're here to celebrate!" Desmond declared. "You're here to enjoy the labors of all your hard work."

"And then what?" Elsa asked.

Desmond made a downward motion with his hands. "Slow down, witch. First, we must get you ready for the celebration tonight. There will be time for questions later."

Sahira glanced at her friends as Fath shifted on her shoulder. She had no idea what getting them ready or the celebration would entail, but it wouldn't surprise her if they trussed her up like a pig and shoved an apple in her mouth.

CHAPTER TWELVE

THE CASTLE WALLS consisted of white brick, most likely harvested from somewhere in this realm. In the dim light of the lanterns hanging on the wall, the golden flecks within those bricks twinkled and danced as Desmond led them down a hallway on the first floor.

The clicking of Zeth's claws ceased as he took in their surroundings. Now, silence hung heavily in the air.

The only thing that interrupted it was the occasional scuff of a boot or a low murmur from those dressed in the vibrantly colored clothing. None of those in white spoke, and the guards rarely did.

At least a dozen or so of the more elaborately dressed immortals looked more irritated by their presence than elated, like Desmond and some of the others. She was beginning to realize those dressed all in white were the servants, the guards were in blue, and the ones who wore the vivid, elaborate clothes were the ones who ruled here.

Beside her, Orin walked so rigidly that she was certain he'd break if someone tried pushing on him. She resisted her impulse to touch him again; even if they already knew there was something between them, they might not know the details.

They can't know the details. You *don't know the details.*

It was true, but she still couldn't give them any more possible ammo against them, and she hoped he didn't do anything stupid. When she first arrived in the Cursed Realm, she wouldn't have doubted he could keep his emotions under control, but not anymore.

He'd always been so cold and calculating. Somewhere along the way, that changed.

There was something far more volatile about him lately. The Cursed Realm had changed him, and in doing so, she worried it might be a stoic *dark fae* instead of a *demon* who set off a catastrophic chain of events.

When Orin remained under control, Sahira shifted her attention back to her surroundings. Everything inside the castle was pristine. Not one speck of dust marred any surface, and no motes danced in the air.

Being inside the castle made her acutely aware of how filthy she was with her torn, dirty, and blood-stained clothes. She yearned to run a finger over the walls, leaving dirt streaks everywhere, but she kept her hands fisted at her sides.

Glancing back, she expected to see someone following them with a broom and mop, but none of their still too-large entourage carried cleaning supplies. They did have swords, spears, knives, and daggers, though.

When she briefly met Elsa's eyes, fear shimmered in their chestnut-colored depths, but her friend didn't look like she was about to spiral out of control. But maybe she was as on edge and as good at hiding it as Sahira.

While they followed the crowd through the halls, Sahira became acutely aware that none of these gilded freaks touched the walls. Despite the size of the group and their immaculate cleanliness, none of them so much as brushed a shoulder against the walls.

It only made her itch to smear her handprints over them more. Her nails dug into her palms to keep herself from doing so.

Questions surged to the tip of her tongue, but she held them back. Desmond had made it clear he wasn't answering questions yet. She wondered if he'd answer them or if this was another twisted game.

They entered another hall where, on their left, sunlight streamed through the windows lining it. The right side consisted of closed doors.

At the end of the hall was another closed door. Someone scurried forward to open it before Desmond arrived. They stepped back to let Desmond descend a set of stairs.

Sahira's pace slowed as they approached the doorway, but they were the next ones to follow him through. They could be walking toward their deaths, and she didn't know how to stop it.

Desmond took a right and then another as he led them deeper into the castle. The sound of running water reached her a second before a woman in white opened another door for Desmond.

White marble surrounded him as he turned to face them and threw up his arms to indicate the cavernous room. From her angle in the door, she couldn't see much beyond him, but water trickled from somewhere, and white surrounded him.

"Here we are!" He lowered his arms and made a sweeping gesture around the room. "Please, come in. You are our guests, after all."

"Is that what we are?" Orin inquired. "Or are we your prisoners?"

Desmond laughed. "You're very much our guests, my distrustful, dark fae friend. Please, come in, relax, and enjoy."

Sahira exchanged another glance with Elsa as Orin and Zeth glared at Desmond. *Please don't do anything,* Sahira inwardly pleaded.

They had no chance of getting away now, the two of them had to see that, but if they bided their time and learned more about these immortals, an opportunity might present itself... or so she hoped. But that opportunity wasn't now.

When she started forward, Orin seized her arm to halt her. His hand was like a vice as it encircled her flesh.

"Don't worry, Orin. We won't harm anyone, especially not your little witch," Desmond assured him.

Her and Orin's eyes narrowed on the man as they assessed him. He saw too much of their relationship, and Orin was giving them away, but she didn't think there was anything left to give away... Desmond already knew so much about them.

"Come now," a soft, melodious voice interjected with the same accent they all possessed. "Stop teasing them, Desmond, and let them get the pampering they deserve."

A beautiful woman with gold-speckled skin, black hair to her waist, and warm brown eyes glided through the crowd to join them. She smiled at all of them before descending the stairs to join Desmond in the room beyond.

"Ah, my lovely wife has finally arrived," Desmond said as the woman lifted a cheek to him; he kissed it. "Where have you been, dear?"

"Someone had to ensure our esteemed guests will reside in the luxury they deserve while here," the woman replied. "I stayed to oversee the readying of their rooms."

She turned back to them and smiled, but her smile wasn't anywhere near as chilling as Desmond's. Sahira wasn't fooled by it and didn't think anybody else was either. If she was with this man, then she was a ruthless shark.

"I'm Sheree," the woman greeted in her pretty voice. "My husband and I rule this land and would like to welcome you to Epoch." She quirked an eyebrow when none of them said anything, but her smile didn't falter. "You must all be exhausted, and you could certainly use a good bath... as well as a massage or ten."

A titter ran through the crowd, but Sahira didn't find her words amusing.

"As our much-awaited guests, please call us Sheree and Desmond." Sheree waved her hand at them as she stepped closer to Desmond. "Come with us."

With no other choice, Sahira squeezed Orin's hand on her arm and started to move forward again. Before she could take a step, he pulled her back a little and stepped in front of her.

This place hadn't dimmed his commanding or protective tendencies any. With a sigh, Sahira followed him down the steps and into the room.

As she took in more of it, she realized this wasn't the place where someone would drown them.... It was where they were to be *cleaned*.

CHAPTER THIRTEEN

DESMOND and his wife closed the doors behind them when they left the pool atrium. In drifting waves, steam rose from the water in the center of the room. The pool was at least forty feet long and twenty feet wide, but it didn't take up half the space.

Gold specks glittered on the white brick floors and walls. Designs and patterns etched the bricks.

Orin spotted a sun, moon, and stars but didn't see an hour-glass anywhere. It was a good thing because, if he did, he'd take his sword and hack away at the bricks until nothing but shards remained.

Lush, green plants lined the windows that made up the entire left side wall. The right side had a dozen or more doors lining it.

From overhead, the sun's rays spilled through the glass to dance off the crystalline water. The water was probably the only thing in this place that didn't sparkle with gold.

The humidity inside the room caused his clothes to cleave to his skin as sweat trickled down his nape and beaded across his forehead. Dozens of guards descended the stairs and moved throughout the room until they stood shoulder-to-shoulder with each other. Some of them carried bows with arrows notched and at the ready.

"So much for a peaceful race," Zeth muttered.

"You have nothing to fear from them if you don't try to attack us," one of the women said. "They are only here for our protection. We realize you're scared, have been through a lot, and are ready to fight, but we cannot have that."

"How do you know what we've been through?" Pip inquired.

The woman's eyes darted away as more guards entered the room and approached them.

"Hand over your weapons," the biggest guard at the front commanded.

Orin glowered at the man. He could envelop himself in shadows and might be able to cloak the others too.

He could grab Sahira and have her disappear with him, but she'd fight him and wouldn't leave the others. Maybe she'd realize they could always return for them and not fight him.

The likelihood of that happening was about the same as him putting on a tutu and doing a pirouette, but he wasn't leaving here without her. When some of the arrows swung in Sahira's direction, Orin sucked in a breath as he stepped in front of her.

"Back off," he warned the guard through his clenched teeth.

The man's eyes bore into Orin as the guard held out his hand for Orin's sword. "Give me your weapons."

"If you hurt her, it will be your last regret."

"I never regret anything. Now, give me your weapons."

Before Orin could decide what to do, Sahira handed over her spear and the dagger strapped to her side. On her shoulder, Fath also handed over his spear and small sword.

"Sahira," Orin hissed.

She shot him a look and then glanced pointedly around the room at the hundred or so guards in there with them. Their eyes met and held again as they stared at each other, and she nodded toward the guard.

Elsa and Loth followed suit, but Zeth hesitated before finally relinquishing his spear, sword, and a knife strapped to his ankle. The guard continued to hold his hand out to Orin, and Pip didn't move.

The brownie would follow his lead, and if anyone was susceptible to death, it was the tiny creature with a fierce heart. And he shouldn't give a shit about that, but he did.

He really disliked that he'd developed a conscience. He scowled at Sahira, the cause of his sudden inability to leave someone to their fate, before breaking eye contact to look at the guard again.

"When will we get our weapons back?" Orin asked.

"When our Lord decides you're trustworthy," the man replied.

So never.

A muscle at the corner of Orin's eye twitched at the man's reference to a Lord. They'd just destroyed one Lord who believed he was equivalent to a God, and now, they were in the presence of another one in this realm.

Desmond and Sheree weren't a king or queen like Cole and Lexi, but a *Lord* who believed himself above all others. That *never* ended well.

"And Desmond is your Lord?" he inquired.

"Yes, as is Sheree."

Orin's eyebrows rose at this. *So, she isn't a Lady, but a Lord too. That's a lot of ego in one realm.*

And he should know, as he had a lot of ego, but at least he wasn't a pretentious douchebag like these cheap, gold knockoffs.

Orin gritted his teeth and handed over his sword. He was certain he'd never see it again. "Aren't you lucky to have *two* Lords."

"You're lucky, too," the pretty woman beside him said. "You've survived where so many others have failed. And tonight, you'll celebrate; we all will."

"Celebrate what?" Zeth asked.

"Life."

"I had a life before I came here. I want to return to it."

The woman bowed her head. "Of course. And I'm sure our Lords will see that you do."

Orin was just as sure Desmond and Sheree had no intention of seeing any such thing. Still, he handed over his other weapons while Pip relinquished hers.

In the end, there was no choice. They were too outnumbered in this place and still couldn't open portals. They were stuck here until they learned more and found a weakness; once he did, he'd see them all dead.

CHAPTER FOURTEEN

WHEN THEY FINISHED DISARMING THEMSELVES, the guards fell back to give them space as women, dressed all in white, swarmed them.

"Please relax."

Orin glared daggers at the woman trying to peel his cloak from him. For weeks, he'd been looking forward to shedding his filthy clothes, a hot bath, relaxing with a drink while stuffing himself, and hopefully getting his dick sucked.

This place was *not* where he imagined any of those things happening, and he wasn't about to be agreeable with their captors. And that's exactly what these things were. They acted like gracious hosts, but they were wardens.

Loth climbed off Sahira's shoulder, and she shrugged out of her cloak. The woman working with her handed it to another woman whose nose wrinkled as she held it away with two fingers. Another woman held out a large can, and she tossed it in.

When the woman grasped her shirt and started lifting it over her head, Orin sneered at the guards watching them. Modesty wasn't something most immortals bothered with, but he didn't want any of these assholes looking at her.

The woman working to strip him muttered something before rising to plant her hands on her hips. "If you're going to stand there like a tree, then I can't get this done."

"Don't you think we should have some privacy?" he demanded.

Though Sahira and the others all gawked at him, he was more stunned than them that those words had left *his* mouth. He didn't care who saw him naked, he never had, but the idea of these golden freaks looking at Sahira made his eyelid twitch.

The woman working on Sahira glanced between the two of them. Something passed across her face before she pointed at one of the massive room's doors.

"Those rooms are all private baths," she said.

"Then let us use them," he grated through his teeth.

She didn't look at all fazed by the anger in his voice as she turned away from them.

"What are you doing?" Sahira hissed at him.

He chose to ignore her, mostly because he didn't have a clue. Them seeing her naked shouldn't bother him, but it did—a *lot*.

With a clap of her hands, the woman drew the attention of every gold-tinged dickhead. "It's time to retreat to the bathing chambers."

Sahira's attention lingered on him as one of the women grasped her elbow and steered her toward a door. Another woman led Loth to the door to the left of Sahira's.

Determined not to let her out of sight, Orin ignored the woman still grasping his shirt as he stalked across the room after Sahira. He only made it a few steps before six guards moved forward to block his way.

"The bathing chambers are only for *one*. Two are not allowed," the overgrown waste of sperm in the front stated.

Orin snorted. "I seriously doubt that rule has been obeyed over the years."

A smile tugged at the man's mouth before he suppressed it. Orin had no doubt the guard had broken the rule a few times.

"You can get down now," another woman said to Pip.

Orin almost snatched the brownie back when she started sliding down his arm. He didn't like separating from them. Maybe it would have been better if they all stayed out here....

There was no maybe about it; he should have kept his mouth shut and sucked up his rage over Sahira being naked in front of them.

With any other woman, such a thing never would have bothered him. He wouldn't have thought twice about it and barely remembered most of his past partners, but as much as he hated admitting it, she was special to him.

Pip kept her chin high as she followed another woman to a door further down the hall. Orin started after Sahira again, but the woman rested her hand on his elbow as the guards continued to block his way.

"This way," the woman said.

Orin pulled his elbow away from her, but she didn't seem to notice as she led the way over to the door beside Sahira's room and opened it for him.

When she went to enter with him, he stopped her. "I thought only one immortal was allowed in at a time."

The sultry smile she gave him caused disgust to curdle in his stomach. "I've been given special permission to go in with you."

"By who?"

"Sheree told us we were to make you *especially* happy."

She must have given them this order when she'd remained behind to oversee the readying of their rooms.

"Then you shouldn't come in." He plucked the scrub brush from her hand. "I can bathe myself."

"But I can scrub your back for you."

Orin refused to be a pawn in this forsaken realm. The only games he played were the ones of his own making. Besides, while he always enjoyed a good fuck, the only legs he wanted between were Sahira's. And he wasn't about to have sex with a woman because someone commanded her to offer it.

"I can wash my own back," he assured her.

Before she could protest, he entered the room and closed the door behind him. The red robe hanging on the back of the door swung from the motion.

A large, claw-foot tub sat in the center of the white brick room. A bar of green soap and a glass container of white liquid, most likely shampoo, sat on a small stand on this side of the tub.

On the other side was a plate of fruits, cheeses, and loaves of bread on a table, as well as a bottle of chilled, open wine and a glass. His stomach rumbled, and his mouth watered at the food.

He was starving, and it had been a while since he'd consumed fruit or had a decent meal. Instead of eating, he walked over to the brick wall and pounded his hand against it.

"Sahira! Can you hear me?"

"Yes." Her muffled voice came through the wall.

"Are you okay?"

"Yes. Are you?"

He'd be a lot more okay if he could see her, but that wasn't an option right now. Resting his hand and forehead against the wall, he breathed deeply as he reassured himself she was okay and that, for now, these things weren't trying to kill them. He was sure that would change at some point, but they seemed to have some time before then.

"I'll see you soon," she called.

"Scream if you need me."

"I will."

Orin glanced at the door as he debated wrapping himself in shadows and rushing out of there. They'd know he left the room but wouldn't see him.

They would come at him, though, and if he somehow managed to evade all the guards, the others would all remain behind. If he fled, they'd probably take them and lock them away, which meant he'd have a tougher time getting to Sahira, and there was no way he was leaving her behind.

Plus, he had no idea what abilities these immortals possessed. They might have something he was unprepared for, which could mess up his escape.

With nothing else to do, he started stripping. For now, he would play their game, which they would soon regret, as he *never* lost.

CHAPTER FIFTEEN

LEXI WAS OBSESSED with *The Wizard of Oz* as a little girl. First, she watched the movie and then watched it a thousand more times before devouring all the books in the series.

Sahira had never cared for their portrayal of witches in the movie, and she certainly wasn't afraid of water. How bad had that evil witch smelled if she couldn't wash her armpits?

But, because Lexi would sit there, beaming at the TV while dancing and singing along to the songs, she'd eaten a lot of popcorn while trying not to lose her mind. Plenty of times, she'd questioned if the Scarecrow could pull some straw out of his ears or stuff some in there to keep himself from hearing. She'd envied him if he could.

Being in Epoch reminded her of the scene where Dorothy and her friends first arrived in Oz. The people had taken them in where they primped and shone them to perfection, all while singing along. Sahira couldn't get that song out of her head as the dagadon spent hours doing the same to her and her friends.

After the tub, she donned the yellow robe on the back of her door and emerged from the bathing room. She discovered Orin already waiting for her, his black eyes glittering with malice and his body rigid while he leaned casually against the wall beside her door.

If anyone believed he was calm, they weren't paying attention, as he vibrated tension. He did relax a little when he saw her and the foot he'd propped against the wall lowered to the ground.

Elsa and Zeth emerged from their rooms, and after a few more minutes, the brownies had all gathered around too. Once they were all together again, the dagadon escorted them out of the atrium and toward a large spa area, where they separated them again and gave massages.

Afterward, the dagadon sat them in barber's chairs where they cut their hair before shaving, waxing, and grooming them like dogs going to a show. They separated them again and stuffed them into clothes.

Okay, maybe not stuffed, but the dress they put on Sahira was a little snug as they buttoned it into place. The same women stayed with Sahira throughout it all, as did all the guards, but she'd given up asking questions.

She'd tried peppering them with questions during her massage and got only silence in response. Then, she decided to try slipping them in on occasion while they were grooming her, but it was like talking to a wall.

Frustration and disappointment over still being trapped here tumbled inside her, but she kept it hidden. She refused to let the dagadon see how badly she struggled to hold it together.

Once they finally finished getting the buttons into place, two women turned her to face the mirror. Despite her complete antipathy over all this, Sahira's eyes widened on her reflection.

She hadn't paid attention to the dress as the women put it on her, but now, it was all she could see. The dress consisted of sheer, black material layered on top of more sheer fabric that allowed her skin to still show through.

The final layer had bright yellow flowers that reminded her of sunflowers, but these had a red center. The flowers strategically covered her breasts and groin area as they spilled across the bodice and toward the ground. What they didn't cover revealed her skin beneath.

They'd taken her hair and pulled it half up and away from her face while the back spilled around her shoulders. They'd then curled all of it.

"It's beautiful," she admitted.

Sahira swayed her hips back and forth. As she did so, the skirt flared a little before falling straight to the floor again.

"Is it acceptable?" one of the women asked in a flat monotone.

Sahira felt like irritating the emotionless woman, so she smiled. "It will do… for now."

Anger flashed through the woman's eyes, but she concealed it again before turning away and opening the door to a large dressing room. Sahira stepped outside to discover Elsa already waiting for her.

They'd also chosen a black dress for Elsa with a sweetheart neckline and red bodice that hugged her curves. The black skirt fell open to reveal her thighs as her friend strode toward her. They'd pulled her chocolate-colored hair into a knot on her head; coiled strands fell free to frame her pretty face.

"You look beautiful," Elsa said.

"So do you."

Did they dress us up to kill us? She suspected she wasn't the only one with this question on the tip of her tongue.

Another door opened, and Loth emerged. The brownie pulled at the lapels of his brown suit as he glared at the guards filling the dressing area. When he spotted them, he kept hold of his lapels as he strode toward them.

"Ladies," he greeted.

"You look very handsome, Loth," Sahira told him.

His smile didn't reach his eyes. Pip and Fath emerged next.

Fath also wore a brown suit, but Pip was in a maroon dress. She didn't look happy about it as she tugged at the collar.

"I don't think I've ever seen Pip in a dress," Loth remarked.

As was his way, Fath remained quiet but watchful while their friend approached. A few more minutes passed before Orin emerged from his room.

Sahira suspected Orin had taken so long because he was being difficult as he liked to do. This was confirmed by the scowls on the women's faces when they followed him from the dressing room.

Sahira barely managed to keep her mouth from dropping, but she couldn't stop the extra thump of her heart as it hit her rib cage. She'd always known he was handsome, no one could deny it, but he also looked debonair in the perfectly tailored tuxedo that hugged all his lean muscles.

His freshly cut hair revealed the tips of his ears. His shaved skin shone, and the smile that could incense her, as easily as it melted her heart, was in place while he glided forward.

When his eyes fell on her, he faltered a step, but his smile never did as his head tilted to the side in that endearing way he had of examining her. As his eyes raked over her, hunger blazed in their black depths.

That look caused her to sway instinctively toward him as her nipples puckered and an ache spread between her legs. It had been too long since she'd been with him.

She was still angry at him for all the games he'd played with her, but she *yearned* to touch him again and to have those arms around her. He could make her feel safe while she forgot all about this place for a bit.

Shaking her head to clear it of her wayward musings, she reminded herself that others surrounded them. Otherwise, she might have rushed over, grasped his hand, and dragged him into one of the dressing rooms.

Her gaze flicked toward a closed door as she briefly contemplated it before returning to reality. No way would that be allowed; they had a role to play here.

She wasn't entirely sure what that role was, but they were actors on a stage to entertain these immortals. When their entertainment value wore off, it would become an issue.

Orin stopped before her and extended his arm. "You look beautiful, my enchantress."

A shiver ran down her spine, and though it shouldn't, being called *my* by him made her happy. She was still irate with him for everything he'd done, but things were different between them; she didn't know how or what it meant, but they were.

However, he was still a dark fae and *Orin*; he could easily stomp all over her heart and not realize it. She had to be so incredibly careful with him.

He's also completely fucked in the head.

His admission in the bathroom had proven it. He had no idea how to handle the possibility he might have feelings for her, so Orin continued playing games by pretending he'd slept with other women.

The hurt he'd inflicted when he drank beer from that nymph's chest, the night after they first had sex, was still a dagger to her heart. She reminded herself that even if he did care for her, his inability to process those feelings might send him running into the arms of another, instead of embracing *her*.

Still, she couldn't stop herself from hooking her arm through his. "You look very handsome tonight, Orin."

"I look handsome every night."

She chuckled as her fingers gripped his arm. Leave it to Orin to remain overly confident and a bit of an ass while they were pretty prisoners in a gilded cage.

Another door opened, and Zeth finally emerged. He looked handsome in his tux, but the sleeves didn't go to his wrists, and his pants stopped at midcalf. The jacket looked like it would split apart if he yawned.

Two women fussed around him as they pulled at the holes they'd cut around the hooks in his shoulders. "We'll have something tailored for you tonight. It will be ready tomorrow," one of them said.

The woman meant this to be reassuring and helpful, but the looks on the other's faces mirrored the defeat Sahira felt. These women expected them to still be here tomorrow.

CHAPTER SIXTEEN

THE BANQUET HALL was an enormous room with ten chandeliers hanging from the ceiling. The glass chandeliers reflected the light, making it seem like it was raining on them.

The table sat fifty immortals with space for more. All the immortals at the table wore colorful, elaborate clothing that stood vividly out against the white room.

A hundred or so Golden Ones stood along the walls, all dressed in white. They waited with pitchers, glasses, napkins, platters, and other assorted things.

Wherever they didn't stand, a guard filled the space. They numbered more than double that of the dagadon dressed in white, and more of them filled the doorways.

White brick made up the walls, and glass doors ran down the entire right side of the room. Those doors opened onto a garden full of wildflowers of every imaginable color.

Warm, twilight air drifted through the doors, carrying those flowers' sweet, floral scent. Mixed in with the flowers were trees that reminded him of the weeping willows on earth, except these blazed red and orange and looked on fire in the setting sun.

The servants escorted them to the empty chairs near the head of the table. Sahira sat to his left while Elsa settled in across from her and Zeth across from him.

They brought three small chairs forward and placed them on the table for the brownies. Pip sat beside him, while Loth and Fath settled in near Zeth.

To his right was a table full of golden immortals he didn't know. To his left, Desmond sat at the head of the table; beside him was his wife.

"Good evening!" Desmond declared. "You must all feel so much better after a day of pampering."

"They certainly smell better," the man next to Sheree quipped.

He had dark brown skin and wore his black hair in braids to his shoulders. His navy blue eyes were cold and calculating as he studied them. Orin smiled as he lifted his goblet of wine and tipped it toward the man he'd gladly see gutted.

Desmond's smile faltered as he shook his head. "Ignore Renaldo. He's just grumpy because he lost."

Renaldo gulped some of his wine.

Lost what? Orin didn't voice the question. He'd learned these immortals had no intention of telling them anything until they were ready.

When they first sat, the chatter at the table died off, but now it returned as the freaks resumed eating and talking. After going hungry for so long, Orin should be happy to see so much food overflowing his plate; he wasn't.

There was so much food here, yet little to spare in the Cursed Realm. But, for all he knew, they might not be in the Cursed Realm anymore.

That tunnel might have been a portal leading them somewhere else. Even if he couldn't open a portal, that didn't mean these things hadn't created one from the Cursed Realm into Epoch. Or they could still be in the Cursed Realm, and these golden dicks called it Epoch.

At least they hadn't entered or left Purgatory as Sahira had hypothesized. It had been an interesting premise but not one he believed; and while it could still be a very small possibility, he was sure it wasn't.

He didn't speak as he watched all of them, with the knife they'd given him to eat with fisted in his hand. Clearly, the ones at the table ran this place and had all the power. Those standing against the wall were here to serve or to make sure Orin and the others didn't try to kill the assholes who ruled here.

He trusted these assholes as much as a dragon not to hunt and eat. He suspected that beneath their golden exteriors, something far more sinister lurked within these bastards.

Desmond laughed loudly and almost shouted as he repeatedly lifted his goblet to cheers with the rest of the table. Wine sloshed out of his cup, but whenever a drop hit the golden surface of the table, someone rushed over to clean it.

Desmond didn't wipe his face as he pursed his lips and twisted his head back and forth while someone else did it for him. Orin had grown up in the lap of luxury, but if he'd asked someone else to wipe his face, his father would have done it for him, and that would *not* have been a pleasant experience.

The man had loved all his children. He'd taught them how to lead and to expect others to do as they commanded, but he'd also instilled respect in them.

Orin expected obedience from everyone except for his family. However, he didn't treat those who worked for his family as little more than animals.

Their helots weren't there to cater to his every whim or wipe *his mouth.* He wasn't a child, but Desmond, and all the others at the table, acted like very spoiled ones.

He hadn't thought much of Desmond before this dinner and thought less of him as the night progressed. As the floor-to-ceiling clock in the corner of the room and the one hanging over the doorway they hadn't entered through ticked away the hours, more wine flowed, and Desmond's face grew increasingly redder from the alcohol.

After so long without consistently knowing the time, Orin's gaze kept returning to those clocks. He still had no idea how much time he'd spent in the Cursed Realm and Barren Lands, but the tick of the second hand fascinated him.

Desmond grew more boisterous to the point where Orin's teeth grated together in irritation. Many of the *Lord's* friends became drunker and more celebratory, while others sat sullenly as they picked at their food and rolled their eyes over the antics of their companions.

A drunk Desmond was annoying, but maybe he'd be their way out of here. If this buffoon was a complete mess, it might allow them to break free.

CHAPTER SEVENTEEN

Across the table, Orin's eyes locked on Renaldo's. While his leader was increasingly animated, Renaldo remained stoic and sipped his wine.

Desmond might screw up enough for them to escape this place, but Renaldo wouldn't. And when Orin shifted his attention from Renaldo to Sheree, he found her studying him from clear brown eyes unaffected by drink.

Neither of those assholes would allow Desmond's debauchery to become a liability. *They'll fuck up somehow*; he was sure of it.

Beside him, Sahira remained watchful while barely touching the food on her plate. Leaning over, he whispered in her ear, "You should eat. This might be the only time they feed us."

When her head turned toward him, a thrill shot through him, and his cock stirred when their lips nearly touched. Her honey scent teased his nostrils as her beauty struck something deep inside him.

"What if they put something in it?" she whispered.

The possibility had occurred to him too, but starving themselves over a chance of something happening wouldn't help them. Besides... "Does it matter? They already have us."

Sahira gulped before spearing a vegetable and chewing it. Satisfied she was getting at least a little nutrition, Orin sat back to watch the night progress.

After a couple more hours, when the servants cleared the meal away to replace it with dessert, Desmond leaned forward to speak with them. "I bet you're ready to learn why you're here."

Orin remained outwardly nonplussed while inwardly, he screamed for answers. He waited a few seconds before turning his head to look at the grinning, red-faced man.

"I think it's time," his wife said in the sweet voice Orin loathed.

"In the Cursed Realm, or here in Epoch?" Elsa inquired.

"Both!" Desmond threw up his hands, and a cheer ran through the happier people at the table while the sullen ones continued looking miserable.

Does their unhappiness mean we might have some allies here?

Orin kept his focus on Desmond because that's clearly what the man wanted, but from the corner of his eye, he watched Renaldo. Disapproval etched the man's face as he stabbed a piece of pie, shoved it in his mouth, and chomped on it while watching Desmond from narrowed eyes.

When they were first seated, Orin was certain they'd never get help from anyone in this room, but maybe he was wrong. There was a divide here, and he was very good at finding weaknesses and digging in until he tore them apart.

"First!" Desmond declared with a clap of his hands. "Let's bring forth the prizes."

The prizes?

Orin's brow furrowed, and the sound of the floor-to-ceiling doors opening at the other end of the room caught his attention.

His head turned toward Sahira and the rest of the gold-tinted freaks at the table as the white wooden doors swung open.

At least fifty gold-flecked immortals, all dressed in white, were led into the room. They walked with their heads bowed and their hands clasped before them. The men had their hair shorn close to their skulls, while the women wore their hair in braids wrapped around the top of their heads.

"What is this?" Sahira whispered.

The woman beside her replied, "The prizes."

"For what?"

"The winners."

What does that mean? Orin pondered as the immortals stopped walking and turned to face the table. They'd aligned themselves perfectly from the head of the table to the end of it.

"Very healthy," Desmond declared. "You've all made wonderful choices. None of us should be disappointed by our winnings." He gestured to the line. "Go on, Sheree, my love. Pick the ones you would like."

A sinking feeling settled in Orin's stomach as the woman rose and walked toward the line of immortals.

CHAPTER EIGHTEEN

"WHAT IS GOING ON?" Elsa inquired.

"The losers must settle the bet we made," Desmond said. "We always place a wager on who will survive, who will retreat, and who will die when someone *finally* leaves Ground Zero."

"Ground Zero?" Zeth parroted.

"I believe you call it Belda's town. And she has taken quite a shine to ruling it; she's very democratic for a lycan."

"How the fuck do *you* know that?" Orin demanded.

Beside him, Sahira stiffened as Desmond's smile faltered. Irritation flickered through his pale blue eyes.

"We don't talk like that at the dinner table," Desmond said.

Orin was about to tell him that he didn't give a shit about how they talked at the table but bit the words back. These things surrounded them, somehow knew far too much about them for his liking, and Sahira sat at his side.

He had a meat knife for a weapon, but that was all. The shadows dancing around him beckoned him to slip into them, but even if he could somehow get past the guards, he couldn't leave Sahira or Pip. The little rodent had grown on him.

If he were completely honest with himself, he wouldn't leave *any* of them behind. They'd gotten this far together and *would* leave together.

He inwardly cursed himself for being a moron and allowing himself to be weakened by all of them. He was very aware that a couple of months ago, he would have left their asses, but times had changed.

Unfortunately, he didn't think those changes were for the better, as they might get him killed.

Orin sipped his wine as Sheree walked down the line of immortals, carefully inspecting each of them. When she pointed to three, some people standing near the wall hurried forward to lead them away.

Sheree returned to the table and straightened her dress before sitting. "They'll be fine additions to my servants. Thank you, Renaldo."

When Renaldo's scowl deepened, Orin understood why half the table looked so sullen... they were losing their servants. Or, more likely, their slaves.

All these new arrivals were chosen by their owners and brought here to be claimed by all the smiling immortals. His fingers clenched on the base of his goblet as anger rose inside him. He didn't like any of these assholes, but *no* one deserved to be treated like this.

He glanced at Sahira as another woman rose to inspect those gathered near the wall. She also picked out three, who were led away by some of the other servants.

Sahira was rigid beside him, her jaw set and eyes unblinking as more immortals rose to claim their prizes. Orin lowered his hand but didn't release his knife as he secretly vowed to gut these twisted freaks.

The sullen immortals at the table only became more miserable while they led away more of their servants. He'd mistakenly considered they might have allies in them, that for whatever reason, they didn't approve of Desmond's antics with *them,* but *this* was the real reason behind their surly demeanors.

There would be no help for them from anyone at this table.

"How do you know about Belda's town?" Orin asked as they took more immortals away.

He loathed Desmond's smile as he fixed it firmly back in place. "Because *we* created what you call the Cursed Realm."

Orin's fingers twitched on the knife handle, and Zeth's claws clicked before he stilled them. Sahira's hand found his knee and grasped it, but while her touch normally soothed him, it did no such thing now.

Desmond had confirmed these freaks were the reason for everything they'd endured these past months. Visions of carving out his eyes filled Orin's mind, and he found himself smiling back at the soon-to-be-dead man.

"And what do you call it?" Pip inquired, her tiny voice barely carrying above the crowd.

"Ground Zero is Belda's town, but you were all players in The Tournament."

CHAPTER NINETEEN

DESMOND REVEALED this as if the word tournament would tell them all they needed to know about why they were here.

And while it did give Sahira some insight into all of it, she was still so confused that she didn't know how to react to this revelation. Or maybe she didn't want to understand.

"The Tournament of what?" Zeth asked.

Desmond waved his hand at them. "The Tournament of immortals, The Tournament of the bravest, The Tournament of those who were courageous enough to venture outside the bounds of safety and onto bigger and better things! It can be whatever you wish to call it, especially since *you* are our first winners."

Sahira didn't feel like a winner, but she held that back. "How did you create such a thing?"

Desmond lifted a finger and waved it like she was a five-year-old, misbehaving child. "Uh-uh, little witch. We can't reveal all our secrets."

Beneath her hand, Orin tensed as a tremor ran through the corded muscles of his thigh.

"You and your friends have your secrets, and we have ours," Desmond continued.

And apparently, this man somehow *knew* all their secrets. Orin had called her little witch while in the Cursed Realm; was that why Desmond said it now?

She had a feeling that was *exactly* why. This asshole didn't do or say anything without knowing exactly why.

"What kind of immortals are you?" Elsa asked.

Desmond gulped some of his wine. Sahira's stomach turned when a servant rushed to wipe his chin. If she were that man, she'd shove the napkin down Desmond's throat until his neck bulged.

"I believe some immortals call us the Golden Ones," Desmond continued when the servant finished dabbing at his mouth.

Sahira's fingers tightened on Orin's thigh, and he rested his hand over hers. Strength flowed through her when their fingers entwined.

Orin could envelop himself in shadows and try to slip away; he'd most likely succeed. She didn't know why he hadn't done so yet, but she was glad he was still here.

"Others," Desmond continued, "call us the dagadon."

"You're supposed to be a myth."

Desmond's head fell back, and he laughed loudly, as did his wife. Smiles tugged at the mouths of those sitting here, acting like someone had taken their puppy.

"Obviously, we're not," Sheree said.

Sahira studied the colorful immortals sitting at the table, and the servants dressed so plainly. "The dagadon were said to have something to do with time; were the hourglasses meant to represent you?"

"Oh no," Desmond said. "They are *very* clear clues as to how you're supposed to leave Ground Zero and enter The Tournament."

She briefly contemplated lifting her knife, leaning across the table, and slicing the smile off that smug prick's face. She'd never get to him in time to inflict any damage, and if she did, the guards would probably kill her and her friends. But she yearned to destroy the hideous perfection of this asshole's face.

"It's very disappointing that so many of you either weren't smart enough, or brave enough, to figure it out," Sheree said.

Zeth's claws clicked again.

"I mean, it's quite obvious Ground Zero is the start, and you must follow the clues to get to the end."

The hell it is, but Sahira didn't argue with Desmond's crazy bitch of a wife.

"The brownies did have a bit of an unfair advantage as they entered into the second round of The Tournament, but alas, they were too small to venture far on their own," Desmond said. "It was a nice bonus to have them join your crew."

"Our friend, Gior, died while traveling here. We've lost many others, too," Loth said.

Desmond shrugged. "In a game of wits where only the best survive, there will always be losses. The weakest aren't meant to survive. It's simple evolution."

The looks on the brownies' faces all screamed murder as they sat on the table.

"What if we had decided to leave the town another way?" Sahira asked.

"Then you would have wandered until you died or returned. But thankfully, you were smart enough to figure out a building was missing and went in the right direction."

"So, the hourglass is also supposed to be an eight to indicate there should have been eight original buildings and not seven."

Desmond threw his arms in the air. "Now you're getting it!"

Oh, she was getting it all right. She was getting the murderous impulse to carve his eyes out and shove them up his nose. "Do the arrows mean anything?"

"Well, they were showing you that you were getting closer to the end, little witch. X marks the spot, after all."

This man really believed they'd laid out good clues for them to follow. He was more insane than Sahira had originally thought, and considering she believed he was batshit crazy, this wasn't a good sign.

"Why did the buildings and towns have fewer things as we progressed through *The Tournament*?" Orin said the words *The Tournament* like they left a bad taste in his mouth.

"We weren't going to continue to make it easy for you," Sheree said.

Sahira barely managed to keep from gawking at the woman. *Easy!* Nothing about their journey had been easy. *Nothing!*

She'd *agonized* over what those symbols meant and which direction they should go when they left Belda's town. Uncertainty had plagued every step of their journey across the Barren Lands and through those other towns, and these scumbags had the nerve to believe they'd made it clear for them and that it was *easy*.

Her fangs tingled with the compulsion to rip out all their throats as she downed some more wine in the hopes of dulling her fury. It didn't help.

CHAPTER TWENTY

"Now what?" Orin asked. "Do we get to leave?"

"Of course," Desmond said a little too loudly. "But first, you *must* give us a chance to celebrate you! You are our first winners, and we've waited *centuries* for you!"

Sahira believed him as much as she did that the sky would turn green and fall on them.

"All of this... *all* of it was for a tournament?" Elsa asked.

Desmond waved a hand at the dwindling number of slaves. Most had already been selected by those sitting at the table. Evidently, there was a hierarchy to these elite immortals, as the ones toward the end of the table were the last to get their chance to choose.

"It is also for fun," Desmond said. "We wager on everyone finally brave enough to venture into what you call the Barren Lands."

"And what do you call them?" Orin inquired as he sipped his wine.

If it wasn't for the tension in the thigh beneath her hand, she could almost believe he was as relaxed as he portrayed, but she knew the truth.

"Round one."

"So, you place bets and exchange servants every time someone leaves Belda's town?" Sahira asked.

She really wanted to call them slaves because that's what they were to these ruling monsters who, in some ways, were more twisted than the Lord who once ruled Dragonia. At least that maniac was corrupted by the power of a throne that didn't belong to him.

These lunatics enjoyed tormenting people and watching them die. And worse, they saw nothing wrong with it. They wanted entertainment, and the Cursed Realm's immortals provided it.

Her head throbbed, and she looked to the servants lining the walls as they led the last slaves away. The dagadon were all so exuberant when they emerged from the tunnel of skulls, but they couldn't *all* think this was good. They couldn't *all* enjoy watching so many suffer and die.

Could they?

"We thought the scarog beetles would drive more immortals from Belda's town. Instead, they accepted that some of them would die once a year," Desmond said.

"Denial that it could actually be *them* was a motivating factor," Renaldo said.

Sahira resisted rubbing her temples as their words hammered at her skull.

"How do you control those things?" Zeth asked. "How do you get them to come in and leave like they do?"

When Desmond waved a finger at him like he had at Sahira, Zeth's claws scraped the table.

"Secrets, demon. We all have our secrets," Desmond told him. "Now, please, watch the wood."

Sahira stopped breathing as a low growl issued from Zeth. Desmond's condescending words had finally caused the demon to snap and his instincts to surge to the forefront.

Desmond's smile didn't falter as a sinister gleam lit his eyes. This bastard was seeking to provoke them into an attack.

When Zeth started to rise, the guards lifted their spears as they stepped closer. Elsa seized Zeth's wrist. "Your son," she hissed.

Orin grasped Sahira's hand in his. A flicker in the shadows alerted her that he was preparing to draw them forth, but they couldn't leave the others behind, and she didn't see how they could get out of this room with so many guards surrounding them.

Zeth stood, trembling as his yellow eyes raked Desmond. He didn't have to say the words; Sahira knew he'd marked the dagadon leader for death.

After a few more tense moments, Zeth finally settled into his seat again. Desmond didn't bother to hide his sigh of disappointment.

"Anyway," the man continued. "We shall celebrate your survival and conquering of The Tournament for a week at least. Then you shall be set free."

"A week?" Sahira practically squeaked.

These things expected them to stay here for a *week*! No, she wouldn't do it… but she didn't have a choice.

Orin could cloak them all in shadows, and they *might* be able to slip past the guards and back into the town, but then what?

There was no food out there and nowhere for them to go except back to Belda's, where they would be monitored, hunted, and destroyed. If the Golden Ones did somehow control the scarog beetles, and they must, they might be able to unleash them on the town at will.

Not to mention, they'd have to make it back through *all* those trials first. And she didn't have it in her to battle the spiders, geysers, and sand monsters again. Not to mention, they didn't have the food or water to get them through it either.

They couldn't escape via a portal, and the dagadon were

dangling freedom before them. She didn't trust them, but what choice did they have?

Unless they somehow managed to kill Desmond and all his freaky friends, they had no choice but to remain here, where they were far outnumbered. And if they did slaughter everyone here, they'd still be trapped in this realm.

The pounding in her head intensified as tears burned her eyes, but she refused to shed them. They'd come this far and succeeded where so many others had failed; she wasn't about to give up now... even if it seemed hopeless.

CHAPTER TWENTY-ONE

THEY HAD to suffer through two more hours of Desmond's company before the very drunk *Lord* of Epoch finally declared an end to the night. He and Sheree rose from their seats, and while they'd barely acknowledged each other all night, he draped an arm around her shoulders.

She helped walk his staggering ass out the doorway where the *prizes* were all taken earlier. Some of them had returned to join the line of servants standing along the wall; each stood behind the new dagadon who had claimed them.

Orin suspected these assholes traded them fairly regularly, and this was nothing new for them. Still, his lip curled in revulsion over it.

"See that our guests are taken care of," Sheree commanded without looking back at them.

It was ridiculous she referred to them as guests when they were clearly prisoners, but it was all part of their game. The seven of them may not be in a dungeon, and bars didn't surround them, but they were far from *guests*.

When some of the women who'd helped clean and dress them rushed over, almost all the guards accompanied them. He didn't know many *guests* who would have such a large contingency surrounding them, but his idea of a guest and Sheree's were different.

"We'll take you to your rooms," the woman who tried to follow him into the bathing chamber said.

Orin squeezed Sahira's hand before releasing it and standing from his chair. When they were ready, the servants led them out of the dining hall through the doors Desmond and Sheree didn't walk through.

From the main entrance, the servants led them to the floating staircase and the second floor. Guards surrounded them as they followed the flow of servants down a white brick hallway.

Most of the white doors lining the hall were closed. The only bit of color in the hall was the wood frame surrounding those doors and the sparkling, magical lights in their golden sconces.

Near the end of the hall, the servants separated, and seven of them stopped outside seven doors. Following their lead, seven guards moved to open the last seven doors in the hallway.

"These are your rooms," the woman who had offered herself to him said.

The three brownies grouped closer together. "We're staying with each other," Pip declared. Loth and Fath nodded their agreement.

It would probably be best if they *all* stayed together, but there was no way he was sharing a room with the demon. He'd saved Zeth's life, but that was where he drew the line. Besides, Sahira would eventually get over being mad at him, and he wasn't about to have company when she returned to his bed.

And she *would* return.

"Of course," another woman murmured, and the guards closed two doors.

"You are free to roam the castle," the woman from his bath said.

"What about outside?" Sahira asked.

"There are guards outside too who will be happy to show you around should you decide to explore out there," a guard gruffly replied.

So no, Orin decided. And he suspected the second they exited their rooms, they'd have a contingent of guards ensuring they didn't go anywhere alone.

When a woman placed her hand in the small of Elsa's back, she handed her a small bag and waved for her to enter her room. Sahira stepped forward as if to follow but stopped as the woman clasped the knob and started to close the door.

Sahira craned her head to see more into Elsa's room and waved to her. Orin couldn't see if the witch waved in return.

Zeth entered the room beside Elsa's while another woman placed her hand on the small of Sahira's back and steered her back across the hall. They were all handed small bags that Orin suspected contained what little the dagadon had decided they could keep of their things.

Sahira moved woodenly as she stopped outside the door to the room next to his. Their eyes briefly met before Sahira gave him a small smile and strolled into the room.

Unable to tolerate the idea of having her out of his sight, he almost went after her, but a woman leaned in to close the door behind her. Orin stopped himself from continuing after her. She was already gone, and they'd only stop him; a confrontation wouldn't accomplish anything now.

The brownies vanished into the room on the other side of Orin's, but he remained outside his door. "What are our chances of ending up in the dungeon?"

He wasn't surprised when his question was met by silence as they all stared at him.

"Do you need help readying your room?" the woman asked.

He didn't want any of these assholes in his room. Without looking back, Orin strode inside; he turned to shut the door, but the woman leaned in and grasped the handle.

"Have a good night," she told him, handing him a bag too.

Orin didn't bother to respond as the door closed with a click. He was about to turn away when he spotted something white floating in the air.

The woman must have dropped it when she was closing the door. Before it hit the ground, Orin snatched it from the air and discovered it was a scrap piece of folded parchment.

He glanced at the door before unfolding it to discover she'd written a note inside....

Meet me in the garden at 2 a.m. Destroy this.

He stared at the note before crumpling it in his hand and taking it into the bathroom. He tore it into tiny pieces before flushing the toilet. The small pieces of parchment floated on the water before being sucked down the drain to somewhere far away.

Satisfied they were gone, he opened the bag and discovered his birth control potion tucked inside. Closing it again, he leaned back to survey his surroundings. Like with everything else in this realm, white brick surrounded him.

It was so white and clean that the lights, and their golden holders above the sink, were almost too dazzling as they reflected off the pristine surfaces. The tub beside him was also a clean, sparkling white and large enough to fit two or three immortals.

When he was sure none of the note would resurface, Orin left the bathroom and turned off the lights. The main bedroom was also completely white, though a red comforter covered the king-size bed, and the clock in the corner had a gold face and wooden base. Of course, it was all flecked with gold.

Gold drapes covered the windows, but like the bathroom and almost everywhere else in this place, the walls were bare of any adornments other than the light fixtures. A door across the way looked as if it connected with Sahira's room, while the one to the far left of his bed must go into the brownies' room.

Orin contemplated knocking on Sahira's door, but there was still more to explore here. He crossed over to the drapes and pulled them open to reveal two French doors and the balcony beyond.

Grasping a handle, he pulled one of the doors open and stepped into the cool night air. He strode over to the edge, and, seizing the railing, gazed down at the garden below. He couldn't make out much of the details, as most of the vast space was lost to the night, but it overflowed with plants silhouetted by the low-hanging moon.

The door to the balcony beside his opened, and Sahira stepped out. Her eyes found his across the ten feet separating them.

CHAPTER TWENTY-TWO

"IT'S BEAUTIFUL," she said. "The whole place would be more beautiful, if it wasn't so sterile, white, and occupied by lunatics."

The corners of his mouth twitched toward a smile. "It's too white."

"I'm scared to touch anything."

"So am I. What do you think about all of this?"

A gentle breeze tugged at her hair, causing strands of it to dance in the night. He hadn't believed it possible, but she looked more beautiful bathed in the moon's faint glow.

He tore his attention away from her when two guards prowled out of the garden and crossed paths as they patrolled the area. Sahira didn't speak until they were out of view again.

"Oh, I think we're fucked. How about you?"

"Right up the ass, without any lube and no safe words to stop it."

Sahira grimaced. "Lovely description."

"Sums it up perfectly."

"I'm afraid it does."

"The question is, how do we get out of it?"

She sighed as the guards stalked into view again. "I don't know."

When the patrol was gone, Orin rested his elbows on the railing and clasped his hands before him. "Neither do I."

"There has to be a weakness here somewhere; we'll find it."

"We will."

She kept one hand on the railing as she turned to face him. "Good night, Orin."

"Good night, Sahira. If you need anything, you know where I am, or you could always come over and join me now. I guarantee your night will be a lot more fun if you do."

Her lips pursed as she studied him before replying. "Have you figured your shit out?"

He frowned as he recalled her words in the bathroom of the pub after he'd confessed she was the only woman he'd been with since her arrival in the Cursed Realm. *"You have to decide what you want, but just so you know, I won't sit around and wait for you to figure it out. This is your shit to deal with, Orin, not mine."*

Had he figured it out? He certainly hadn't had time to think about her words, their relationship, or much of anything before being thrust into this nightmare. All Orin knew for sure was he would protect her, he liked her more than any other woman he'd ever known, and she belonged in his bed.

But that wasn't enough for her. He wasn't sure what would be enough for her either.

Is she looking for a relationship? Because he didn't do those, and staying faithful wasn't a possibility for him.

Yet, without meaning to, he'd remained faithful to her without any commitment or bonds between them. He hadn't realized that until now.

He'd always expected to move on to other women at some point, but he could have had the dagadon woman today and chosen not to. It didn't matter that he couldn't stand or trust her; he'd never had to do either to fuck a woman. Why start now?

But he had started and had no idea what any of it meant.

"I'll take that as a no," she said when he didn't respond. "I don't think they'll bother us anymore tonight. They have a much bigger game plan for us. I'll see you tomorrow."

Unfortunately, he agreed with her but didn't say so. When she turned and walked away, he buried his disappointment as she entered her room.

He'd much prefer she was safe with him, but while much had changed throughout this day and night, she was still mad at him, and they both required time to process whatever this was between them. Although, he wasn't sure he'd ever understand it.

But, until something changed, he might as well get some rest. He had a feeling tomorrow was going to be a long day.

Orin returned to his room and locked the door behind him. He pulled the drapes closed, stripped out of his clothes, and climbed into bed.

He had no intention of going to meet that woman in the garden. While he was a little hungry for the sexual energy that fed a dark fae, he only wanted one woman, and she wasn't waiting for him in the garden.

CHAPTER TWENTY-THREE

THE NEXT MORNING, a group of women bustled into Sahira's room as the clock in the corner chimed ten. She'd already been up for a couple of hours, prowling around the space, but there wasn't much to see beyond the white walls, the large bed with its deep blue cover, and a small bathroom.

The closet was full of colorful clothes, but none were as elaborate as the dress she wore last night. She'd enjoyed a shower and scrubbed herself before finally rinsing off and stepping out.

Afterward, she'd chosen a pair of black pants and a yellow blouse that buttoned to her neck, but she left the last buttons undone to breathe better. After she was dressed, she removed the protective spells she'd placed over the doors. There was no way anyone would come through those doors during the night without her knowledge.

More than a few times, she prowled to the door separating her and Orin. She'd reach for the knob before telling herself he had to come to her and heading back the other way.

She couldn't forget the look in his eyes when she'd asked him if he'd figured his shit out last night. It was clear he hadn't and was as confused as always, but those crow-black eyes had simmered with a hunger that made her skin prickle with awareness.

She'd almost thrown all caution to the wind and gone to his room. They had no idea what would happen to them here; she might as well embrace life while she could, but she was *so* tired of the endless back and forth between them.

And she was still *pissed* he'd tried to make her think he was having sex with all those women when he wasn't. She'd always known Orin liked his games and often toyed with others, but that was beyond messed up... even for him.

So, she'd stayed here, aching and alone as she tried to sort everything out in her mind. But she had no idea what to make of any of this.

Now, with a group of women bustling around her as they held up clothes before pulling them away and fussing with her hair, Sahira found her temper becoming surlier by the second.

She kept her exasperation hidden while they worked, and the guards looming in the doorway made it clear they wouldn't tolerate anything less than complete obedience from her. Finally, the women settled on a deep maroon dress, and Sahira removed her clothes.

When the women tugged the dress over her head, the bodice hugged her upper body while the skirt fell close to her legs. The material was more lightweight than it looked and as soft as silk as it shimmered in the light.

This place was a giant hellhole with a bunch of monsters running it, but they made beautiful clothing. *One bonus for the psychopaths,* she decided.

The dress also had pockets, which was another bonus for the crazy, game-playing, liked-to-bet-their-own-kind immortals. She dipped her fingers into the pockets and wiggled them while contemplating casting a spell to make one of these women spill their guts about this place.

The guards in the doorway caused her fingers to clench

instead of working their magic. They would immediately stop anything the woman had to say... probably by killing her.

Sahira didn't trust anyone in this realm, but she suspected these servants in white were as much a prisoner as she and her friends. She wouldn't be the cause of one of them dying unless they gave her a reason, and then she'd gladly kill them too.

When the women shifted their focus to her hair, Sahira waved them away. "I'll do it."

She ignored their protests as she twisted it into her customary bun and took the pins they produced to keep it in place.

"Oh, we could have done something far more lovely with it," one of the women said.

"I've had enough of being lovely," Sahira retorted.

A few women raised their eyebrows, but the others hurried away.

"This way," the one she'd spoken with said irritably.

Sahira rolled her eyes at the woman's back. Did they really expect her to be happy about all this?

They'd been thrown into Hell and raked across its coals while in the Cursed Realm and Barren Lands. Did these idiots think all this primping and the elaborate meals would make up for that, or were they putting on an act for the guards?

With a sigh, she followed them from the room. She was eager to see her friends and learn more about this place. The more they knew, the better their chances of finding a weakness and breaking free.

Orin emerged from his room as one of the guards shut the door behind her. He'd brushed his short hair back from his face to expose its elegant angles; it emphasized how handsome he was.

He wore body-hugging, black fae pants and a white tunic with green edging. The contrast of the white against his black eyes and hair made them stand out more.

Her stomach flipped as desire burst through her. Damn it,

why did he have to be so good-looking, irresistible, and such an asshole?

But none of that mattered as the Golden Ones surrounded them while their friends emerged to join them in the hall.

"Our Lord has a fun day planned for you."

Sahira glanced at the woman who had mostly worked with Orin yesterday. Her white-blonde hair hung in a plait over her shoulder as her dark brown eyes surveyed him. The woman wiped an invisible speck of dust from his shoulder before brushing by him to lead the way down the hall.

Sahira fell into step beside Orin as Zeth and Elsa fell in before them, and the brownies trailed behind. They were led down the staircase, along another hall, and into a smaller dining area, where they were served a breakfast of eggs, meat, fruits, and bread.

As many guards as possible filled the room and stood against the wall to watch them. Coffee flowed endlessly as Sahira alternated between it and a sweet juice she'd never tried before, but it was delicious.

Despite her rumbling stomach, the food felt like a weight going down her throat, and she barely did anything more than pick at it. When they finished, the servants led them out of the room and into the garden.

Sahira had seen them last night and again this morning, but being amongst the trees overflowing with flowers and shrubs of every color imaginable enchanted her. They strolled beneath a thick canopy of limbs laden with yellow leaves that created a tunnel for hundreds of feet.

She could almost forget they were trapped here as birds flitted from one colorful plant or tree to another. The larger birds were vivid shades of red, yellow, and orange, while the smaller ones were mostly blue or yellow. She hadn't seen any birds since arriving in the Cursed Realm and loved seeing them now.

"I missed birds," she whispered.

"So did I," Orin said, "especially crows."

There were no crows here, but hearing the songs of these birds warmed Sahira's heart. The guards hung back as the servant women guided them through the trees; their simple white dresses stood out starkly against the colorful garden.

They passed a massive fountain with two horses rearing. Their front legs nearly touched as the beasts fought each other. The statues were as golden as the fountain beneath them.

As they walked further into the garden, a distinct clicking sound caught her attention. At first, it was too far away to be more than a curiosity, but the deeper they moved into the colorful, lush garden, the louder the noise became.

"What is that?" Elsa inquired.

CHAPTER TWENTY-FOUR

LIKE ALWAYS, they ignored her as no one answered the question. Sahira tried to place the noise; it sounded familiar, but she couldn't quite put a finger on it.

Finally, the meandering dirt path they traversed opened onto a field where the sun hung high in the clear blue sky. Green grass stretched on for at least an acre before it ended in perfectly manicured, ten-foot-tall hedges that lined the entire area.

Sahira couldn't see beyond those hedges, but she could now see the source of the clicking as two men, dressed all in white, parried back and forth with their fencing swords. It had been years since she'd seen a fencing match, and while she'd always enjoyed them before, this wasn't going to be one of those times.

At the start of the match, their white clothes were most likely pristine, but now slashes of red and big circular blotches of blood marred them. The men didn't wear any protective gear as they danced back and forth across the lush lawn.

Their movements should be elegant and entrancing, but this bout was brutal. Sahira winced as one of them struck another blow, and a fresh stain of blood spread across the surface of the other's clothes.

Whenever someone landed a blow, a small gasp or murmur of disapproval ran through the crowd sitting on a stage. Gathered there were all the brightly dressed dagadon. Their colorful clothes stuck out against the green grass, hedges, and the white of the servants surrounding them.

Sahira resisted tearing the maroon dress from her. She didn't want any part of *that* crowd.

The dress grew tighter by the second, and she swore the bodice was crushing her ribs. She closed her eyes and took a steadying breath while listening to the battle progressing before them.

Feeling like she could breathe a little easier again, she opened her eyes. One of the fighters lunged forward and sank the tip of his blade into his opponent's shoulder. The man cried out as he staggered back, freeing himself from the weapon.

This was going to be a battle to the death. And what a drawn-out battle it would be as the points of their fencing swords were too small to inflict enough damage to kill instantly.

Unless someone managed to strike a lucky blow straight to the heart, and even then, it might not kill these immortals. They might be like the dark fae, who could only die from a sword composed of fae metal.

The swords weren't thick enough to chop off someone's head, so these fighters must go until one collapsed from blood loss or exhaustion. *And then what happens? Does the other continue to poke and hack at them until they die?*

Sahira gulped back the breakfast rising in her throat. She wished she hadn't eaten what little she choked down.

"This way," the blonde-haired woman said.

Sahira dug in her heels when she realized the woman was heading toward the four empty seats at the front of the stage. They were to be front and center between Desmond and Renaldo.

When she didn't move with the others, Orin placed a hand on

her back and nudged her forward. "I can't watch this," she whispered.

He kept his hand on her back as he bent to murmur in her ear. "Then close your eyes, but you have to join them."

Sahira started to refuse, but she couldn't cause a scene here. They would know how much this bothered her if she did, and these assholes would *relish* it. They'd probably drag out two more fighters and make her sit through that too.

Taking a deep breath, Sahira somehow managed to get her feet to move again as a small cheer ran through half the crowd while the other half groaned. *They're betting on this too.*

She really shouldn't have eaten as the once comfortable warmth of the day suddenly felt oppressive, her stomach lurched, and sweat trickled down her nape. She didn't look at the fighters as she walked but focused on those empty chairs.

She could get through this if she remained fixed on them and the strength of Orin's arm as it slipped around her waist. When her gaze shifted to Desmond, she discovered the monster watching them with amusement.

And it wasn't *her* who amused him, as his attention was mostly on Orin. Oh, she was sure the prick enjoyed how much she disliked this, but her interactions with Orin entertained him far more.

The dark fae prince wasn't supposed to care about the feelings of others. *No* dark fae did unless their feelings were involved too.

And while Orin didn't understand his feelings for her and was fighting them, they were what made him so damn stupid when it came to his games with her. Instead of admitting he *might* like her, he pretended to screw a parade of women.

However, though he was an emotional disaster who had no idea how to handle possibly caring for someone else, his actions said he *did* care. When they first met, he would have left her standing there to fend for herself, but he didn't do that, and he didn't take away the comfort and support he offered her. Instead, his hand flattened against her belly.

But Desmond would use Orin's feelings and uncertainty against him once he figured out how to do so. She was beginning to realize Desmond enjoyed his games as much as Orin; he just had much more help.

CHAPTER TWENTY-FIVE

"COME, JOIN US!" Desmond called cheerfully as he waved at the empty seats beside him.

His eyes were a little bloodshot, but that was the only indication he had too much to drink yesterday. A goblet of something sat before him, but Sahira couldn't see what it contained. At Desmond's side, Sheree kept her nose in the air while watching the show.

Orin sat beside Desmond, and as Sahira settled into her seat, she spotted the three small chairs on the shelf running across the front of the stage. When lifted onto the shelf by her and Elsa, the brownies reluctantly climbed onto the chairs as Elsa sat beside her and Zeth next to her.

Sitting stiffly in her chair, Sahira worked to keep her face impassive as the match continued and a bunch of cruel assholes surrounded them. Her skin crawled with revulsion as she focused on the hedges beyond the fighters, but she couldn't shut out the sounds of their battle.

"What is going on here?" Orin asked.

Sahira felt it was obvious, but who knew how Desmond would respond? When the brownies turned to study the crowd,

Sahira almost scooped them into her arms to cradle them protectively against her but kept herself from moving.

It would only piss off the small, prideful creatures if she did, and she didn't want these monsters to realize how much they'd all grown to care for each other.

Who are you kidding? They already know.

That thought, and the certainty accompanying it, only made her chill and nausea worse.

"Another tournament." Desmond beamed as he waved a hand at the fighters. "Like with all of you, only the strongest will survive." He paused to study Orin with a pensive expression. "I bet you would be fantastic out there, Prince."

Sahira's hands clenched in her lap as panic sent her heart into hyperdrive, but Orin laughed as he lifted the goblet a servant set before him and sipped it. Sahira ignored the drink placed before her, as did the others.

"I'm afraid I wouldn't be much entertainment for you," Orin replied. "I don't do graceful sword dances; I destroy."

Desmond roared with laughter and slapped his thigh. "I must agree. You are not one for subtlety, are you, Orin?"

"Only when it benefits me."

"Your brother is now king of the dark fae, or so I've heard."

Sahira was *very* curious to know how he'd learned this if they couldn't leave the realm, or maybe it was just *them* who couldn't leave, but she doubted it. If the dagadon could leave, someone would have seen them. It was impossible for immortals such as these to go unnoticed in the realms; their sparkle didn't exactly blend in.

She didn't ask her question. These things would never give up their secrets.

"That was a nice way to say you know more about me than I do about you. I'm not the only one who isn't into subtlety," Orin said.

Sahira gulped, and despite her every intention not to

acknowledge the man sitting beside Orin, her head turned toward Desmond as she waited to see how he would take Orin's words. For a minute, the two alphas sat, sizing each other up before Desmond broke into that spine-tingling grin again.

Desmond lifted his goblet in a salute toward Orin before taking a sip. "You are not. I also hear there is a new leader in Dragonia."

How? Sahira inwardly shouted as her nails bit into her palms. *How do you know this?*

"You hear correctly," Orin confirmed, looking completely nonplussed by Desmond's insights into things he shouldn't know.

"She's your niece, from what I understand," Desmond said to Sahira.

She stared back at him as she recalled all the conversations that had swirled through Belda's pub. They exchanged a lot of information with every newcomer who entered the realm.

Those trapped in the Cursed Realm were thirsty for knowledge of the outside world; they peppered every new arrival with questions. Desmond could have gleaned all this information from those conversations, but that meant the dagadon had been listening to them the whole time.

Every time she believed the Golden Ones couldn't unnerve her more, they proved her wrong.

"Yes, the new queen is my niece," Sahira confirmed.

"I bet you're both very missed," Desmond murmured.

Sahira didn't know what to make of his words. Did he plan to try ransoming them to Lexi and Cole? They seemed to have everything they could need in Epoch, but Desmond was a cruel, greedy douchebag, and those types were never satisfied with what they had.

"I trust you all slept well," Desmond continued as another groan and cheer ran through the crowd.

The change of conversation didn't throw off Sahira; Desmond liked keeping others on their toes.

"Yes," Orin said. "After what we've been through, it was good to feel safe again."

Sahira rolled her eyes. Eventually, exhaustion had won out, but she'd spent most of the night tossing and turning as she waited for someone to bust down her door, throw her in a dungeon, or feed her to spiders.

She had her alarms set, but that would only let her know someone was coming and slow them down, but she'd never fend them all off before they captured her. And she was sure none of the others had slept well in this place either.

Orin and Desmond grinned at each other. Neither of them was a lycan, but they were both alphas who enjoyed fucking with the heads of others. This could end very badly for all of them.

CHAPTER TWENTY-SIX

"You must be ravenous, Prince," Desmond said. "I know the dark fae have certain *appetites*. When we return to the palace, I'll have some of my men escort you to one of our fine bordellos. Many of my men enjoy frequenting them."

Sahira stiffened, and while Orin didn't so much as flinch at the words or falter in his smile, tension radiated from him. Zeth and Elsa were riveted on them, but the brownies continued to examine the crowd filling the stands.

Would he go? He'd only been with her since her arrival here, but they had no promises with each other. He was a dark fae who thrived on sex with different women, and he had no idea what he wanted from her.

Plus, this question was another of Desmond's games. He was trying to see how much he could push Orin one way or another while testing the bounds of their relationship. Inwardly screaming against all this, Sahira didn't breathe as she waited for his response.

"That's a very fine offer," Orin said while Sahira's pulse thundered in her temples, "but my appetites have been sated for a bit."

Sahira released her breath as she tried to remain as casual as possible while inwardly sobbing with relief over his response. As much as she hated to admit she cared for him as much as she did, it would have devastated her if Orin said yes.

Desmond's and Orin's eyes locked, and then the dagadon Lord shifted his attention to her. It took everything she had not to look away from his penetrating, nearly colorless gaze. After a tense minute, Desmond laughed and clasped Orin's shoulder.

"You had to kill time somehow on your travels, I'm sure."

Orin chuckled. "Yes, I did."

Sahira buried a flash of irritation over his words. Their relationship, whatever it was, was none of Desmond's business, but that didn't matter to the leader of the Golden Ones because he had *made* it his. Desmond would turn that screw until it snapped; then, he'd use the pieces against them while entertaining himself.

"We have many fine women in our bordellos," Desmond continued, "and men, too, if that is also your thing."

Orin nonchalantly drank more of his wine. "I've always preferred women."

"So does your witch, or at least the full-blooded one, from what I've heard."

Sahira's head turned toward Elsa, who stared at Desmond with eyes that narrowed as her mouth pursed. Beside her, Zeth looked confused and irritated by Desmond's shocking insights into their lives.

Sahira's mind spun back to the memory of her and Elsa standing inside the library in the brownie town. Elsa had made it clear she preferred having sex with women.

It was yet another insight these things knew about them… but, like Cole being the dark fae king and Lexi being the queen of Dragonia, it was revealed in a place with a symbol.

Sahira was becoming increasingly certain those symbols had somehow allowed the dagadon to listen to them. They might have even *watched* over them.

When she'd touched the symbols, she felt no magic running through them, but that didn't mean it wasn't lurking beneath the surface. It could have been something she couldn't tap into.

They had no idea what the dagadon could do, and while she often felt the power of others in things, it wasn't a given that she would. If the power was old and had been there for years, its lingering, residual effects would have dwindled to nearly nothing.

Given the centuries Belda had spent in the Cursed Realm, there was a good possibility any magic residue vanished years ago. Those symbols were more than clues about how to enter The Tournament; she was sure of it.

Her fingers fisted as she shifted her attention back to the battle. She instantly regretted doing so as the fighters sparred with increasingly sluggish movements. Their uniforms were more red than white now.

She stared at Elsa, who was still glowering at Desmond. She willed her friend to see her until Elsa finally did.

With a subtle shake of her head, Sahira wordlessly told her to look away. After a reluctant moment, Elsa finally did.

When one of the fighters fell to his knee, half the crowd cheered and then grumbled when he staggered back to his feet and blocked the next blow. Sahira stared over the men's heads while she waited for this to end.

Orin sipped whatever was in his goblet, but none of the others touched theirs as the fight continued endlessly on. Finally, after what felt like hours, one of the men went to both his knees.

This time, he didn't get up.

He remained on his knees for less than a minute before toppling forward. The blood loss had weakened him considerably, but he wasn't dead, as his breaths ruffled the short grass.

A cheer went through half the crowd while the other half grunted. They all chugged some more of their drinks while some laughed and slapped others on their shoulders.

They exchanged money as those who bet on the winner collected their spoils from those who lost.

"You got me this time, Renaldo," Desmond said as he handed the man a chunk of gold.

Renaldo lifted the gold piece in the air to examine it. "I'd prefer to have my servants back, but this will do."

"And you might win them back if we ever have someone brave enough to enter The Tournament again."

To her right, Sahira spotted a woman dressed all in white. Tears streamed down her cheeks as she noiselessly wept. She clasped her hands before her as she gazed at the downed man on the field.

The anguish on the woman's face caused Sahira's heart to twist. She inwardly pleaded to Hecate that she was wrong and they'd lift the man from the grass and take him somewhere to heal.

Her pleas were eradicated when Desmond called, "Bring in the dogs!"

"The *dogs*?" Sahira blurted.

"The poor things must eat."

CHAPTER TWENTY-SEVEN

WHEN THE IMPLICATION of his words sank in, Sahira nearly bolted out of her chair. Orin's hand coming down on hers kept her in place. She turned to look at him, and his eyes burned into hers as she felt him willing her to stay seated.

But this was the last place she wanted to be. Before she could say or do anything, the low snarl of animals made the hair on her nape rise.

Sahira gulped as she turned toward the six massive men standing behind those chains as thick as her thighs. At the end of those chains were three beasts, so big she couldn't tell if they were dogs or small horses.

Two handlers tried to control one beast as the animals snarled, snapped, and dragged the men forward. Each man was at least six feet tall and two hundred pounds, but the dogs pulled them along as if they were no more than children.

With their short gray hair, colossal shoulders, and claws that could eviscerate with one swipe, the dogs had heads twice the size of an immortal's. The scent of the downed man's blood excited them; they lunged and jerked against the chains as spittle flew from their mouths.

Their lower jaws jutted out beneath their upper ones to reveal razor-sharp teeth. The two canine teeth on their lower jaws jetted at least three feet into the air.

These weren't dogs; they were monsters.

"Holy shit," Elsa murmured beside her.

Sahira's fingers constricted on Orin's. She should stop interacting with him and cut off any sign they might care for each other around Desmond, but it wouldn't do much good. The man had already seen and knew too much.

It was also too late for her when it came to the others. Desmond knew they all cared for each other and would do whatever it took to ensure they survived. He would use that against them all.

The dogs were almost to the man lying on the ground when their handlers released the chains. With a savage howl, the beasts lunged forward and sank their teeth into their victim.

Sahira winced and bowed her head as she tried to drown out the victim's screams by screaming louder in her mind. No matter how loud she shouted, she couldn't block the man's agony.

After far too much time, the shrieks finally stopped, but the bone crunching continued. Beside her, Elsa trembled like a leaf in a hurricane, and while the brownies kept their attention on the crowd, Pip couldn't hide the sheen of tears in her eyes. Loth and Fath didn't bother to conceal their disgust.

Sahira didn't realize she was crying until a single tear landed on her hand. The cool drop shimmered in the light before she freed her hand from Orin's to wipe it away.

She brushed her fingers over her cheeks but felt nothing else there. She couldn't let these vicious bastards see her cry. They'd only see it as a weakness.

And they *devoured* anyone they believed was weak.

CHAPTER TWENTY-EIGHT

SAHIRA DIDN'T WANT to look, but her eyes flickered back to the bloody remains of the immortal the dogs tore apart. Done with their initial feast, each beast had retreated with a limb to snack on.

Bile rising in her throat, her gaze shifted to the crying woman on the sidelines. Her shoulders hunched up as she openly sobbed with her head in her hands. None of the servants standing beside her offered her any comfort.

Instead, they stood shoulder to shoulder with their gazes forward while they watched the immortal, one they all *must* know, be devoured. *How can they show so little emotion?*

Because they're probably used to this.

Sahira gulped as the other fighter limped past the servants and into the garden. No one offered to help him, and Sahira suspected that if he fell, the dogs would devour him too.

She'd give anything to be back in Belda's town, with no answers and frustration mounting daily. That town was a form of torture designed to drive those who encountered it insane, but it wasn't full of monsters.

These *things* probably hated Belda because she'd kept her

town from dissolving into complete chaos where immortals savagely murdered each other daily. That was perhaps what these assholes hoped to have happen, but Belda had proven them all wrong. Sahira was incredibly proud of the lycan who had thwarted these heartless beings without knowing it.

Why they didn't stop Belda, she didn't know, considering they had a way to control the scarog beetles, but they'd allowed the lycan to continue ruling her town. And if the symbols allowed the dagadon to somehow monitor the towns, they didn't get the pleasure of the pit... which they would have enjoyed.

They must have allowed Belda to continue for a reason. Most likely because, even with her control over that town, immortals still wandered into the Barren Lands, where they could place bets on them.

"If that is all for today," Zeth said as if none of this fazed him, "I wouldn't mind walking the garden again."

"Ah yes, the garden is lovely this time of year," Desmond said. "My wife and I shall join you."

Sahira yearned to get as far from this man as possible, scrub her skin until it was red, and cry in the shower, but she didn't say anything as she rose. When Elsa stood, she rested her hand on the shelf; her legs trembled before she steadied them.

The brownies rose too. When Sahira held out her hand, Loth and Fath scrambled onto it, up her arm, and across her shoulders, where they each settled on a different side.

Pip leapt onto Orin's arm and climbed up to sit on his shoulder. She didn't have a weapon, but she looked ready to claw the eyes out of anyone who came near them.

They filed out of the stands, and guards fell in around them as Desmond and Sheree strolled into the garden with Orin at Desmond's side. Though Orin acted genuinely interested in what Desmond had to say, Sahira wasn't fooled into thinking Orin liked this man or his wife.

Orin could be cruel and had hurt her many times, and he'd

kept Del imprisoned and locked away from her and Lexi, but the dagadon exhibited a different level of cruelty. She didn't know how he could stomach talking to them, but then, Orin always enjoyed a good game, and he was playing theirs.

Still, she couldn't look at them as they spoke of the trees and plants while meandering through the garden. Beauty surrounded her, but she barely noticed any of the details as she took strength in Loth and Fath's presence on her shoulders while Elsa and Zeth walked beside her.

Lunch, a tour of the grounds afterward, and another big dinner all passed in a blur. By the time Sahira could retreat to her room for the night, she was ready to collapse. She'd barely eaten anything for the past two days, and while her stomach rumbled, the idea of putting food in it also made it rebel.

An entourage of women in white followed her into her room and helped unbutton the elaborate dress they'd changed her into before dinner. Elsa, Zeth, Loth, and Fath had also all retired for the night, but Orin and Pip remained at the table.

Because of this, she had more women than normal crowding into her room. She almost screamed at them to get out but bit back the words. She wasn't as good at playing the game as Orin, but she still had to pretend at least a little.

If she didn't know any better, she would think Orin was beginning to like this realm and its hideous occupants. A small part of her questioned her conviction that he wasn't.

The woman who normally worked with Orin went to her closet, disappeared inside, and returned with a robe and night-gown. She dumped them both on the bed, turned, and stalked out of the room as if Sahira were nothing more than an annoyance to tolerate.

Sahira retreated into the bathroom, where she showered for far longer than normal while scrubbing her skin clean. She'd give anything to escape this realm and forget everything she'd seen here, but she had no idea how they could break free.

From everything she'd seen, they were more trapped here than in Belda's town. When she finally finished in the shower, she dried herself off and trudged out to the bedroom.

She pulled on the nightgown and the robe. When she slid her fingers into the robe's pockets, they brushed against something inside.

Frowning, Sahira pulled out the small parchment and opened it to read…

Meet me in the garden. 2 a.m. Destroy this.

CHAPTER TWENTY-NINE

ORIN SIPPED his wine and set it down while the dagadon laughed loudly. Their faces were flushed from too much drink as they swayed in their seats. Though he also cast his voice to yell like he was a drunken mess too, he had a high tolerance for alcohol and barely felt its effects tonight.

He would have preferred not to drink, but that wouldn't go unnoticed by those who poured the goblets. So, he drank far more than he would have liked, but staying sober was easier when his and Sahira's lives were on the line. Not to mention the others.

Almost everyone else had retreated, but Pip remained on his shoulder, sipping wine from a tiny chalice they must have forged the second the brownies entered this realm. He would do whatever it took to protect her too.

Desmond's boisterous laughter rebounded off the walls. The others were much happier tonight too. Apparently, watching some poor soul getting tortured by dogs was a mood enhancer for these cheap, gold knockoffs.

"Tell me, Orin," Desmond said as he turned to face him.

Wine sloshed out of his goblet and onto the table. It had

barely landed on the smooth surface before someone scurried forward to wipe it away.

Orin plastered on a smile as he twirled his drink between his fingers and waited to hear what the red-faced man had to say. On his shoulder, Pip shifted before settling into place again.

"What was your *least* favorite part of The Tournament?" Desmond inquired.

Next to Desmond, Sheree watched him with fascination. He had yet to see these two do more than kiss on the cheek.

Cole and Lexi didn't make him want to run screaming from the room with their love, but it was obvious. These two acted more like roommates than lovers but were never apart.

A few hundred years with one immortal probably leads to a lot less affection and sex.

He inwardly shuddered at the possibility of being tied to someone for centuries and living a sexless existence…. Sahira's amber eyes swam through his mind, and something inside him softened. Maybe it wouldn't be so bad if it was with her and the sex had only gotten better between them, not worse.

Are you really thinking this? Orin lifted his goblet to stare at it. Maybe the wine had gotten to him more than he realized.

Shifting his attention back to the strange couple beside him, he studied them as he tried to puzzle them out. Had Desmond forced Sheree into this marriage?

It would be highly unusual for an immortal to do such a thing, as marriage was sacred to them, but from what he'd seen of Desmond, the man had no respect for anything. Orin doubted he drew the line at marriage.

It made sense if he had somehow coerced her into this, as Sheree was exceptionally beautiful. Desmond was the type who sought only the best for himself.

"Yes, please do tell," Sheree said as she sipped her wine.

Orin recalled Desmond's question about his least favorite part of The Tournament. He wasn't about to tell him, and the suddenly rapt table, that his least favorite part was the uncertainty… the constant not knowing if they were making the right choices. The uncertainty had gnawed at him like a mouse on cheese.

He also wouldn't tell them he'd feared he couldn't get Sahira out of there alive, or they'd all die while wandering the Barren Lands. That would only make them happy.

Instead, he said, "The spiders. I don't like spiders."

A laugh went around the table, and a few women giggled as they eyed him over their goblets. Orin pretended not to notice while trying not to sneer at them.

"That was such a fun idea," Sheree said.

Orin kept his astonishment hidden. "You created the spiders?"

"Oh no," Desmond said. "They've always lived in this realm; we just trained them to stay in one place. At first, we had to feed them to keep them there, but once their queen built a web, they settled into the area, and we stopped feeding them.

"They've had a few meals from Belda's town, but not many. And as their numbers have grown, they've spread out further while mostly eradicating whatever wildlife lived in the area, but for the most part, they're content where they are.

"Admittedly, there had gotten to be a few too many of them, but you helped solve that problem. You lowered their numbers again, so they won't require as much food to keep them in place."

"We destroyed their web; what will keep them from moving?"

"We're aware," Desmond said with a smile, "and are monitoring the situation."

Orin took that to mean they'd started feeding the abominations again. He wouldn't press for more information; getting these freaks to talk was much easier when they weren't firing questions at them.

So, he sipped more wine and listened to their laughter while all those dressed in white remained near the wall and the guards watched over him. Eventually, and after far too many hours, the night ended, and Orin rose as Desmond and Sheree left the room.

The large clock hanging over the doorway the couple exited through indicated it was nearly one in the morning. He stifled a yawn as Pip leaned against his cheek, and a small snore issued from her.

With guards trailing his every move, Orin strode back to the main hall and ascended to the second floor. He didn't look back at the guards as he stopped outside Pip's door and poked her to wake her.

She sat up and yawned loudly before slumping against his cheek again. He opened the door.

"Time for bed," he said. "I'll see you in the morning."

She glanced at the guards before whispering in his ear. "How long do you think they'll toy with us before they kill us?"

"Not long."

Pip crawled down his arm to drop onto the floor. Without a backward glance, she sauntered into the room. Orin shut the door and continued to his room; he entered and closed the door behind him.

Leaning against the door, he studied the space as he replayed everything that happened today and tonight. So far, he'd found no weaknesses in this place, but they had to be there.

Even if we don't find any, we have to leave soon.

There was no getting around that. Today had been a display for Desmond, a show of how far they would go to entertain themselves and destroy another.

After the Barren Lands, Orin hadn't required that show, none of them did, but the dagadon enjoyed putting it on for them. Eventually, they would get bored of only putting on shows and look to do something more... with *them*.

They'd have to plan an escape from this place soon.

Tomorrow night, he'd cloak himself in shadows and see what he could learn from the palace and the grounds. He might return to the tunnel to see if they could return to the Barren Lands.

It was far from their best option and certainly not the one he'd expected to make when they started this journey. However, it was preferable to being eaten by dogs or tossed to the spiders.

And if they left here, they'd have to go back through those spiders. This time, they'd have fire ready to fight those monsters and, hopefully, an easier time getting through them now that they'd destroyed their web. He dreaded the geyser field the most.

He'd lied to them at dinner. That endless, *exhausting* hell had been far worse for him than the spiders, but he'd kept the truth hidden from the pricks below. They didn't deserve to have it.

His attention shifted to the door leading into Sahira's room. He contemplated knocking on it but didn't want to wake her if she slept.

Sleep was a precious commodity in this place, and they all needed to rest as much as possible to prepare for whatever the dagadon had in store for them. He had a feeling they'd soon be getting a lot less sleep.

CHAPTER THIRTY

THE CLOCK in the corner of her room said it was 1:55 AM when Sahira slipped on the black cloak she found in her closet. With amazingly steady fingers considering the anxiety battering her, she buttoned it into place.

When she finished, she strode over to her balcony doors and inched back the drapes to peer outside. The guards were walking past, and she watched them continue before quietly opening a door and slipping outside.

She'd heard Orin return almost an hour ago and had contemplated knocking to have him join her for this excursion but decided against it. If this decision led to her death, she wouldn't take anyone else with her.

Besides, he'd been down there for a while, drinking with all the others. He was probably at least buzzed, if not drunk, and might not be in the best condition for this. She would have far preferred his shadows to obscure her as she moved through the night, but she could do this without them.

At the edge of the balcony, she leaned over to look down. They were on the second floor, but it was still a good thirty-foot fall, as the ceilings below were high.

Thankfully, next to the balcony, thick green ivy scaled the wall to the roof, where the neatly clipped plant ran around the top of the building. She'd tested the ivy earlier between the guards' patrol and was fairly certain it would hold her weight.

Or at least it had better hold her; it was also the only way she would get back into her room.

Closing the door, she stepped back into the shadows of her balcony and flattened herself against the wall. Sahira hated that she couldn't put a protective spell over her room while gone, but she couldn't risk not getting it down in time for her return.

With her fingers digging into the cool, white brick, Sahira searched the night as she waited for the guards to emerge again. She'd spent a lot of time out here earlier, watching as the patrol ensured the grounds remained safe... or, more likely, that *they* stayed in their rooms. The dagadon had said they were free to explore the area, but she was sure they'd have an entourage with them if they tried.

Over time, she'd learned the guards went by at one-minute intervals. Sometimes, it was a couple of seconds more and some-times a couple of seconds less, but most times, it only took a minute before they stalked past again.

She was certain they continued to another destination, as she'd seen twenty guards walk past throughout the night. There could be other guards in the garden waiting to grab her if she descended, but she hadn't seen them or any signs, such as fright-ened birds or wildlife, to indicate there was something in the woods with them.

Hiding in the shadows of her balcony, Sahira held her breath as two different guards emerged. As they walked toward each other and passed within a foot before moving on toward their next destination, Sahira started counting.

She ensured they were out of view before swinging herself onto the ivy. She swiftly lowered herself to the ground with a deftness born of desperation and a keen awareness of the passing time.

She was still ten feet away from the ground when she released the ivy and jumped off. Her cloak billowed as the air rushed up around her.

Before she hit the ground, she bent her knees to absorb some of the impact. She landed without a sound, and her hand rested on the cool earth as her gaze darted around, but still, nothing moved.

With the seconds ticking away, Sahira rose and sprinted toward the sanctuary of the trees and shrubs. Thirty seconds had passed since she last saw the guards and when she dashed into the garden.

The moon's dim radiance barely lit her way as she waited for someone to seize her, a guard to step in front of her, someone to shout to release the dogs, or for a monster to pounce on her back, but nothing stirred amongst the plants.

If someone happened to be meandering the path tonight, and if Sahira had enough warning, she could cast a glamour over herself to look like one of the Golden Ones, but she didn't dare to stop and do so now. She was fairly sure she'd gotten far enough away that the guards wouldn't hear her, but she wasn't taking any chances.

She was almost to the horse fountain when a figure partially emerged from between a tree and a bush with brilliant purple, drooping flowers. Sahira recognized the woman from her room before she slid back into the shadows.

Turning off the path, Sahira's steps slowed as she eyed where the woman had vanished. She was crazy for doing this, but did she have any other choice?

This woman might know something or be able to help them or might be leading her to her death, but at least it was *something*. She followed the woman between the tree and the bush with flowers the color of the sky and leaves resembling flames.

She spotted the woman ahead as she bent and pushed aside some branches before slipping into what looked like an alcove. Sahira didn't hesitate before ducking down to follow her.

Once inside, the woman released the branches, and they descended back into place with a small swoosh. Blackness encompassed her before a light flared.

CHAPTER THIRTY-ONE

STARTLED BY THE UNEXPECTED FLAME, Sahira stepped away from the candle and found herself in a small space of drooping branches and leaves that brushed her face. But the surrounding area wasn't what unsettled her; it was the *three* Golden Ones standing across from her.

The one in the middle, a tall, thin man with a hawkish nose and stooped shoulders, held the candle. When a strand of his wavy brown hair fell into one of his blue eyes, he pushed it away.

To his right was the woman who had left her the note and had mostly worked with Orin. Her white-blonde hair was tucked beneath the black hood of her cloak, and her dark brown eyes reflected the candle.

Another woman with auburn hair and brown, bloodshot eyes was on the other side of the man. Sahira recognized her as the woman who had cried over the man eaten by the dogs.

"I'm glad you came," the woman who brought her here said. "I tried to get the dark fae to meet with us last night, but he never showed. It's dangerous for us to be out here like this."

Sahira ignored her accusatory tone as she focused on the first part of that statement. "You tried to get *Orin* to meet you?"

"Do you know any other dark fae in this realm?"

"Excuse me if I'm unfamiliar with who does and does not live here. I've been trapped here, tortured, attacked, starved, dehydrated, and exhausted to the brink of death to get here. I'm sure I haven't met everyone here."

She almost added, *you stupid bitch*, but was outnumbered here and not in the mood for a fight.

The woman opened her mouth to respond, but the man held up a hand to silence her. "Easy, Aurora. We're not here to argue; we're here to join forces... or at least we hope so. I'm Clive." He waved at the woman Sahira disliked. "This is Aurora." He shifted his hold on the candle to wave at the other woman. "And this is Alda. We might be able to help you with some of your questions."

Sahira folded her arms over her chest as she eyed them. "And why would you do that?"

"Believe me, we understand hating this place and everything about it. I'm sure you've noticed that they treat us servants poorly too."

Poorly was too kind of a word for how they treated these immortals. Worms on fishing hooks were treated better.

"We're also trapped here," Clive continued.

"Are you now?" Sahira inquired, not sure if she believed him.

"Not quite as badly as you; we don't have guards watching us. We can go through the tunnel and into the Barren Lands, as you call them, but we are not free to leave Epoch. No one is. Like you, we're unable to open portals too."

"Laurent left here to warn you about what you would face if you arrived," Alda said. "There was something about all of you that was different, and we all believed at least a few of you could make it. We'd hoped he could stop you, and maybe you could all figure out how to end this. Did you see him?"

Sahira's arms fell back to her sides. "Someone left here and made his way toward us?"

"Yes. He wouldn't have stayed in any of the towns for long. He knew better than that."

Sahira recalled the scorched immortal they'd discovered on the edge of the geyser field. "We never got to talk to them and have no idea what they looked like, but someone died on the geyser field before we arrived there. We saw proof of him passing through the other towns."

Clive's shoulders sank further as his head bowed. Alda rested her hand on his arm. "Your brother was a good man."

"He's just one more victim of the Elite," Clive muttered.

"So was mine."

"Is that what you call Desmond and his ilk, the Elite?" Sahira asked.

"Yes," Aurora answered.

Sahira met Alda's bloodshot eyes. "Your brother was the one they let the dogs kill today?"

When the woman winced, Sahira regretted her question, but she had to know as much as possible about these immortals. She trusted them as much as she trusted fire not to burn her, and there was a very good possibility she was playing with fire by being here.

"Yes," Alda whispered in a voice choked with tears. "He didn't deserve that."

"No one does," Sahira said. "Is it something they often do?"

"The Elites like to play their games," Aurora answered, "and we're always their targets, but they don't usually kill us."

"If they killed us every time they fucked with us, there would only be them left in Epoch," Clive said. "Today was more of a show for you, to exhibit what they're capable of doing."

Sahira rubbed the bridge of her nose. "We didn't need it; we're *very* aware of what they're capable of doing."

Alda sniffed. "It was fun for them."

"So, they're the Elites; what do they call all of you, commoners?"

"That and serfs, low class, or servants," Clive said.

Aurora's mouth pursed. "Or garbage."

Sahira's eyebrows flew up. "They call you *garbage*?"

"They call us whatever they want to."

"There are far more of you than them; why not rise against them?"

"They have the guards on their side; they're all treated *extremely* well and have the weapons. How do we fight that?" Clive asked.

Sahira had been asking herself the same question for the past two days.

"And some of us are too afraid to fight and would rather have things continue this way."

"Many have had their spirits completely broken," Alda whispered.

Judging by the woman's dejected appearance, Sahira suspected she was on the verge of being one of them. Closing her eyes, she rubbed her temples as she pondered their words.

Though she hated it, she understood why many in this realm were too beaten to rise against their vicious rulers. Years of abuse had inured them to it. Some, if not many, were born into this, and it was all they knew.

"There's no reason for the guards to change things," Aurora said. "They get whatever they want here."

"I see," Sahira murmured.

"And this is the only way of life we know, though many of us have heard stories from our parents or grandparents about better times. Those times were millennia ago, and none of those who knew anything different are still alive."

"I'm sure the Elites had something to do with that."

"They did," Clive confirmed.

The Elites weren't stupid. They were cruel, powerful, and heartless but not stupid.

"How did they become the *Elites*?" Sahira asked.

Clive shrugged. "They've always been that way. Well... not always. Most of the Elites now aren't the original ones who settled this land but are the descendants of those originals."

"You have no enemies here, at least not from what I've seen. How did *any* of them die?" Sahira asked.

"How, indeed?" Alda murmured.

Sahira pictured Desmond's shark-like smile as she came to her own conclusion. "They were in the way and killed because of it."

"Or they knew too much."

Chewing on her bottom lip, Sahira contemplated this revelation. "The other Elites are probably walking a tightrope, hoping they don't get killed too."

"Maybe, but they don't act like it. It's been thousands of years since they died; I think they're pretty secure in their roles now."

Sahira lowered her head to rub her brow as a dull throb started behind her eyes.

"They possess a *lot* of power," Aurora said. "They'll slaughter us if we try to fight them."

"Don't you have the same powers?" Sahira asked.

Clive shook his head. "We don't have the guards, and they have the stones."

CHAPTER THIRTY-TWO

"THE *STONES*?" Before any of them could reply, Sahira held up her hand. "Wait. First, let's start at the beginning. You're the dagadon; not much is known about you other than you can manipulate time. Can you do that?"

"Yes, but not to the extent they are manipulated here and throughout Epoch. We can't stop others from opening portals... at least not without some help," Clive replied. "We can manipulate time so it slows down or speeds up to disorient our opponents. It doesn't affect a fellow dagadon."

Sahira glanced around their small space, but what she really saw was Belda's town and all the immortals trapped there. "Then how does the Cursed Realm exist?"

"Because of the stones. Many millennia ago, our ancestors settled in this valley. The outer reaches of this land, the places you traveled through, also existed, but this valley was lush, beautiful, and safe. When they arrived, they discovered a set of stones. Those stones manipulated and increased their powers into something far different and stronger.

"Over time, the Elites used the stones to twist this realm into a place no one could escape. We've been told this is best for all of us, that we're safe here and no one could come after us," Aurora explained.

"Why would anyone come after you?" Sahira asked.

"They told us the Golden Ones were once hunted for our ability to cast gold."

"So *that's* why gold flecks everything here," she muttered.

"Yes. It is pretty but useless," Alda said. "But it seems others would crave our gift and use it to make them wealthy."

"That's always possible, but many immortals have gifts others crave. Witches and warlocks can cast spells and control the elements, the arach control the dragons, and the dark fae have power over the shadows and elements. We all have something another species covets, but we don't all *hide* because of it."

"We've been told the dagadon were once nearly hunted to extinction," Clive said. "Do you know if this is true?"

"I've never heard that, but I always believed the dagadon were nothing more than a legend told as fascinating bedtime stories. I don't know if the dagadon being hunted is true, but it's doubtful. If immortals started doing that to each other, we'd *all* have to live in constant fear, and *none* of us want that," Sahira said. "Besides, you certainly don't come across as a weak race. It would have taken a *lot* to hunt you to near extinction."

"Even if all the other races ganged up on us? Or the arach unleashed the dragons on us?"

"If that happened, then *no* one would have been able to harvest your magic or gold. You're useless to them if you're dead, so what would be the point?"

They all exchanged glances before Clive spoke. "We don't know. They never informed us about that."

"I also don't understand why they chose to hide instead of fight. You're clearly not a pacifist race."

"We will do what is necessary to survive."

"Then why hide?"

They all looked at each other, but when their gazes fell helplessly on her again, she knew they didn't have an answer. And she imagined much of what they'd been told were lies. Hecate, she yearned to punch that smug smile off Desmond's face.

"Okay, tell me about these stones," Sahira said. "How did they help create the Cursed Realm, and how do they keep all of us from opening portals?"

CHAPTER THIRTY-THREE

"They're called the Augmentation Stones," Clive said.

Sahira searched her memory for any such thing. She'd spent most of her life learning as much as she could about the magical world and its offerings but couldn't recall ever reading or hearing about these stones.

"I've never heard of those," she admitted.

"Until coming here, you believed *we* were a myth," Aurora said. "Just because you've never heard of them doesn't mean they don't exist."

"I never said they didn't exist," Sahira retorted. "I'm saying I've never *heard* of them and don't know what they do."

"They amplify and twist powers into something different and stronger," Clive said. "In Epoch, they've taken our ability to manipulate time and twisted it into something more powerful and malignant. It's why *no* one can open a portal in or out of Epoch. Those stones turned the magic of the original Elite into something malignant, but they allowed it to happen."

"It sounds like they welcomed it," Sahira muttered.

"They did."

"Okay, so originally, Epoch was established to supposedly keep your people safe."

"So they say."

"And what you're telling me is that no matter what, there's no way out of here for us? That even though he said we would be able to leave, Desmond knows we can't."

"Yes," Clive confirmed.

Sahira had suspected as much, but she hated to hear it stated so confidently. "What does he plan to do with us?"

"Do we look like we're privy to the Elite's plans?" Aurora asked. "We're as much cannon fodder for them as all of you."

Her eyes narrowed on the woman who was ridiculously hostile, considering *she* left the note that brought Sahira here. "You're servants; you hear things. You've lived here for centuries, if not more, so you know how they act. Let's not pretend you're completely in the dark about all this."

The woman glared at her, and Sahira returned it until Clive spoke again, and her attention shifted back to him.

"We really don't know. I'm sure it's nothing good, but we didn't expect them to put you in the castle and treat you with such high regard either."

"That was Sheree's idea," Alda said. "That's why she stayed back when everyone else went to greet you. She kept a handful of servants with her to ready the rooms, and I was one of them. She thought it would be fun."

That can't be good, but then, nothing here is.

"Wonderful," Sahira muttered, but she'd have to worry about the implications of that later. Right now, she required more information. "Why were the towns established? Was it just for The Tournament?"

"That took many years of planning," Alda said. "Our ancestors lived there while building each of the separate towns. They established their own homes there for a bit."

Sahira's eyes widened at this revelation. *"That's* why there was evidence of other buildings in Belda's town."

She remembered learning this detail and not understanding it then, but she did now. She hadn't bothered to see if there was evidence of other buildings in the different towns; what would be the point? But there must be.

"Shit," she whispered. "Okay, so they built the towns and came back here after?"

"Some did. Some didn't survive to make it back," Clive said.

"Of course they didn't."

"They also left clues for any immortal who arrived to guide them from the town and into The Tournament."

"Their clues were garbage," Sahira muttered.

The corners of Clive's mouth twitched toward a smile. "We all agree, but the Elites instructed our ancestors to leave them. They mostly wanted to screw with the heads of other immortals."

"They succeeded. So, they built the towns just for The Tournament?"

"Yes. The first immortals who entered a portal into Epoch and became trapped here usually arrived where they erected Belda's town. The brownies are the only ones who have entered The Tournament in a different location. It was quite astonishing when they did so; everyone talked about it for weeks."

"The Elite did *not* like that," Alda said. "They hadn't expected it, and it took some fun out of their game."

Score some points for the little guys for keeping these bastards on their toes.

"In the beginning, our ancestors didn't pay much attention to the immortals who arrived in those outer lands. They had guards and knew they were there, but with no food, many wasted away until they were incapable of moving. The beasts who live here eventually devoured them.

"After a while, the Elites grew bored and decided they needed entertainment. That entertainment came in the form of the immortals who arrived here. They ordered the building of the first town where most of them arrived, on the shore of the lake and near the river.

"They put up seven buildings to help those new arrivals survive, left behind some farm animals, planted crops, established the symbols as clues, and waited. They even gave them books in case they were bored."

"So you can control throwing your gold dust because there was no sign of it in Belda's town?" Sahira asked.

"We can."

"Did they put trapdoors into all of those seven buildings or just the pub?"

"All of them."

Sahira had suspected as much. "And they use the symbols to monitor and learn about the immortals trapped in those towns or traveling through The Tournament."

When Aurora's jaw dropped, Sahira rolled her eyes at Aurora's shock that she'd already deduced this much.

"How did you know that?" Clive asked.

"I pay attention to what's said... like servants do," Sahira stared pointedly at Aurora when she said this.

Aurora's eyes narrowed on her, but she didn't speak.

"How much can they see and hear through those symbols?" Sahira asked.

"They can't see anything, but they hear everything inside the buildings with symbols."

Sahira struggled to keep from blushing as she recalled what she'd done with Orin and their conversations in some of those buildings. They'd been private conversations that were no one else's business but were probably known to everyone in this realm.

Her fingers dug into her palms as her teeth scraped together while she kept her temper restrained. These monsters had done so many things to violate all of them, this was little compared to that, but it still infuriated her.

"They probably didn't expect them to build other homes," Sahira murmured, "and assumed they could eavesdrop on them all the time."

"Probably not, and while they gave them enough to survive there, they didn't expect the immortals to settle in and make it home either. Enough of them still traveled out to make it interesting for the Elites," Alda said. "They bet on *everything*."

Everything was a game to these immortals. The Cursed Realm and their suffering were nothing more than fun for the Elites of Epoch. She didn't know what to think or how to process that.

"What about the scarog beetles? How do they only arrive once a year and have such a set time limit?" she asked.

"They celebrate that day here," Alda said. "It's called the Bloodletting. The Elites gather everyone in the realm to listen and watch as the scarogs descend on the town. Even though they designed the buildings to withstand an attack from them, we all know at least one immortal, and usually *more*, will perish. They take bets on who will die."

CHAPTER THIRTY-FOUR

"AGAIN WITH THE BETS," Sahira muttered.

"There's little else for them to do here," Clive said. When Sahira shot him a look, he held up his hands in a pacifying gesture. "I'm not condoning it. I'm just saying it's how they entertain themselves."

"If the symbols are only for hearing, how do they watch?" Sahira inquired.

"The dagadon have some control over animals too. On the day of the Bloodletting, the Elites combine their powers to take control of the beetles. Through their eyes and ears, we can see and hear what happens to the unfortunate souls unable to evade them."

She was almost one of those unfortunate souls, but thankfully, Orin saved her from such a fate.

"And when the Bloodletting ends, they send the scarogs back?" she asked.

"Yes. They far prefer the caves located miles away from Belda's town. They remain there, hunting the smaller creatures who live in the caverns until the Elites get bored and decide to have another Bloodletting. They'd probably do it more than once a year if it wasn't for the fact they'd lose too many immortals and make it more boring for them," Aurora said.

"And Hecate forbid we have *that*," Sahira said. "Is it the same with the spiders? Did they also watch us through the spiders?"

"Yes," Clive said.

The more she learned, the more she hated the dagadon. "Did they somehow watch us on the geyser field?"

"No," Alda said. "They had to wait and see if you made it to the next town."

"Good." Sahira shifted her attention to Clive. "So, they knew your brother was trying to find us. That means they know they have followers who aren't happy with how they run things."

"They're not stupid; they know many of the servants are unhappy."

"I wouldn't be so certain. Arrogance goes a long way to making others blind to what they don't want to see."

The three of them exchanged an uneasy glance. "There's nothing we can do about it, and they've done nothing different, so all we can do is continue as if everything is the same," Clive said.

"So why are you telling me all this?" she inquired. "What do you expect to happen?"

"Originally, we intended to tell the dark fae," Aurora said. "We felt his ability to move through the shadows might help us, but the stupid man never arrived, so we settled for you, as you seem to have some control over him."

At first, Sahira was irritated by the woman's *"so we settled for you"* comment, but she couldn't stop laughing at the woman's final words. "No one has any control over Orin. *No one.*"

"Some influence then." Alda couldn't keep the hopeful tone from her voice.

Sahira had about as much influence as the moon over Orin,

but she kept that to herself. They might stop talking to her if she said so. "What do you want him to do?"

"Find the stones and destroy them," Clive said. "If he destroys the stones, he'll ruin the spell, and we can *finally* be free."

From what she knew of the dagadon, having them roaming the realms might not be such a good idea, but if they didn't do something soon, she and all her friends would die. She didn't doubt it.

It didn't matter that she didn't trust these beings; they had to find the stones and break the spell. If all went well, they'd also take out many of these monsters before leaving here.

"Do you know where the stones are?" she asked.

All three of them shook their heads.

"How do you expect us to do anything without some insight into where to start?"

"They can't be in the castle," Aurora said. "I've been inside every room and know *every* nook and cranny; they can't be there."

"So have I," Alda said, "and I agree."

"And what about hidden passages, such as the ones your ancestors created in the towns? We weren't given any hints about their existence?" Sahira demanded. "What did they expect to happen if Orin and I didn't know about the one in the pub?"

"I'm sure they planned to take bets on if you would continue into oblivion, stay there and die, or come up with another option," Clive said. "There is no other way into Epoch as all the hidden rooms filter into what was once a cave. The tunnel you walked through, and the town, were all part of the cave."

"More bets." Sahira pinched the bridge of her nose. "Could there be hidden passages in the castle?"

Aurora bit her bottom lip as she pondered this, but the woman couldn't be so stubborn, or stupid, as to deny the possibility. "Yes," she finally admitted.

"Fantastic," Sahira said. "Because we didn't find the one that brought us here; Radagast did. Without him, we wouldn't have known it existed. Which means there could be any number of passages in the castle that we're supposed to wander around trying to find."

CHAPTER THIRTY-FIVE

"THE DARK FAE can hide in the shadows," Aurora said as if Sahira were stupid.

"Yes, but if he's wandering around in the shadows searching for hidden doors and finds them, then he might alert someone to his presence. And without a place to start the search, it's like looking for a needle in a haystack."

"You have a place, the castle."

It would take a miracle for Sahira to walk away without punching Aurora tonight. "That's the *fucking* haystack," she bit out through her teeth.

"He'll have to make sure no one is around while he's exploring."

"Such a simple answer from a simple girl," Sahira retorted. "Because there aren't guards, servants, and Elites crawling all over that place."

Aurora's face reddened as they glowered at each other. "*You* made it out."

"I made it past *two* guards. Who knows how many are still in that castle because they are *very* aware of what Orin can do."

Clive rested his hand on Aurora's shoulder and pulled her

back a step as he spoke to Sahira. She relaxed a little but still scowled at Sahira, who chose to ignore her.

"I know it sounds daunting and impossible, but it's the only hope we have," Clive said.

"What if the stones aren't in the castle?" Sahira asked. "This is a vast land. Is he supposed to search the whole thing before they toss us in the dungeon, feed us to the dogs, or send the scarogs after us?"

"He's the only hope we have," Alda whispered. "Your arrival is the first thing that's changed in this realm in thousands of years. That has to *mean* something; you *must* be able to help. We can't keep living like this."

Neither could she, but Sahira didn't point that out, especially since her life expectancy was probably far shorter than theirs in this place.

"What's with the town?" she asked. "Why the houses and the sliding figures?"

"Just another part of the game," Clive said. "I bet it's creepy when you don't know what's happening."

"It is," Sahira said.

She crossed her arms over her chest as she contemplated everything they'd revealed tonight. She didn't trust these three. This could all be a new game they were playing, one the Elites were aware of, but she didn't see what other options they had than to try to find those stones.

"Are they listening to us in the castle? Are there symbols in the rooms?" she asked.

She'd done a cursory search for trapdoors and hadn't seen any symbols in the process, but she hadn't taken as much time as she should have to examine every centimeter of her room.

"No," Alda said. "The Elite all live within those walls; if they start spying on each other, it would be revealed, as there's only *one* place where you can listen to everything happening throughout the towns. The symbols are all interconnected."

"Could Sheree have put the symbols in there when you readied the rooms for us?"

"No. It would have taken too long to carve them and connect them to the system. Plus, she watched over us like a hawk, and I never saw her move out of any of the doorways."

Sahira wanted to believe the woman, but she would tear her room apart the first chance she got and tell all the others about this development.

"Okay," Sahira said. "Then we'll try to stay on Desmond's good side, and hopefully, he'll decide to keep us around for a little longer if we do."

"It's not Desmond you have to worry about; it's *her*," Clive said. "*She's* the one with all the power, and the only Elite left who helped establish this realm. She'll do everything she can to keep us here and under her control."

"Who, Sheree?"

"Yes."

Sahira hadn't expected this revelation. "But Desmond acts as if he rules this land. Did she cede some of her power to him when they married?"

Aurora released a bitter laugh. "They're not married."

"*What?*"

"That must have been something they came up with to tell you, another mind game to play," Clive said. "But they're not married. *She's* the one with the true power and the only one who knows where those stones are."

"Sheree is the true evil here," Alda said.

CHAPTER THIRTY-SIX

SAHIRA CLIMBED the ivy and returned to her room. Once there, she worked as quietly as she could to search it. She pulled all the clothes out of the closet, ran her fingers over the wall, and examined the white brick.

She looked under her bed, lifted the mattress, and examined the floorboards before doing the same to the bathroom. Once satisfied that she'd covered everything, including the sparse furniture, she went to the door separating her room from Orin's.

She undid the bolt on her side of the door and hesitated before knocking. According to the clock on the wall, she was only in the garden for less than half an hour. She'd spent another hour going over her room.

He'd stayed up late with the dagadon and was drinking when she left him. He was most likely sound asleep, but that's not what stayed her hand.

She didn't care if she woke him... she cared there might be someone else in the room with him.

He hadn't been with anyone else since she arrived in the Cursed Realm, but that could change. If he opened the door to reveal another woman in there, she might lose it.

She'd had about all she could take in this realm and couldn't handle that blow on top of everything else. However, she had to tell someone about everything she'd learned, and since Zeth and Elsa were across the hall, and the brownies were on the other side of Orin, that left only him.

Plus, *he* was the one she wanted to discuss this with. She cared for all the others, but he was something more to her.

She couldn't analyze what it meant that he was the first one she sought to turn to with this information. The first one she *always* wanted to turn to.

She was aware of what it meant for her. The only problem was, he was so fucked in the head, it would most likely end in disaster for them.

With no other choice, she knocked on the door. And when he didn't immediately answer, she hit it a little louder. She couldn't bang too hard, or she might attract the attention of the guards in the hall, but she wouldn't have another chance to talk to him until tomorrow night.

She had no doubt the dagadon servants would swarm in on them again tomorrow morning. Thankfully, they weren't early risers, so she might be able to catch an hour or two of sleep before the farce of why they were here started all over again.

Sahira tried the knob. It twisted in her hand, but the door remained bolted on his side. She knocked on the door again, and this time, though she kept it low, she didn't stop.

After thirty knocks, the slide of a bolt came from the other side before the door swung inward to reveal Orin. He ran a hand through the tussled black hair framing the elegant planes of his face.

His arrival at the door threw her back to Belda's pub and another time when she woke him in the middle of the night. Then, she'd been convinced he was attacking her while she slept.

She later found out it was Radagast, but she'd accused Orin

of it first, and he'd looked as delectable then as he did now. Why did the man *always* look so tempting? And *why* was his favorite state nude?

"Couldn't you put some clothes on before you answered the door?" she demanded.

His sleepy-eyed look vanished as he scowled at her. "Excuse me for not preparing for company at *four-thirty* in the morning."

Irritated with herself for wanting nothing more than to step closer, slide her arms around his waist, and kiss him, Sahira glowered in response. She crossed her arms over her chest to keep from touching him as she rocked back on her heels.

Unable to stop herself, her gaze flicked beyond him to the bed. The blanket and sheets were thrown back, but she didn't see anyone else.

She hated the relief that flooded her. *You're in so much trouble.*

Sahira didn't bother denying it as she shifted her attention back to his lean frame with its chiseled muscles. Black ciphers ran across his upper chest and arms before ending at his wrists.

She suspected he had more of the dark fae markings—the sign of how powerful they were—but hadn't seen them and probably never would. Orin wasn't the type to let down his defenses enough for that to happen.

If he ever did.... She let the hopeful pondering trail off as she decided not to let her mind travel down a route that would never happen.

"Is there a reason you woke me up?" he inquired. "Or was it just to bitch at me?"

Her glower deepened as she grasped his wrist. Ignoring the thrill of electricity and excitement that ran through her at the feel of his warm skin, Sahira pulled him into her room.

Since she hadn't examined his room yet, she said, "I'm feeling a little lonely."

She looked back at his disheveled bed again before pulling his door closed and locking it. When she turned back to him, all of Orin's sleepiness vanished as he grinned at her.

CHAPTER THIRTY-SEVEN

WHEN HE REACHED FOR HER, she slapped his hands away and danced back a few steps. Before he could say or do anything, she placed a finger against her lips. He frowned but didn't speak as he tilted his head to study her.

Sahira waved her fingers in an intricate dance while whispering the words to cast a silencing spell that wouldn't let anything they said go beyond them. If the dagadon were listening somehow, this would probably make them suspicious, but they had to know Sahira and the others didn't trust them.

Maybe this would confirm for them that Sahira suspected they were listening. But hopefully, they'd assume she sought to keep their sounds of passion from the guards in the hall.

When she finished, she lowered her hands. "Now we can talk, and they won't hear us."

"We can talk later. You just told me you were lonely."

"I lied. We have to talk."

"Talk?"

"Yes. You know that thing where immortals and humans exchange words in conversation."

"I know what *talking* is, but I have far better things in mind, and you know what those things are. You enjoy them too. I know that because I've heard you scream my name while begging for more."

She rolled her eyes as she tried to suppress the heat and enticing memories his words elicited. Oh, she'd begged, and he'd gladly given it to her. "Keep your dick in your pants."

"I'm not wearing pants."

"Metaphorically, then."

Amusement shone in his eyes. "I don't do metaphorical."

"Orin!" She threw her hands up in exasperation. "Stop being an asshole!"

He sighed before looking at his erection and patting its head. "Sorry, old friend. She got us all excited to *talk*."

She rolled her eyes again. "You're such an ass."

"I'm the ass? You're the one who keeps waking me up in the middle of the night to yell at me. I'm not the best when it comes to social etiquette because I usually don't give a fuck, but yours is *far* worse than mine."

Knowing they could banter like this all night and get nowhere, Sahira decided to plunge into why they were here. "Earlier tonight, I received a note telling me to meet someone in the garden at two."

The twinkle of amusement left his eyes as his gaze flicked to the clock in the corner of her room. "You didn't go, did you?"

"Of course I did."

"What were you thinking?" he exploded.

When she first met Orin, the amount of emotion he revealed was similar to a rock, and almost all of that emotion was amusement at the expense of others. Now, she'd seen him angry far more times than she'd believed possible.

He'd directed that anger at her before, and it was back again now. Orin wasn't as irate as he was in Belda's pub after realizing she'd fed from Zeth and believed she'd slept with the demon, but he was still steaming.

"*Why* would you do something so risky?" he demanded as he stepped toward her.

Sahira planted her feet, refusing to back away as she lifted her chin and glared at him. "I was thinking I might get some answers."

"You're not to go anywhere in this realm by *yourself* in the middle of the night, *ever*."

She planted her index finger in his chest and poked him. "And *you* don't have any right to try to command me, *ever*."

"Someone has to look out for you. You're clearly not using your head."

Sahira regretted her decision to tell him about what happened tonight. She hadn't expected him to be thrilled with her, but.... "I'm not a child. I'll do whatever I want and make my *own* decisions. You chose not to go without discussing it with me, so why would I tell *you* about *my* choice to go?"

Orin folded his arms over his chest as he rocked back on his heels. "Who left you this note?"

"Aurora, the woman who usually works with you. When you stayed behind to drink with Desmond, she came to my room to help the others."

"And she told you she left me a note too?"

"Yes."

He ran a hand through his disheveled hair. "Who did you meet?"

"Aurora and two other servants, Clive and Alda. Alda was the one crying during the dog attack earlier; the victim was her brother."

Orin showed no emotion over this revelation. It was so strange to her how some things could set him off so much, yet he could remain completely unbothered by other things... like dogs tearing an immortal to pieces and the suffering of his poor sister.

"And what did they have to say?" he asked.

CHAPTER THIRTY-EIGHT

ORIN GROUND his teeth together as he struggled to keep his temper under control. He hadn't gone into the garden because of *her*, but now she was telling him that she'd traipsed her ass out there to meet strangers at two o'clock in the morning. *Alone!*

He wanted to throttle her as badly as kiss her, and it took everything he had not to shake some sense into her thick head. While she spoke, some of his irritation faded as disbelief and fury over her revelations replaced it.

When she finished telling him everything she'd learned and what the servants wanted from him, his gaze focused on the balcony doors and closed drapes. He should have been the one to meet with and judge them while they spoke. He was very good at picking out a liar.

"So they can manipulate time," he murmured, "and it doesn't work against another dagadon."

"They also have some control over creatures and magical abilities."

"Any weaknesses?"

"The Elites and guards are too arrogant for their own good. They don't see us as a threat."

Orin smiled grimly. "And they're completely wrong in that."

"They are."

He looked at her again. "Do you believe there really aren't any symbols in this building?"

"I searched every inch of this room when I returned from talking with them and found nothing. If the dagadon all started spying on each other, it would get ugly, and even if they are all crazy, they know it won't be good if the Elites turn on each other."

"True. How do we know those servants are telling the truth?"

"We don't. What they said tonight could all be part of some game the Elites put them up to. Everything they said could have been a lie; I knew that while speaking with them, but I had to hear what they said."

"You shouldn't have gone alone. You should have gotten me first."

"You stayed up late with Desmond and his psychopathic non-wife. Plus, the note was left for me."

"I was trying to learn more about the ruling couple... or apparently, *not* a couple."

He'd always enjoyed his games, but the dagadon were truly fucked. *I wonder if they know what's real and what isn't anymore.*

Probably not.

"Okay," Sahira said. "So, we're learning more about them, at least."

"Do you think those stones really exist?"

Sahira shrugged. "It makes sense. The dagadon are powerful, but they don't have the strength to shut down a whole realm without some help to boost their strength. If they had those kinds of powers, they wouldn't have to fear being hunted and destroyed by other immortals."

"That could have all been a lie too."

"I know." She bit her bottom lip. "Maybe they were playing

one of their games and became trapped here. Or maybe, this is what the Elites want. What do they have to complain about? They have everything they desire here: money, wealth, entertainment, and a *ton* of power."

Orin rubbed the scruff on his chin while pondering her words. "I'm going to have to start looking for those stones."

Sahira looked at the clock. "There's not enough time tonight. There's no guarantee you'd be back before they come to get us. Besides, where would you start? This place isn't the biggest castle I've been in, but there are a *lot* of rooms, and any number of them could contain a hidden room.

"The trapdoor in my room at Belda's pub was so perfectly hidden *no* one knew it was there for centuries. And the servants tonight said there were other trapdoors in *all* the towns. As far as we know, no one ever found those either. What are the chances we'll find a hidden room in this place?"

"No one was looking for those rooms. I'll be looking for them now."

"You can't go out there on your own."

He snorted a laugh. "Isn't that what *you* did?"

"One of us had to go. And why *didn't* you go when you got the note?"

"Because Aurora was also instructed to have sex with me, or maybe she was willing to do it, as most women are."

"Oh, she was willing," Sahira muttered.

"How do you know that?"

Her eyes narrowed as her tone turned hostile. "I just do."

He didn't know what happened in that garden, but it was clear Sahira didn't like Aurora. "If I'd allowed it, she would have fucked me in the bathing chamber, and I turned her down. I wasn't going to encourage her by meeting her in the garden."

"Why did you turn her down?"

He blinked at her as if she'd spoken a foreign language. For a second, he almost believed she might have.

Did she really just ask him why he didn't go screw another woman under a bush? After everything they'd been through, she should already know the answer.

But when she continued staring at him, he realized the stubborn, maddening woman expected an explanation from him.

Unable to control his temper, he threw his hands in the air. "You've *got* to be kidding me! Are you being purposely obtuse, or do you just enjoy *pissing*. Me. Off?"

When her eyes widened, he shook his head and restrained himself from shouting at her again. Yelling wouldn't solve any of this, but he didn't know how to get through to her.

"I don't…. I'm not sure what to say," he told her. "I told you I haven't fucked any other women since you were trapped here. Aurora made it *very* clear she was willing to have sex with me. Maybe she was trying to talk to me then, but I wasn't going to let her in that room."

When Sahira started to speak, he held up his hand to hold off whatever she might say. "And not because I didn't trust myself with her. I didn't *want* to fuck her. I don't know what else you want from me, Sahira. I've told you the truth about all of it."

"How am I supposed to know that for sure? Just like these *things*, you've done nothing but play games with me since I entered the Cursed Realm. You manipulated me, used me, and purposely tried to make me think you were having sex with other women to hurt me. You think I'm wrong for doubting you, when *you're* why I do."

Orin closed his eyes and flinched when she compared him to the dagadon. He *never* wanted to be like them, but to her, he was. And he'd *never* meant to hurt her.

There was a time when he didn't think he could trust her, but he'd been wrong. He trusted her with his life; she'd become so important to him, and he couldn't lose her.

He'd always believed caring for others was a weakness; it

wasn't. Yes, it might get him killed because he would do whatever it took to keep her alive, but she didn't weaken him.

If anything, she made him stronger because he would savage this realm, and everyone in it, to ensure her happiness. She was fuel for the fire already inside him.

"I'm sorry," he said. "I really am, but I can't take it back. And I never meant to hurt you."

"You didn't mean to hurt me? What did you *think* would happen when you started acting like you were having sex with a bunch of other women?"

"I didn't know, and that's what I was trying to find out," he admitted.

Am I really saying this? But he was, and he wasn't going to stop.

"I was trying to see how you'd react."

"Why?" she demanded.

"Because I wanted to know how *you* felt!"

CHAPTER THIRTY-NINE

SAHIRA BLINKED at him as his shouted words sank in. First, had he *really* just apologized? To her? She didn't think he knew the word sorry, never mind actually *use* it, but she was sure she'd heard it come from his mouth.

She started to respond, but no words came out, so she stood there, gawking at him. Finally, she found words again. "Why did you want to know how I felt?"

He scowled at the wall over her head before lowering his gaze to the floor. "I was trying to see if that night, our first night, felt as different to you as it did to me."

Sahira's breath sucked in when he lifted his head and their gazes locked. In his eyes was a vulnerability she'd never expected to see from Orin as he stared pleadingly at her.

"I would take it back if I could, Sahira." He ran a hand through his hair and tugged at the ends of it. "But I can't change the past. I wish I could. All I can do is assure you that you're not a game to me anymore."

"What am I to you?"

He lifted his hands helplessly before they fell back to his sides. "A friend."

She'd once told him he had no friends, and she'd firmly believed it. Outside his family, Orin was a man who didn't forge bonds with others, but when he said this, she believed him.

For Orin to consider her a friend was a big step forward for him. However, she craved more than friendship from him.

"Someone I care about," he continued.

His gaze focused on the balcony doors as his brow furrowed. He seemed to be piecing it together while he spoke.

"Someone I can't lose." When his eyes shifted to hers again, confusion and something more shimmered in them. "I... I care about you, Sahira. I may not have all my shit together like you want and deserve, but that much is true. I *care* about you."

She had no idea what to say.

"And before you ask," he continued, "I don't know what it means because it's never happened to me. But I promise you, this isn't a game; it's the absolute truth. I'll do whatever it takes to make you believe me."

She could only stand there and stare at him with her mouth hanging open, which she was sure made her look like an idiot. Orin loved his games, but truth emanated from his voice and eyes; he was desperate for her to believe him.

Standing there, she knew the truth. She wanted more from him. She wanted *love* because that's what she was willing to give him.

At one time, she believed he could never care about anyone beyond himself and his family, but she'd been wrong. He cared for her, too, and was saying things she *never* would have believed possible for him.

"I know you want something more, a better understanding of it all, or maybe a commitment...." His words trailed off as he tugged at his hair again.

The distress emanating from him pulled at her heart, but she was still too stunned to move or speak.

"Or maybe you don't. I don't know what you want either,

Sahira. I was trying to find out by making you think I'd slept with those other women, and it just... it made you furious with me when you learned the truth.

"There are no more games between us. They ended a long time ago. They didn't end as soon as they should have; that's my fault, and I regret it. I don't know what you want from me or what I can give you, but I can assure you that I'll get you out of this alive, and there won't be any other women while whatever this is between us is going on. It will be *only* you."

Sahira still couldn't find words as hope and resignation radiated from him. He wasn't promising her forever; hell, she'd never considered forever from him. She knew she was falling in love with him and had believed she was tumbling over that deadly cliff by herself... until now.

He might not be as far gone as her in his feelings... or maybe he was. He was a fucked-in-the-head dark fae, after all. She imagined that when they started falling for someone, they turned into a complete mess and fought it every step of the way, like him.

And maybe he'd never completely fall. Maybe he'd never be able to give her anything more than this, and she would walk away with a broken heart, but she was walking into it with eyes open.

Maybe they wouldn't have forever, but they could have now. Besides, given their current situations, now could be a day, a week, or mere hours.

Was she going to keep fighting with him over semantics while a guillotine hung over their heads?

"I'm sure you're exhausted." He turned away and reached for the bolt. "I'll let you get some sleep."

Like she could sleep after all of this. As he started to open the door, she finally shook off her paralysis and strode toward him. She wrapped her fingers around his arm.

She knew what she was doing and what might come from this, but she didn't care. She would have now.

And she would have him.

CHAPTER FORTY

"Stay," she whispered.

Orin studied the determined countenance on her face as she uttered the word he'd longed to hear, but she couldn't hide the fear in her eyes. He hated that fear because it wasn't for this place or the uncertainty of their future; it was because of *him* and the uncertainty of everything they were to each other.

It was a fear he couldn't ease with promises he couldn't make. But he would do everything in his power not to hurt her or prove that fear correct, even if doing so went against all his instincts.

When he touched her face, her hand fell from his arm as his fingers caressed her cheek. He'd already memorized every curve and contour of this woman, but he couldn't stop exploring her.

Is there anyone as beautiful as Sahira? He didn't think so.

His hand slid back until he found the knot she'd tied into her hair, and with deft fingers, he undid it. The mahogany waves cascaded around her shoulders and spilled down her back.

Her delicate yet proud face lifted as he slid his fingers through the silken waves. Always, with women, sex was the first thing on his mind. Sure, he enjoyed teasing and playing with them, but he'd never savored them as he did her.

He intended to remember every detail of her and this night.

Her breath caught a little, and red glinted in her amber eyes as his finger nudged the tip of a fang until a bead of blood shimmered on the end. He smiled when she licked the blood from him.

Undoing the button of her cloak, he dropped it on the floor. They would talk again about her decision to go into the garden alone, but not tonight. Tonight was for *them*.

Beneath the cloak, she wore a black shirt and dark brown pants. When he started unbuttoning her shirt, she didn't move while watching him leisurely reveal her tantalizing, creamy skin.

He was tormenting himself and loving every second of it as he bared more and more of her to him. The shirt fell open when he finished with the buttons, revealing the lacy black bra beneath. She hadn't chosen this; it wasn't something Sahira would wear, but his mouth watered at the tantalizing view of her nipples against the lace.

Unable to resist, he skimmed his knuckles across one of those nipples and smiled when her breath sucked in. "You're so exquisite, *my* enchantress."

The sexy smile tugging at her lips caused his already rigid cock to jump in anticipation of being deep inside her. His fingers grazed her arms as he pulled the shirt off and tossed it aside.

While he enjoyed the bra and how little it hid from him, it wasn't her. She only wore it because the dagadon had put it on her.

She gasped a little when he didn't bother to undo the clasp but instead grasped the back and tore it free. They'd never put it on her again.

When he removed the straps, he revealed her beautiful, firm breasts and dark nipples. Settling his hands on the curve of her tight ass, he pulled her a step closer before taking one of those nipples into his mouth.

Not only did she smell of honey, but she tasted of it too. Sweet and savory, she was warm and yielding as her back arched and the ends of her hair caressed his hands.

For the first time, she touched him as her fingers threaded through his hair to rub the tips of his ears. He shivered with pleasure when she found the sensitive spots.

With one hand, he found the button on her pants and undid it. He was reluctant to stop tasting her but planned to do so in another way as his mouth trailed down the valley between her breasts, flat belly, and lower while he pushed her pants to the floor.

He removed one boot and the other before helping her from her pants. Settling his hands on her thighs, he looked up to watch her while nudging them further apart.

Passion clouded her eyes, and he smiled before bringing his mouth to her hot, wet center. Sahira's fingers threaded through his hair while he licked, tasted, and teased until her legs quaked and her hips thrust toward him.

When he sensed she was on the verge of coming, he broke away, rose, and grasped her ass again. He lifted her until her legs locked around his waist.

With every tortured step he took toward the bed, she rubbed against the head of his shaft. He gritted his teeth against the urge to plunge in and fuck her until they were both too spent to move, but somehow, he resisted.

Settling her on the bed, he lowered himself but still didn't enter her. Instead, his mouth found hers again as his fingers stroked her clit.

Her hips rose to meet him as her excitement grew again, but when he pulled away once more, she moaned her displeasure and nipped his bottom lip. Orin smiled as her lengthened fangs told him she was starting to lose control... just how he liked her.

With deft movements, he rolled her onto her stomach and kissed and licked his way from her nape to her toes.

"Orin," she panted.

"What is it, little witch?" He slid his hand between her legs once more. "You are so wet and tight."

She lifted her hips toward him, begging him to ease her. "That's because I want you."

Those words sent a firestorm of emotion and desire racing through him. All he had to do was lift himself a little more, and he could be inside her.

Instead, he settled against her back and lifted her wrists over her head to pin them on the pillow. "The sounds you make and the way you whisper my name make me so hard I can barely think."

"I can solve that problem," she said with another wiggle of her hips.

Somehow managing to keep himself from unraveling and giving in to her, he shifted her wrists into one hand and moved his other toward her clit again. The stroke he gave it caused her to buck beneath him.

"Do I make you as wild as you make me?" he asked.

Her words came out as pants as he teased her. "More so."

Despite the tension growing inside, he chuckled and bent his lips to her ear. "I doubt that. Are you going to beg me for release?"

Her head turned on the pillow. "Is that what you want me to do?"

"No. I want to hear you say I'll be the only man you're fucking from here on out."

Despite the quiver in her body and need for release, she stubbornly set her chin. "If you say the same thing."

"I already told you that while this is happening between us, there will be no others. You've made no such promise."

He didn't realize how much that bothered him until now. He

was on the verge of finally being inside her again, and his cock ached from the blood filling it, but he'd walk away if he didn't hear those words.

"Say it, Sahira."

"You're the only man I'll fuck," she promised. "As long as *I'm* the only woman *you* fuck, no one else will have me."

"You're right about that," he growled as he finally entered her.

When her inviting sheath enveloped him, he groaned. She was so exquisite it was as if she were made for him.

She made him feel better than anyone ever had, but it was more than that. Being inside her was like coming home. He never wanted to leave as he thrust deeper, harder, and longer while her fingers dug into the pillow.

He was so close to release, but needing to see her again, he pulled out and rolled her over. When he joined with her again, he claimed her mouth in a kiss that demanded everything from her, as his body did.

He wouldn't take anything less than everything from her and would make sure she gave it to him. As power swirled between them, he feasted on the energy their sex created, sating the dark fae hunger, but when it came to her, he didn't think he'd ever be completely satisfied.

He'd always clamor for more.

Knowing she had to be hungry too, he broke the kiss and turned his neck for her to feed. His hands compressed on her when her fangs sank into his throat. Together, they made each other stronger as they cried out in ecstasy while also demanding more.

He didn't know when they finally separated, but he was exhausted and panting for air when he drew her into his arms and held her. It would be a long time before he let her go again.

CHAPTER FORTY-ONE

EVERY TIME HE DRIFTED AWAKE, Orin would reach for her and smile when rewarded with her presence. Sometimes, they would have sex again; other times, her presence soothed him, and he fell back asleep.

It was midmorning when he woke again to find her nestled securely against him. He'd woken with other women before, but never to discover his arms locked around them and his nose buried in their hair so he could inhale their scent.

He did so now, and when he did, he smiled as his hand flattened on her belly and slid a little lower.

"Haven't you had enough?" she murmured.

"I'm a dark fae; there's no such thing as enough. Are you done with me?"

Her mouth twitched toward a smile, but the circles under her eyes spoke of her exhaustion. His hand stilled on her before returning to her belly as he pulled her closer. Yes, he'd like to ease his rigid cock again, but it could wait.

"I didn't say to stop," she said. "Just let me sleep through some of it."

He burst out laughing before bending to kiss her cheek. "No one sleeps through anything I do."

"Hmm," she murmured as her eyes closed. "Let me be the judge of that."

He decided to do exactly that as he explored her body while listening to small shifts in her breathing. She kept her eyes closed, but her legs parted for him. When he climbed on top and planted his hands on either side of her head, he bent to nibble on her bottom lip.

"You're still awake," he murmured.

She cracked an eye open. "Am I? I think you'll have to do something a little bit *more* to make sure of it."

"You're a saucy little enchantress."

When he entered her, she cried out, and her fingers dug into his back as her legs encircled his waist. Grabbing her by the hips, he rolled over to settle her on top.

It was where he far preferred her, so he could watch as delight played across her features and her breasts swayed enticingly when her head tipped back. She was beautiful, and she was *his*.

He was fascinated by her as she circled her hips and came with a loud cry. With her muscles contracting around his shaft, he followed her over the edge as tingles ran down his spine and his back arched off the bed.

It was a good thing he'd brought his potion for birth control with him on this journey. Otherwise, she might end up with his babe inside her, as he knew she hadn't come prepared.

Would that be so bad?

The shock accompanying the idea left him immobile as she slumped against him before rolling to the side. He'd never considered children before, *never* wanted to be a father or tied down by kids.

But as his hand rested against her flat belly, he couldn't help thinking he'd enjoy seeing her heavy with *his* child. *What is wrong with me?*

Many immortals would say *many* things were wrong with him, but he'd always been perfect the way he was. *Everyone changes.*

It was true, and while he'd never seen a reason to change before, he'd gone and done so anyway... because of her. And now, just maybe, he'd like to be a father.

But such a thing wouldn't be possible while stuck in this realm. He threaded his fingers through hers while her breathing and pulse slowed.

"I'm glad I finally got to fuck you in a *real* bed and not some mattress on the floor or rocks," he said.

She laughed before lifting her head and folding her hands on his chest to rest her chin on them. "I didn't think conditions mattered to you."

He grinned at her. "Oh, nothing will stop me, and I'd already decided I'd fuck you on a bed of nails, but I'm also a prince who appreciates luxury."

He loved the way her eyes twinkled with amusement. They warmed his heart and soul, which he'd never believed possible.

He brushed the hair back from her face as he relished her beauty. *I'm a lucky man.*

After everything he'd done to her, she had every right to hate him, but for some reason, she was smiling at him like he was the greatest thing in the world. He'd do anything to ensure that didn't change.

He lifted his head to kiss her as a knock sounded on the door. "Ignore it."

She met his lips, and the kiss deepened while the knocking grew louder. With a groan, Orin fell back. "Fuck off!"

Sahira chuckled. "The muffling spell is still intact."

She waved her fingers in an intricate pattern as she worked to release the muffling spell and alarm she set before they first fell asleep. When she finished, she rested her hands on his chest again.

As more knocking sounded, Orin yelled at them again. This time, he got a reply. "Desmond has requested you all join him for brunch."

"Now they'll know you spent the night here," she said.

"We're not hiding anything about our relationship from them, Sahira. We never have."

"I know, but he's going to use it against us."

"Yes, he will."

And the only thing he could do to stop it was find a way out of this place. So far, that hadn't proven to be a simple feat, but he *would* do it.

When the doorknob rattled, Orin shifted Sahira and tossed a blanket over *his* witch. Leaping to his feet, he made it to the door as it started opening.

He grasped it before it could swing too far and scowled at the woman before him. It wasn't Aurora, but he recognized the woman as the one who dealt with Sahira the most.

"I didn't say you could come in," he snarled.

When the woman took a startled step back, a guard loomed up behind her. "Your presence has been requested, and you will honor the command," the guard barked.

"We'll get *ourselves* ready."

The woman shoved a dress and undergarments into his hands. "Aurora has your things."

With those words, she hastily retreated, and Orin slammed the door shut. He turned to find Sahira sitting up in bed with an eyebrow quirked at him.

"You didn't have to scare the woman," she said.

"They have no right coming in here... unless you give them permission."

"We have no rights here."

He couldn't argue with that as he lifted the black dress.

Colorful butterflies interwove the bodice and skirt, and dozens of buttons ran up the back.

"I can figure this out," he said.

"Really? Because I'd guess you're only an expert in taking them off, not putting them on."

Before lifting his head to her, Orin braced himself for her irritation; instead, she smiled again. Rising from the bed, she glided over and kissed his cheek.

"Come now, dark fae, I'll teach you something new," she said.

"I'm always up for something new, Enchantress."

She smiled as she sauntered into the bathroom with her hips swaying.

CHAPTER FORTY-TWO

BRUNCH WAS STRANGE, with Desmond and Orin talking while they sipped wine. Sheree was there too, but none of the other Elites joined them at the table tucked into an alcove away from the kitchen.

The table was nowhere near as big as the one in the main dining hall; it only had seating for ten. The brownies were perched on top of it in their tiny chairs while the rest of them sat near Desmond at the head of the table.

Normally, Sahira only picked at the food they served her. The idea of feasting on anything these creatures offered made her stomach turn, but it also rumbled incessantly after her night with Orin.

She was tired and somehow wide awake as she fought to keep a grin off her face. A big, toothy smile was entirely out of place here, but despite the guillotine blade scraping her neck, she couldn't completely tamp down the smile tugging at her lips.

She'd never experienced anything like last night. Not only was the sex fantastic—it always was with Orin—but there had been a different level of intimacy between them. She'd never felt as close to any other man as she did with him.

She'd opened up to him more than ever before as they also talked and laughed between sleep and sex. No matter how much she'd tried to deny it, there was something special between them, something unique, and while death loomed over them, so did the possibility of something more....

If they could get out of here.

Trying not to let something that could prove impossible put a damper on her mood, she refused to focus on that. She wanted just *one* day of happiness in this forsaken Cursed Realm.

She tried not to look at Sheree too often while they ate. She'd barely paid attention to the woman before and couldn't start now, but she was acutely aware of her cutting her food with dainty perfection while sitting beside Desmond.

Desmond was once again too loud and too *much*, but she'd gotten used to his boisterous persona. It might be the only thing about the man that wasn't a lie.

She nibbled on her toast and looked across the table to Zeth and Elsa. They'd have to find a way to fill them in on what she learned last night. The brownies wouldn't be a problem, as Orin also shared a connecting door with them.

When Sahira glanced at Orin, her heart skipped a little. He was so handsome as he laughed at whatever Desmond said. If she didn't know any better, she'd think that laugh was real, but he despised this man as much as her; he was just far better at playing Desmond's games.

She had no idea what the future held for them, but right now, Orin was hers, and she loved it. She also loved *him*.

There was no denying that anymore. Somewhere along the way, this arrogant, oblivious, manipulative, sometimes extremely cruel man had wormed his way into her heart. Most likely because while he was *all* those things, he was also loyal, smart, brave, and not quite as callous as he liked to portray.

He'd probably deny all of that, but he'd proven it to her while they traveled across the Barren Lands. He'd saved Pip from the geysers and hadn't left Zeth behind for the spiders to eat.

Somewhere during all that, she'd fallen in love with a man she once considered an enemy and as trustworthy as a crocodile with an empty belly. If they somehow survived this, she had no idea what would happen between them... or with her family.

Her heart sank a little at the reminder Orin once imprisoned her brother. Del *loathed* Orin; she didn't know if they could ever get along or if her brother would ever forgive her for this.

He might see it as a betrayal to him, and he'd be right. Orin had let her and Lexi believe Del was dead when he knew the truth; he'd kept him locked away from his family. She shouldn't ever forgive him for that, but she did.

They were both completely different than when they first met; things had changed, and while she didn't doubt Orin was still ruthless when necessary, he wasn't the same. But could Del see that, and would he be willing to try?

Sahira gulped, and acid churned in her stomach at the possibility of losing her brother, her best friend. She couldn't let that happen, but what if she had to choose between him and Orin?

Closing her eyes, Sahira took a deep breath as she tried to calm her rising anxiety. She was getting *way* ahead of herself here. They couldn't get out of this realm and had no idea what the future held.

Maybe she and Orin wouldn't have forever, and maybe next week, or six months from now, she wouldn't want that, but they had *now,* and she was looking forward to every second of now... minus the creepy Golden Ones, murder, and all the uncertainty.

That reminder put a damper on her mood, but she still munched on a piece of toast laden with strawberry jam. Her stomach thanked her for putting something in it. Apparently, her stomach didn't know manipulative, murderous assholes surrounded her.

When she finished eating, she pushed her plate aside and

sipped coffee while studying the white wall across from her. She pondered the events of last night as Desmond and Orin continued speaking.

The servants had given her what might be some helpful information, but it didn't guarantee them a way out of this place. Plus, they couldn't know if any of the information was true. Still, it was something, and they'd have to follow up on it.

Finally, brunch ended, and Desmond stood. "Sheree and I would like to show you something."

CHAPTER FORTY-THREE

AN UNEASY FEELING ran through Sahira, and the jam soured in her stomach. She didn't know what this man planned to show them, but it couldn't be good. *Nothing* with him ever was.

She hoped she didn't throw up her brunch before this was all over. Her gaze darted to Sheree, who sat with a serene smile as she gazed at Desmond with adoration. That smile bothered her more than Desmond's words, and if she didn't know better, she'd think that look was real.

She's too good an actress.

"Come now," Desmond encouraged when no one moved. "The day is wasting."

Sahira swallowed the lump in her throat as she set down her napkin and rose with the others. The brownies scampered up her, Orin, and Elsa as they assumed their normal positions on their shoulders.

When Orin's fingers brushed hers, she knew it wasn't an accident but an attempt to comfort her. She almost clasped his hand but restrained herself. These two had to know Orin was naked in her room this morning.

But the two of them having sex was one thing, and while she

was sure they also knew they cared for each other, holding hands was a different level of intimacy. The dagadon would use everything they could against them, but Sahira couldn't keep loading the gun.

But then, they probably already had it fully loaded and cocked.

Still, Sahira didn't take his hand as they followed Desmond and Sheree down another white hallway with guards all around them. Sheree could look at Desmond like she loved him, but as they walked side by side, Sheree kept her hands clasped before her and her head held high. Their body language wasn't that of a couple in love, and they couldn't hide it.

Desmond's pale blue eyes glistened when he turned to Orin. "Do you like to hunt, my friend?"

"It's been many years since I've been on a true hunt unless you include those I hunted during the war against the Lord," Orin replied.

Desmond laughed. "Of course they count! But I'm talking a true hunt with men being men."

It wouldn't surprise Sahira if Desmond started thumping his chest and grunting. If men were all like him, *she'd* hunt them.

"I've always enjoyed a good hunt," Orin said.

"Then we shall go on one this afternoon. You, me, Loth, Fath, and Zeth!" He turned to one of the guards. "Have the captain of the hunt prepare for one this afternoon."

"Yes, my Lord."

The man sped away and disappeared around one of the turns. She glanced back at Zeth, who was scowling at Desmond. Had Desmond included him simply to push the demon's buttons?

If Zeth exploded, it would give them an excuse to imprison or kill Zeth, and she was certain Desmond would take a full contingent of guards with him. Men being men didn't include him not being a coward.

If he were a *real* man, he'd go out there without any guards and see how long he survived with Orin and Zeth. Sahira would take bets on less than a minute.

"I'm sure you enjoy hunting too, Zeth," Desmond continued.

"I do."

The low grumble of Zeth's voice caused the hair on Sahira's nape to rise. The tone of his voice left no doubt he'd enjoy hunting Desmond the most.

What would happen if they all went out there, Zeth's inherent demon instincts took control, and he lost it on them? He'd managed to keep them suppressed for years so he didn't end up in the pit; he wouldn't take the chance of not returning home to his wife and son.

But would he recall his wife and son if Desmond continued to push at him, or would he try to destroy the monsters who had kept him from his family? And would it get him and Orin killed?

Sahira didn't know the answer, but strawberry jam didn't taste so good when it burned its way back up her throat. She gulped it back down but still tasted it.

When they came to the end of the hall, they took a right and walked past more doors before stopping in front of a white one at the end. "Here we are!" Desmond said brightly.

Sahira was really regretting eating anything when Zeth's claws clicked behind her. Pip shifted on Orin's shoulder while Fath remained unmoving on hers.

She had no idea where they were but didn't doubt she wouldn't like it.

CHAPTER FORTY-FOUR

ORIN BRACED his legs a little further apart as he sought to shield Sahira while Desmond produced a key, unlocked the door, and swung it open.

He didn't expect anything to rush out at them unless they'd trained it to avoid the Golden Ones, but he still expected something to happen. When nothing did, he didn't relax.

They'd been brought here for a reason, and it wasn't a good one.

Sheree went through the door first. Desmond stepped out of the way and waved his arm for them to enter ahead of him.

"Guests first," the man said.

Orin smiled while his hands fisted with the impulse to beat the man to death. It would be such a satisfying, fun thing to do.

Instead, he moved toward the light spilling out of the open doorway. A low murmur of voices came from inside, but he couldn't make out what they said.

When he crossed the threshold, he hesitated enough that Sahira walked into him before catching herself. Orin compelled himself to keep moving into the giant amphitheater.

From where they stood at the top, it was at least fifty feet down to the center of the white brick structure. Stone benches spread out beside him and down toward the center, where a figure eight, or an hourglass, was etched into the white floor.

Orin couldn't stop himself from sneering when he spotted the symbol. He hated it.

On the level where he'd entered, a set of stairs ran down ten feet before stopping at a wall. That wall rose nearly to the ceiling in front of the benches.

Only his position on the stairs and his ability to look down allowed him to see more benches branching off the stairs on lower levels, as they also had walls in front of them. Having barriers to block the view of an amphitheater made no sense, but there they were.

To his left, in front of the wall, a guard sat across from the symbol etched into the wall. It looked exactly like the one they saw in the last town... an hourglass with two of the three arrows making an X while the third was a bull's-eye straight into the center. The bottom half of the hourglass was shaded in.

The Golden One in front of the symbol sat with his shoulders back and his eyes focused on the hourglass, though nothing was happening with it.

When the others were all in the room, Desmond entered and again took the lead. "This level is always the most boring, or at least it *was* until you all entered our lives," Desmond said.

Orin's nostrils flared as understanding dawned on him. *This* was where they came to listen to the conversations of the Cursed Realm.

CHAPTER FORTY-FIVE

DESMOND LED them to the next level, where another Golden One sat in front of an hourglass symbol with an arrow still at the bottom of it. The middle part of the hourglass was shaded in, while two other arrows made an X beside the symbol.

They descended to the next level, which was the same, except for the slightly altered hourglass with only one arrow beside it. They made their way lower until they arrived at the bottom level, where the symbol was completely intact.

Dozens of Golden Ones sat before the symbol to his left. The low murmur of voices he'd heard came from that symbol. When he listened carefully, he detected Belda's more strident tone and the clatter of alcohol bottles, glasses, and laughter.

This was the symbol inside the pub. Thrown off a little by hearing the sounds that were so familiar and so far away, sounding as if they were in the next room, Orin almost touched the symbol.

Maybe they could somehow connect with those they'd left behind. Maybe they could shout a warning and tell them to stay far away.

"They can't hear us through it," Sheree said.

Like the freak she was, she'd materialized from somewhere to the right of him. Even more disturbing was that it seemed she'd read his mind.

"This is the pub," he stated the obvious.

"Yes, and if you walk around our beautiful amphitheater, you will find the library, mercantile, stable, granary, infirmary, and jail."

"Then, let's take a little stroll," Orin suggested.

When Sheree smiled at him, he knew it was because he hadn't been able to keep the hostile tone from his voice and knew they'd struck a nerve with him. After what Sahira revealed about this woman last night, he knew she was the creature waiting to spring its trap. Her sweet smile hid the soul of a monster.

Together, Desmond and Sheree led the way around the amphitheater. As they walked, it sank in that each floor of the arena had a symbol to match the town they represented. The figure eight on this level had all the arrows inside it and no sand.

"So, you *were* listening to us," Elsa said as they stopped in front of the next symbol on this level.

The way she said it led Orin to believe she'd already suspected such a thing, but the dagadon hadn't tried to hide it from them. They'd dangled it like a hook they kept pulling away at the last second.

"I'm afraid it is a necessary evil," Desmond replied. "We *must* know what's going on in the towns and when someone is leaving Ground Zero, but we don't monitor your homes."

He said this as if this lack of eavesdropping made them decent beings. It didn't, and they weren't.

Only because they built those homes after you established the town, but Orin didn't speak those words. They all already knew that truth.

"Well, of course, you must listen," Sahira said sarcastically.

When Orin shot her a warning look, she glowered at him while continuing. "How else could you place your bets."

Orin's eyes narrowed on her. They were already on the chopping block; she shouldn't instigate them further.

Desmond laughed. "Exactly! She gets it!"

Sheree's sweet smile remained as she turned away from them and waved a hand at the next symbol. "This is the mercantile."

Across from the symbol sat a handful of dagadon. There weren't as many seated here as in front of the pub, but they still numbered higher than they had on the upper floors of the amphitheater.

This is insane.

Orin felt like he'd stepped into one of those game shows the humans liked so much, but instead of spinning a wheel or jumping on float-like things, he'd entered one full of powerful magic determined to destroy them all. This game consisted of them being thrown in a cage and given a wheel to run in circles while their captors watched in amusement.

His nails dug into his palms as anger and power thrummed through his veins. When he found those Augmentation Stones, if they existed, and they could finally break free of this realm, he would pulverize the smiles off Desmond and Sheree's faces.

The whole time while he was killing them, he'd have that same shit-eating grin Desmond always sported. And if all went well, he'd make them feast on their insides before he finished. The vision made Orin smile.

They moved on to the next symbol, and the next, and the next. At each one, at least a couple of conversations were going on; all were mundane. Immortals made purchases at the mercantile, and at the stable, a small group discussed if they should sheer the sheep.

Zeth had pretty much run that stable by himself, but a few immortals had replaced him. Someone sang an old pixie ballad at the granary, and Gromuck gruffly discussed how to stock the library shelves.

"A new lycan arrived yesterday," Desmond explained. "They chose to work in the library." With a sly smile at Sahira and Elsa, he continued. "There are two job openings there now, after all."

Neither of them acknowledged his words before they continued. When they'd circled back to the pub, Orin stopped to listen to the voices that had become so familiar to him while he worked there.

He could pick out a dozen different immortals he knew, and it was still early in the day, so the place was quiet. And none of them had a clue of the horrors awaiting them beyond the town.

"What do you think?" Desmond inquired.

Before anyone could respond with what they *truly* thought, Orin spoke. "Fascinating."

Sahira huffed behind him, and Pip squirmed on his shoulder.

"It is, isn't it," Desmond said. "And when someone leaves and things get exciting, we all come down to listen. Unfortunately, we can't hear you throughout most of your journey."

But you used beasts to spy on us. Orin gritted his teeth as he smiled.

"At least not until we get to a new town, and then you know everything again," Loth said.

"Yes! At least not until then," Desmond replied, clapping his hands. "Now that you've seen this little room of wonders, it's time for some fun. Let's go hunting!"

CHAPTER FORTY-SIX

SAHIRA LOATHED the idea of the men going hunting while she, Elsa, and Pip remained behind. And not because Desmond and his fellow dick swingers didn't think a woman could handle a hunt, which was insulting enough, but because the dagadon divided them when only doors had separated them until now.

The stark reality of that churned the acid in her stomach, and once again, the strawberry jam made its presence known as she watched Orin, Zeth, Loth, and Fath ride off with Desmond, Renaldo, the Elite men, and at least a hundred guards. If anyone had tried to convince themselves this was for fun, the presence of those guards ended those delusions.

Sahira lifted Pip and settled the brownie onto her shoulder before looking at Elsa. "Maybe we can stroll the garden."

"Do you think they'll let us?" Elsa inquired.

Sahira glanced over her shoulder to the servants and guards gathered behind them. They wouldn't be allowed to go far without someone watching over them, but she had to talk to these two.

Someone, besides Orin, had to know what was going on

here. She doubted he'd get to reveal it to Zeth, Loth, and Fath while on their *hunt*.

If they could walk far enough away from the guards while in the garden, she could cast a spell to keep their words from traveling to their captors. The guards probably wouldn't notice; if they did, she'd release the spell.

And maybe they'll chop off her hands afterward, but she was willing to take that chance, considering everything happening here. They were stronger as a group, and Pip could let Loth and Fath know what was happening.

On the first night they arrived, when she'd been trying to see into Elsa's room, she'd also glimpsed a door between her and Zeth's rooms. She'd be able to tell him what she learned today... if they came back from the hunt.

Don't think it. But it was a niggling, cancerous worm digging through her mind until it was impossible *not* to think of it. If she focused on it too much, she'd go insane with anxiety and be useless to anyone.

So instead, she focused on her goal of letting Pip and Elsa know what she'd learned last night. They would also have to search their rooms for symbols. Although, after what they'd seen today in the amphitheater, they probably already planned on doing that.

"Can we go for a walk in the garden?" Sahira asked over her shoulder.

The servants all looked at each other, but the tallest guard answered with a grunt and nod. The manly men had all ridden out from the stables to the left of the castle, but to the right was the first hint of flowering shrubs and a different entrance into the garden.

Stepping off the white stairs of the small porch near the stables, Sahira's skirt swayed around her ankles as she strolled toward the blue flowers on a large red bush overflowing the walkway. Elsa walked beside her.

Like she'd suspected they would, all the servants remained while a dozen guards trailed twenty feet behind them. It's what she'd hoped for, but Sahira couldn't help feeling insulted by how little all these assholes thought of them.

If Orin and Zeth were still here, they'd probably have at least fifty guards trailing them, but these idiots saw them as weaker without them. She longed to prove them wrong but couldn't do it now when so many guards surrounded Zeth, Orin, Fath, and Loth.

She'd put them in danger if she tried something now. But when the time came, she'd make sure the dagadon regretted their misconception of her and the others.

"Do you think they'll be all right?" Pip whispered.

"I'm sure they have something planned for today, but I don't think they're ready to start killing us. They've just gotten started with whatever sick game they're playing," Sahira said.

The guards were far enough away that she didn't worry about them hearing her, but she wouldn't have held those words back even if they could. They were the simple truth, and everyone knew it.

"They'll get bored of us soon," Elsa said.

"I'm not so sure," Sahira said. "Yes, they will definitely get bored of us, but we're their new source of entertainment, and it's obvious they *love* to be entertained. Although, their idea of it and mine differ greatly."

"No shit," Pip snorted.

"They might keep us around for a few months before they start killing us. I originally assumed they'd get rid of us in a week or two, but I think we'll have more time. I'm sure there are more than a few nerve-racking hunts and other cruelties in our future."

She suspected one or more of their new games would soon involve her and Orin's relationship. And since they were at the mercy of these monsters, there wasn't much they could do to stop it.

The possibilities of what they could do to them caused her to tug at the neckline of the far too fancy dress these assholes had selected for her. *Stay focused on the now. Worrying about the future is pointless.*

"I hate this place," Pip whispered.

"There's still hope," Sahira said.

She glanced back at the guards, but most were focused on the trees or talking with each other. They wouldn't notice if she waved her fingers in front of her and uttered a small spell to ensure their words didn't go beyond them.

"What are you doing?" Elsa asked.

Sahira finished casting the spell before speaking. "I have to tell you something, but we don't have much time. They didn't notice the spell."

Sahira looked back to ensure this, but none of the guards paid any attention to them. Hecate, these idiots really believed they weren't a threat to them. It was extremely helpful but *infuriating.*

She looked forward again and told them about last night's events as quickly as possible. When she finished, Elsa stopped walking.

"Keep going," Sahira hissed.

Elsa pointed to a tree, remarked on its color, and continued as if that was why she'd stopped. She fell into step beside Sahira again.

"How do we find the stones… if they exist?" Elsa asked.

"I think Orin is the only one who can search for them. He could probably take me with him, but I have a feeling he'll argue against it, and he'll have a point. It would be better if he had someone to watch his back, but he can move faster without me and won't have to be concerned about keeping us both cloaked."

"He can take me," Pip offered. "I'll be *on* him, and I can

watch his back. He won't have to worry about us getting separated or anything like that."

Sahira didn't like the idea of Orin going out there with just a brownie, but she didn't know what else they could do, and it would be a *battle* to get Orin to agree to take her. She already knew she wouldn't win it… but would he take Pip?

Most likely not, but it was an option.

"He could take you," Sahira murmured. "Although, I'm sure he'll fight that too."

Pip lifted her tiny chin. "The stubborn man will lose that fight."

"I hate being unable to help in this," Elsa said.

"Me too," Sahira said. "But we can watch for anything unusual in the castle or on the grounds. That could give Orin a place to start searching for the stones. I'm going to release the spell now. Hopefully, we can talk more at another time."

Sahira waved her fingers in front of her so the guards couldn't see them moving and undid the spell. Commenting only on the beautiful bushes and the possible magical properties of them and their flowers, the three of them continued strolling the garden as if everything was perfectly fine in their lives.

CHAPTER FORTY-SEVEN

THEY RODE miles away from the castle before arriving at a place full of giant trees with vivid red trunks and bright orange leaves that leapt like flames in the sun streaming through them.

Not only had they brought horses and a carriage full of supplies, but six of those massive dogs also accompanied them. Orin had no idea what they were hunting; given the contingent and supplies, it was huge.

For all he knew, the four of *them* were to be the hunted. The possibility had niggled at the back of his mind ever since Desmond declared they would go on a hunt.

When he climbed on the black stallion they handed him, he knew he could be riding into a trap, but they were greatly outnumbered, and fighting it would only jeopardize Sahira. They could be riding out to be the entertainment or leaving the others behind for the same thing to happen.

Orin glanced back toward the castle. They'd ridden far enough away that he couldn't see it nestled deep in its valley.

The idea of leaving Sahira behind had created an anxiety he'd never known before; it scratched at his insides as deeply as the claws of the wendigo that had once speared him. He'd rather experience that again than this inescapable need to return to her.

He was more scared for her than he was for himself. He didn't know what that said about him, her, or their relationship, but it was true.

First, he had to get through this afternoon; it would be long as he was sure some new game was unfolding. And what better game to play than to separate them from each other and let uncertainty reign?

He didn't think death was on the table today. Desmond, Sheree, and all these other Elites were still having too much fun screwing with them. Death would come eventually, but until then, the mind fucks would build until the devastating conclusion.

They still had time to find a way out of this... or at least he hoped so.

If he didn't play along with them, they would use Sahira against him. They were doing so now by separating them, and Desmond was *very* aware of it.

Orin refused to let the man see how much not knowing if Sahira was safe bothered him. When Desmond called a halt to the ride at the edge of the woods, he plastered on a grin and dismounted his steed. He patted the beautiful horse on its neck before handing his reins to the immortal who scampered toward him.

"Beautiful land," Orin said as he studied the fiery trees. "I've been through many realms, but this might be one of the loveliest I've seen."

Inwardly, he rolled his eyes at himself. Had he really used the word *loveliest*?

But that was the kind of thing Desmond would say, and when surrounded by freaks, it was best to act like them.

"Oh yes," Desmond said. "We're *very* blessed here in Epoch."

"Very blessed," he agreed.

When Loth snorted his disagreement, Orin almost shoved the brownie off his shoulder but decided against it. The little rodents had grown on him, but they had to play the game too. It was the only chance they had of all of them surviving.

"What are we hunting?" Zeth asked.

Desmond beamed so widely that *all* his teeth were on display. "I'm glad you asked."

Orin immediately disliked that smile. It told him he was going to *loathe* whatever was coming.

CHAPTER FORTY-EIGHT

"TECHNICALLY, it's not going to be a *we* hunt; it's going to be a *you* hunt," Desmond said. "As in, the four of *you* will hunt while the rest of us take bets to see who wins. We've never played this game, so I'm curious to see how it turns out, especially since you'll be hunting the most dangerous game."

Oh fuck.

Orin had seen much of what this realm had to throw at them and couldn't imagine anything worse than those spiders or beetles, but obviously, something worse lurked within the shadows of these gigantic trees. None of them spoke, as none of them were willing to ask *what* they were hunting.

"Aren't you curious about what you'll be hunting?" a sweet voice asked.

Orin had never seen her arrive, and she hadn't left the castle with them, but the crowd parted to let Sheree pass through them. She wore a dazzling red dress and serene smile as she glided through the group.

Desmond's smile grew as he threw his arms wide. "There's my lovely bride! We couldn't let this glorious event start without you."

Sheree stopped only a few inches away from him. She opened her arms too, but they didn't embrace as they each air kissed the other's cheeks.

He'd never met such pompous, immoral assholes before, and he was a dark fae. They *lived* pompous and immoral.

While they were putting on their show, Orin pictured smashing their heads together to *make* them kiss. He'd keep bashing until their foreheads cracked and their brains oozed out; it would be *lovely*.

It would probably be one of the last things he did, but it would feel so good. The only problem was, he'd leave Sahira vulnerable to what remained of these assholes.

"What took you so long, love?" Desmond inquired as they stepped away from each other.

"It took me some time to decide who else got to play," Sheree said.

Orin stiffened as the crowd parted again. His breath caught in his lungs as he waited for Sahira to walk through the group next. There was no way he was hunting her or anyone else.

Instead of the three women they'd left behind, they led two dagadon men through the crowd. The guards had chained their hands before them and bound their ankles with manacles. Dirt caked their faces and tattered clothes.

"And who have you chosen?" Desmond inquired.

"Two criminals from the dungeons," Sheree replied.

"Fantastic!"

Orin could only imagine what crimes these men committed. They'd most likely refused to jump through some hoop, or maybe they'd sneezed. He was leaning toward sneezing, as that seemed to be how the brains in this land of insanity worked.

"The demon versus the dark fae," Desmond declared. "The brownies can be their passengers, but for this hunt, they won't have anything on the line."

Zeth and Orin exchanged a look. Fury darkened the demon's

yellow eyes and caused his brow to furrow; Orin was sure his face mirrored the demon's even while he tried to hide his emotions.

"The dark fae shall have the brunet while the demon will hunt the blond. We'll give the prisoners a five-minute head start," Desmond said.

"And you will hunt until death," Sheree added.

Her bloodthirstiness was starting to shine through.

"I'm not hunting someone I don't know and who has never done anything to me," Zeth stated.

Sheree turned that sweet, almost childlike smile on him. "Of *course* you don't want to do such a thing. That would make you a psychopath."

Zeth and Orin exchanged a look again; Orin had no doubt the demon would resist this. He also had no doubt they'd be forced to hunt.

Sheree flicked an imaginary speck of lint off her sleeve before focusing on them again. Her brown eyes twinkled in the sun, but no warmth shone in them. "You'll hunt them because if you don't, we'll kill the girls you left behind. I can assure you, there are guards with them right now."

Orin's jaw clenched, and his teeth ground together. Over the years, he'd played many games and done many things to many immortals to get his way.

He'd used Lexi against Del to learn her secrets and kept the man locked away to put his father's armies at a disadvantage during the Lord's war. He'd manipulated Sahira and countless others.

While he regretted what he'd done to Sahira, he didn't regret those other things. He was who he was and did what he believed necessary.

However, he'd *never* been like these golden freaks. He *never* would have done something like this.

Maybe some of those he'd walked over to get his way would

believe his actions were almost as bad as these golden fuckers, but he sure didn't. Then again, some might think he wasn't the best judge when it came to that.

He'd like to believe all those he'd left in his wake wouldn't put him on the same level as these monsters, but what did he know? The possibility made his stomach churn.

One thing was for sure, he wasn't going to let anyone harm Sahira or the others. She was his number one concern, and he'd protect her the most, but they'd all worked together to get to this point.

While he wasn't sure any of them would make it out of this alive, none of them were going to die because he'd somehow failed them. Orin's attention returned to the demon.

He could only hope Zeth felt the same way, but if necessary, he'd kill both the prisoners to protect Sahira. He'd hate every second of it and *despised* being nothing more than pawns to these freaks, but he'd do whatever it took to safeguard Sahira.

CHAPTER FORTY-NINE

"AND IT WON'T BE a fast death for your women. The guards are always allowed to play with their catches." Sheree patted the arm of the large man beside her. She'd touched him more than her fake husband, Desmond. "It's part of what keeps them so happy. And some of them *really* enjoy the screams of a woman. Some get very excited... if you know what I mean."

The guard she was touching smiled. Orin's pulse pounded in his temples as he battled to keep his revulsion for the man hidden.

He stared at the side of Zeth's head as the demon focused all his wrath on the Golden Ones. Zeth had to realize they didn't have a choice.

Every day they survived this place was one more day they could work on getting free. Now that they knew about those stones, they might have a chance to do so. Zeth didn't know this, but he had to realize that killing men they had no connection with was the better option here.

"Pip," Loth murmured.

Orin didn't want to think about what the guards would do to

the tiny brownie. And when he considered what they'd do to Sahira, his blood boiled.

"It's not going to happen," he grated.

He studied the Golden Ones and their contingent of guards. Did he have enough time to slip into the shadows, return to the castle, find Sahira, Pip, and Elsa, and get them out?

His gaze went beyond the large contingent to the numerous horses and hills separating him from Sahira. Without a horse, he wouldn't make it before the dagadon. He was fast, but not that fast.

He could try stealing one of the animals, but then they'd see him go and follow him back. That would severely cut down the time he had to find the others, and if they caught him first, it would only be worse for the women.

This "caring about others" thing was starting to irritate him. He could easily vanish into the woods and avoid these things.

He couldn't escape Epoch, but he'd survive. And eventually, he would get back into the castle, find those stones, and put an end to all of this. If he did such a thing now, the guards would tear Sahira apart.

Shit!

He couldn't even curse himself for allowing this to happen when he only wanted to get back to her and ensure she was safe. He cared far more for her than he ever believed possible and wouldn't lose her.

His gaze settled on the two prisoners who had most likely sneezed the wrong way and were chained for it. Over the years, many had died at his hands, but these would be the ones he regretted most.

All's fair in love and war.

And the dagadon had declared war on them. He had no idea how, but he would be the one to win. Until then, they had to play by the dagadons' rules, but they had forgotten one thing... a pawn could take a king.

Sheree squeezed the guard's arm before releasing it. "So, what shall it be? Will you hunt, or will the guards all take a turn at your women? Of course, I'll be sure you're there to enjoy the show, and we'll have to take bets on who will live the longest, though I'm not sure the brownie will count. I don't think she'd survive one cock inside her."

A low murmur of agreement went through the crowd as Loth released a growl that might have made the dogs piss themselves.

"I'm sure someone would be willing to take that bet," Desmond said.

The crowd snickered, and someone called. "Mitchel would!"

"Of course!" Another man called back. "I always love a good long shot."

"I thought we were your *guests*," Zeth sneered.

"Of course you are! And highly esteemed ones at that!" Desmond went to slap Zeth on the shoulder, but the demon's look caused him to think twice, and his hand fell back to his side. "But guests must earn their keep."

"And we've fed and clothed you some of the best our realm offers. Nothing is free in life," Sheree said.

Unable to stand the sound of their voices anymore, Orin spoke. "I'll hunt them both."

Zeth looked toward him, and Orin saw the understanding and sadness in the demon's eyes. These immortal prisoners didn't deserve this, but neither did any of them. If it were Zeth's wife in the castle, he'd destroy them both too.

"There's no need," Zeth said. "I'll hunt."

Apparently, the demon was also willing to ensure his friends didn't suffer.

"Wonderful!" Sheree cried. "But then, you didn't have a choice. Desmond has already told you this is a competition between you, but the winner gets a prize, and the loser will suffer the consequences."

He was certain he didn't want to know, but Orin had to ask. "And what are those?"

Desmond turned and held out a hand. One of the guards produced a hatchet; its sharpened edge gleamed in the sun as he handed it over. "If you are to lose, then you must also lose something. I mean, one must suffer the consequences of being a failure."

"The loser's hand will suffice," Sheree said. "The hunt doesn't end until both prisoners are dead."

"Fuck," Loth hissed.

That about summed it up. When Orin looked at Zeth again, he was sure the same rage in the demon's eyes also shone from his.

By the end of this day, they'd both commit murder, one of them would lose a hand, and neither had a choice.

CHAPTER FIFTY

ORIN HAD SPENT the past two hours hunting the brunet man through the woods. It was taking far more time than he'd anticipated, but the fact he had dozens of guards tromping through the woods behind him didn't help.

The brunet and blond were set free in separate areas of the woods. The contingent had been divided, so half went with Orin and the other half with Zeth.

They'd trained the guards to protect their Elite, but they definitely weren't trained in stealth. He moved silently while they stomped on every stick, cursed each branch that hit them in the face, and generally sounded like a herd of elephants tromping through the woods.

Disdaining the woods, Desmond, Sheree, and the rest of the Elites remained behind to eat the picnic the servants had started to unpack while Orin and Zeth prepared to hunt. At first, Orin was surprised they weren't coming to watch the show, but then, the hunt wasn't the main attraction for them; the loss of a hand and the ensuing reaction were what they sought.

Orin was determined to ensure he didn't lose, even with the

elephants trailing him. As much as he'd grown to like the demon, he preferred his appendages intact.

He didn't have to be in Zeth's head to know the demon felt the same way. They'd do what they could to ensure the other survived this, but they were also here to win.

So, they hunted, all the while knowing the first to succeed would doom their ally to a life of five fewer fingers.

Orin searched the woods for a sign of where his prey had gone. In the beginning, the brunet plunged heedlessly into the forest, leaving a clear trail of broken branches and disturbed ground in his wake.

He'd slowed, probably because he was malnourished and dehydrated from imprisonment. He'd also become more careful about the trail he left.

Thankfully, Orin had grown up hunting with his father and brothers. Of course, they hadn't turned immortals loose in the woods and tracked them down, but they'd killed some of the fiercest beasts in the Gloaming and throughout the realms.

Sometimes, they'd spend weeks camping together, laughing around fires, sharing drinks, tales, and dangerous exploits. They only took a break to clean themselves before hunting a more elusive and attractive prey... women.

After a night of debauchery, they'd return to the hunt. Those were some of the best nights of Orin's life, and he remembered them fondly, especially now that his father and half of his brothers were dead.

Though he never could have imagined those nights would help him with something like *this,* they had prepared him for it. He was sure Zeth was probably skilled at hunting too, but Orin *would* be better.

Plus, both their targets had been locked away, probably beaten, and judging by the loose fit of their clothes and the sharp angles of their collarbones, not well fed. Either of them could be too exhausted to carry on at some point.

If Zeth's target collapsed first, it would put Orin at a disadvantage and vice versa. Orin hoped the brunet collapsed before the blond, even if it would make killing the poor bastard more difficult than it already was.

He was on the prowl for a man who most likely didn't deserve his fate and was too weak to put up much of a fight. He didn't have much of a conscience, but this nagged at it.

Holding up a hand, Orin turned to glare at the guards when they continued stomping forward for a few more feet before finally stopping. They were useless fucks who had no clue what they were doing.

On his shoulder, Loth shifted as he studied the swaying shadows of the forest. Overhead, the leaves rustled in the rising breeze. It was one more sound he didn't need on top of the guards.

When they *finally* all stopped moving, Orin bent to study the earth. Slight indentations marred the damp soil, and something had disturbed the leaves covering the ground. One of those imprints was a heel.

Not a complete idiot, his prey had shed his boots a mile ago. Running through the forest had to be difficult with bare feet, but now that his target wasn't so heedless in his charge through the woods, he didn't leave as many damaged branches in his wake, and his footprints were less obvious.

But they were still there. Orin tilted his head in the direction the prints went before rising to follow them.

Relentlessly, he tracked the prints through the woods as they moved in a diagonal path toward the right before cutting back to the left. The man was trying to lose him… and failing.

Orin preferred not knowing anything about his victim, but it was clear the man was intelligent and didn't want to die. He shoved those bits of knowledge into the dark recesses of his mind.

He was good at compartmentalizing. It was how he lived with the guilt of being the reason the Lord killed his father.

And while he resented that they forced him into this, his prey might not be completely innocent. Orin doubted he'd done anything to deserve *this* fate, or at least not anything *he* would have deemed worthy of this, but he wasn't the judge or jury.

He was simply the executioner.

Though birds flew from the trees and small animals scattered to hide from them, he didn't see any of the bigger animals who had also left their prints amongst the dirt and leaves. But then, they could probably hear this contingent of guards from half a mile away and fled them.

His prey could hear them too.

After another few hundred feet, Orin stopped and held up his hand again. Again, the stupid twats kept going when they should have stopped.

Orin studied the trees and shifting breeze as he scented the air. He didn't have the nose of a lycan, but, like all immortals, he had a strong sense of smell, and the body odor of his prey was growing stronger as he closed in on the man.

He was close enough to finally ditch these assholes and do what was necessary. He'd be back in time to stop them from sending someone back for Sahira and the others.

"I'll be back," he told them. "All of you dumbasses, wait here."

"Watch it," the head guard growled.

"Oh, I'm sorry. All of you morons who couldn't hunt a rat if trapped in a box, stay here."

They scowled at him, but he didn't care. These dicks barely had a brain between their eyes and were already his enemies.

He no longer had to play the game to find out where all this was heading. The dagadon had made it clear today, but he was going to keep his hand and ensure the safety of the others.

"Listen here, dark fae—" the guard in front started.

"Hold on, Loth," Orin commanded.

The brownie's tiny fingers wrapped into his shirt. Without waiting to hear what the guy with shit for brains had to say, Orin drew the shadows around him and disappeared.

The guards immediately started shouting as they scrambled toward where he'd just stood, but Orin was already moving as he tracked his prey deeper into the woods. He moved faster and with a lot more stealth without the guards, but he had to be fast about this.

He didn't have much time before the guards sent someone back to let Desmond and Sheree know he'd vanished into the shadows. Sahira would pay the biggest price if he didn't return soon, and he couldn't let that happen.

He wasn't going to find the brunet with those guards following him. He had to be fast, and since he didn't have a weapon, he'd have to do this with his bare hands.

The guards shouted as they ran around the woods behind him. He glanced back to discover them in complete disarray as they stumbled around, searching for him before he focused forward again.

He moved swiftly through the trees, keeping the shadows around him as he moved. In less than a minute, he lost the guards who had no idea how to track anything but gained ground on the brunet.

"Hurry," Loth whispered.

"I am."

When he rounded a copse of trees, the sound of running water drifted to him, and the man standing at the edge of a small stream came into view. He had one foot in the air as he prepared to enter the water.

Without making a sound, Orin snuck up behind him as the man's foot sank into the water. He didn't stop to think about what he was doing; he didn't have a choice.

It was this man or a woman he cared for deeply. There was no competition.

Orin didn't hesitate as he grasped the sides of the man's face and twisted his head to the side. The audible pop of his neck snapping echoed through the forest a second before the immortal's body went limp, and Orin released him.

The man crumpled to the ground.

CHAPTER FIFTY-ONE

THE GUARDS WERE STILL STUMBLING around the woods when Orin returned to them. When he released the shadows obscuring him, they gasped and staggered away before correcting themselves.

If it weren't for Sahira and the others, it would be easy for him to kill more than a few of these assholes before slipping into the woods, where he could survive until he found a way out of this realm. Before Sahira, he'd always believed that caring for others was a weakness.

However, Sahira never made him feel weak; in fact, he felt whole and invincible in her arms, yet he was keeping himself in danger for her. What astounded him most wasn't that he remained, but that he didn't regret doing so.

He was here for her, for them, and he wouldn't leave until they were all free. And while the whole situation was a nightmare, he was glad to stay... for them.

Orin dropped the brunet's body on the ground, where it landed with a thud. The guards looked from him to it and back again before the rage clouding their features faded, and a few smirked.

"It's over," he stated.

"She must be a really good fuck for you to return, dark fae."

Orin's eyes narrowed on the guard who'd spoken, but he refused to give the man the reaction he sought. Instead, he smiled as he memorized the man's face; it would be fun to slaughter him later.

"Let them know our hunt is done," another guard commanded.

A dark-skinned man removed the horn strapped to his side and blew into it. The loud, awful noise resonating through the woods scared the birds from the trees, and Loth covered his ears.

The birds soared upward in various colors and screeches as they flew away from the sound. Their small, colorful bodies blocked out the sun before they fled deeper into the woods.

That sound meant Zeth now knew he'd be the one to lose a hand. Regret tugged at Orin, but he'd done what was necessary; done what they *forced* him to do.

"It's time to return," the main guard said. "Get the body."

Two other guards picked the man up and carried him between them as they strode back through the woods. The buffoons were as loud on the way back, but it didn't irritate Orin as much this time; he had nothing to lose anymore.

The guards surrounded Orin as they made their way back through the forest. It took them a lot less time to get out than it did to make their way to his prey, and while Orin was glad to be free of the trees, he was less happy to see Desmond and Sheree again, as well as all their asshole friends.

When he was in the woods, the rest of the Elite women had joined them as all pretense of this being a hunt for the men was over. He assumed they'd come in the carriages now parked behind the horses.

A cheer ran through more than half the crowd while the other half chugged their wine. It was easy to tell who had won their bets and who had lost.

He *loathed* these creatures, everything they were and every-thing they represented was the worst of all immortals. They'd made it so he didn't enjoy playing games anymore, and he hated them for that too.

"It's the dark fae!" Desmond declared. "As I knew it would be. Only a fool would bet against you!"

A murmur of anger ran through those who'd bet against him. Money exchanged hands, palms slapped against backs, and more bottles of wine emerged.

Desmond strode over to Orin and slapped him on the back. "You've yet to let me down, my friend."

Orin bared his teeth in a semblance of a smile, but he couldn't fake it as well as he used to with this man. Loth leaned away from Desmond until he pressed against Orin's face.

This man's touch made Orin's skin crawl, but he refused to move away from Desmond. It would only amuse this gold-flecked abomination.

Something malevolent churned in Desmond's eyes. "Come, sit, and enjoy the celebration of *you!*"

He released Orin's shoulder and strode back toward the thick blankets and pillows the servants had spread across the ground. The Elites lounged on the cushions while eating from the platters overflowing with fruits, cheeses, loaves of bread, and meat.

Servants hurried through their tangle of limbs to refill their goblets. Orin didn't join them on the blankets but stood to the side as he waited for another horn to blow.

All he wanted was to return to the castle and assure himself that Sahira was safe. He had to see and hold her again; only she could erase the memory of this day.

And if they've done something to her?

Then they'll burn in the fires of wrath I unleash on them. Because nothing would stop him then, not even the safety of the others.

"They're going to take Zeth's hand," Loth whispered.

"I know," Orin murmured.

"I wish we could kill them."

"So do I."

Soon, they would pay for believing they had him and the others exactly where they wanted them. Soon, they would learn the wrath of the dark fae, but not until he was sure Sahira was safe.

CHAPTER FIFTY-TWO

He didn't know how much time had passed, but the sun was sinking toward the tops of the trees when another loud horn blew. The birds that had resettled into the trees screeched as they took flight again.

At least another hour passed before Zeth, Fath, and their contingent of soldiers emerged with a blond-haired man's body. Zeth emanated rage as he stalked between the guards surrounding him.

He could put up a fight and take many of them down before they overpowered him, but still, he strode forward with his shoulders back. Unlike him, Zeth hadn't fallen for someone in the Cursed Realm, but, like him, he'd come to care for their friends.

Orin hadn't always liked the demon, but it was clear Zeth was a man who had a strong sense of morals. Zeth knew he would lose his hand, but instead of taking down some of his guards, as he easily could, and trying to flee into the woods where he might escape them, the demon had returned to lose an appendage.

For the first time, Orin was also grateful for the demon. If

Zeth hadn't returned, Sahira, Pip, and Elsa would have paid for it.

When Zeth's eyes met his, Orin bowed his head in thanks. It wasn't nearly enough; when all this ended, and they were free of these monsters, he'd find a way to try to repay the demon for returning.

He didn't know what could compensate for losing a hand, but he'd try.

"Finally!" Desmond exclaimed. "That took far longer than any of us anticipated. I was getting rather bored."

Orin tensed when Zeth's eyes swung away from him, his nostrils flared, and his clawed fingers curved into fists. His black skin rippled as his muscles bulged. If Zeth went for Desmond, Orin would have to intervene, even if he'd prefer not to.

When Zeth bared his teeth at Desmond, he revealed fangs that could easily rip the man's throat out, but somehow the demon kept himself under control. Orin suspected he was thinking of his wife and son, who he loved and planned to return to.

Such thoughts were enough to keep any man in check. Before coming to the Cursed Realm, Orin *never* would have understood that. He did now.

"But thankfully, we have more entertainment ahead of us," Desmond said as he turned back to the Elites. "Every loser must pay."

Orin's teeth scraped back and forth as Loth twisted his hands in his shirt. "I can't watch this," the brownie whispered.

Orin didn't want to watch either, but he wouldn't turn away. Zeth deserved for them to bear witness to this; it would fuel them when the time came to make these monsters pay.

One of the servants brought forth a hatchet and handed it to Desmond. When he held it high, the honed edge gleamed in the sun, and a cheer ran through the crowd.

The Elite who'd bet against him had gotten over their resentment as they practically salivated over the hatchet. Someone brought a tree log from the woods and set it twenty feet away from him. Someone lit a torch to use for cauterization afterward.

One of the guards went to grasp Zeth's arm, but he jerked it away from the man. The demon kept his shoulders back as he strode toward the log with his chin raised and his eyes raking over every one of the assholes on the blankets.

Not one ounce of distress emanated from him; it was all pride. He wouldn't give these bastards the satisfaction of fear. He wouldn't scream when the blade cut through either; Orin was certain of it.

"On your knees," one of the guards commanded.

Zeth refused to do as he ordered. Instead, he slammed his hand on the log and stared defiantly ahead as if he saw none of them.

Orin didn't blame him; he wouldn't kneel for these dickheads, either. Okay... *maybe* he would if it kept Sahira safe, but they'd have to shove him to his knees for it to happen.

Desmond grinned from ear to ear as he strolled away from the Elites with the hatchet on his shoulder. There was a little sway in his step as he leaned from side to side while walking. It wouldn't astonish him if the freak started whistling.

Instead of walking over to Zeth, Desmond sauntered toward him. He was only a foot away when he stopped and held the hatchet out to Orin.

"It's freshly sharpened, so it should cut clean through," Desmond said.

CHAPTER FIFTY-THREE

ORIN FROWNED as the guards closed in on them. One stood so close their arms nearly touched.

Orin's gaze went from Desmond to the hatchet and back as a sick sensation filled his belly. They didn't expect *him* to cut off Zeth's hand, did they?

Of course they do.

He kicked himself in the ass for not seeing this coming and for it taking so much time to sink in. He'd underestimated the dagadon, something he hadn't believed possible, considering he already thought the worst of them, but they'd surprised him with this when they shouldn't have.

This was another part of their sick, twisted games.

"I won't do it," Orin stated.

"Of course you will," Desmond said. "Because if you don't, I can assure you, the little witchy vampire you're so fond of will beg you to save her while *I'm* fucking her."

With those words, Desmond decided to stop pretending he was married to Sheree. *No* married immortals would say or follow through on such a thing; they were entirely devoted to their spouses.

What proved this more was the big smile on Sheree's face. The sick bitch would probably watch.

Desmond gave the hatchet a little wiggle. "One of you will lose a hand today, Prince Orin. And since we all know you won't take yours, you *will* take the demon's."

He couldn't remember a time when he'd been more incensed. It seethed inside his body and pounded in his temples as a scream lodged in his throat.

Desmond's smile widened as Orin glowered at him. His breaths sounded like a bull's as they went in and out through his nostrils.

"Your choice, Prince."

When Orin snatched the hatchet from Desmond's hand, Loth groaned. The image of burying the sharp edge in Desmond's face burst through Orin's mind as he adjusted his hold on the weapon.

Before he could swing it, a guard grasped his wrist. Orin jerked his arm away from the man and sent a scathing look in his direction.

He'd prefer not to have the oaf touching him, but it stopped him from doing something that would have gotten them all killed. Taking a calming breath, Orin tried to ease the rage battering him, but it had taken on a life of its own and refused to be caged again.

However, he could control it. When his gaze swung to the demon's, Zeth gave a small bow of his head.

"It's okay," Zeth said. "Just do it quickly."

His attention returned to Desmond, and when he met the man's pale eyes, Orin smiled. For the first time, a flicker of apprehension ran through the other man's eyes before he buried it.

Desmond wasn't a stupid man. He knew he was staring his death in the face.

Orin kept smiling as he brushed past Desmond. It slipped away while he walked toward Zeth. The demon's chin remained proudly up, but he couldn't hide the sorrow in his yellow eyes.

When Orin stopped before the stump, Fath covered his eyes with his hands before lowering them. A steely look of determination came over his face too. Orin sensed the brownie wanted to run away, but he rested a hand on Zeth's nape as he tried to offer comfort in solidarity.

They would all go through this together, because though Loth said he couldn't watch, he placed a hand on Orin's shoulder. "It's okay," the brownie assured him.

This was as far from okay as it got, but their choices were limited, and as much as he'd come to respect the demon, he'd grown to love Sahira *far* more. He knew that now.

The love had been there for a while, trying to break free so he could see the truth, but he'd been too stubborn to acknowledge it and too determined to cling to who he'd always been. However, that was the past, and Sahira was his future.

He'd found his home with her. He belonged with her, and there wasn't anything he *wouldn't* do for her.

"I'm getting bored, dark fae," Sheree called in a pouty voice, "and I'm not very nice when I'm bored."

The fact she considered herself nice at all showed how delusional the crazy bitch was, but Orin refrained from pointing that out.

"I will see blood, dark fae," Desmond said.

Zeth's gaze didn't waver from his. "The faster you do it, the better."

When the demon held his wrist further out over the log, Orin seized it. He stared at the thick muscle cording Zeth's wrist and arm as he prepared himself for what he had to do.

Lifting his head, he looked over the Elites before shifting his gaze to Desmond and the vast number of guards surrounding them. They were all practically drooling as they devoured this scene.

The servants had also frozen as they looked on with dismay. Some of them had turned away to busy themselves with the carriages. They were used to the abuse and having to witness it, but they still didn't like it.

Maybe there's hope for them.

"Do you have bets on whether or not I'll do this?" Orin asked.

Desmond beamed as he rocked back on his heels. "Now you're getting it, Prince."

"What did *you* bet?" Orin asked.

Desmond held up his index finger and wagged it at him. "Uh-ah, I can't tell. That would be cheating."

"That's true."

"But whatever you choose, I will have a hand," Desmond said. "I already made a spot on my mantle for it."

Orin couldn't stop himself from chuckling. "Of course you have."

As he glanced over the crowd again, he reminded himself that though they were pawns, a pawn could take a king. After this, he vowed to no longer be a pawn in their games.

Knowing what he had to do, Orin looked at Zeth again while he raised the hatchet. Their gazes remained locked as, without a sound, Orin swung it down. The blade cleaved straight through muscle and bone that cracked with a snap.

As Orin had known he wouldn't, the demon never screamed.

CHAPTER FIFTY-FOUR

UNABLE TO SIT STILL, Sahira anxiously paced the lawn near the stables. It had been *hours* since the men rode out for the hunt; she didn't know if they'd return today... or at all, but she couldn't bring herself to leave.

And the guards and servants were no help. She'd asked if they were supposed to return today, but no one answered her.

She'd heard carriages rattle away hours ago, but they'd still been in the gardens, and she couldn't see what was happening. No one would tell her anything about that either. It was all so *maddening.*

Tugging at her hair, she refrained from muttering to herself while pacing. Her endless walking had worn a path through the grass, turning it nearly to dirt.

She brought her hand to her mouth and almost started biting her nails again before recalling that nothing remained to bite. She'd eaten them off hours ago.

Elsa and Pip sat on the stairs, watching her as the sky turned various shades of colors with the setting sun.

"Maybe we should eat something," Elsa suggested. "You haven't had anything since breakfast."

Sahira couldn't think about eating right now, especially since that strawberry jam was still burning her throat. "I'm not hungry."

The thud of horses' hooves vibrating the ground alerted her they were coming before she saw or heard them. As a witch, she was more in tune with the earth and its energy beneath her feet.

So was Elsa as her friend rose from the porch and strode over to stand beside her. Elsa's fingers were warm and strong as they clasped Sahira's wrist.

Sahira braced herself for the worst. There was no way anything good had come of this hunting adventure.

When Pip joined them, she climbed up to sit on Sahira's shoulder. "They're fine. They're all fine."

Sahira wished she could believe her, but she didn't argue as she lifted her free hand and held up her finger for the brownie to clasp. "They're all fine."

Maybe if she said it, it would come true. There was no harm in trying to talk it into being true.

The hoofbeats grew close enough for her to hear them as they thundered across the ground. When they broke over the top of a hill, the large contingent finally came into view.

The blue clothes of the dagadon guards spread across the land as far as she could see; the brighter colors of the Elite's clothing stood starkly out from all the blue.

The wagons that rode out after them came into view with the servants, as did a grouping of carriages. Her brow furrowed at the sight of those carriages.

Did the Elite women join them on the hunt?

She hadn't seen any of them in hours, but they rarely saw them outside the dining room. Why would they keep that hidden from them?

I'm never eating strawberry jam again; she decided as it burned onto her tongue. It was a shame too, as it was a favorite, but she'd never be able to look at it again without thinking of *this*.

The Elite men rode in the front, but the jovial air that surrounded them when they all left was gone. Then, they'd laughed, shouted, and promised it would be the best hunt ever. Now, they all looked like a five-year-old who had their lollipop ripped from their hands midlick.

Heart hammering, Sahira frantically searched for Orin, Zeth, Loth, and Fath but didn't see them. Finally, she glimpsed Zeth in the center of the dagadon guards.

Dozens of guards surrounded him, but his height made him stand out. She couldn't see his face before he rode into the stables and out of view.

"Where is Orin?" she breathed.

"I'm sure he's in there," Elsa assured her. "There were too many of them to see everyone."

Unable to wait longer, Sahira tugged her finger away from Pip and started toward the stables with Elsa at her side. Three of the guards stepped into her path.

"Stay where you are," the shorter one commanded gruffly.

"Why?" Sahira demanded.

The guard didn't respond as he stared over her head. Sahira's fingers dug into her palms as she restrained herself from hitting him.

Finally, after what seemed like hours but was probably only minutes, the Elite and their guards started filtering out of the stables. The women were with them and looked as unhappy as the men.

They didn't speak as they glided toward the porch, but Sheree stopped beside a couple of guards and pointed a finger at the three of them. "Make sure *all* of them stay in their rooms tonight."

Apparently, they wouldn't be attending tonight's feast or

made to pretend this wasn't all a sham anymore. *What happened out there?*

Sheree turned away and lifted her skirt to climb the stairs. Desmond sent them a scathing look that caused Sahira's skin to crawl before he followed his pretend wife into the castle.

Finally, Zeth emerged from the stables with Fath on his shoulder and at least a hundred guards surrounding them. But the overwhelming number of guards wasn't what caused her heart to plummet. It was the blood splattered across Zeth's clothes and face.

But more than that, it was also Orin leaning heavily against Zeth's side as the demon's arm around his waist helped support him while they walked. Loth had a hand against the side of Orin's face while gazing at him.

The brownies had all hated Orin when they started their journey together, and Orin had felt much the same about them, but that had changed along the way. Now, only concern etched Loth's features as he sought to comfort his friend.

Blood also coated Orin, but she couldn't tell if that blood was from him or whatever animal they hunted. *What happened out there?*

CHAPTER FIFTY-FIVE

"ORIN," Sahira breathed.

Releasing Elsa's hand, she sprinted forward to get to him. When one of the guards tried to block her again, she darted to the side and went low to avoid the hand he swung at her.

She'd only succeeded in pissing them off, but she didn't care. All that mattered was getting to Orin and finding out what happened.

Orin's head lolled forward, his black hair tumbled across his forehead, his skin was the color of paper, and his toes dragged across the ground as Zeth carried him. So focused on him, Sahira didn't notice the blackened and bloody rags wrapped around his hand until she was almost to him.

No, not a hand... a *stump* where his hand used to be.

"Orin!" Sahira cried as she arrived at his side.

She clasped his face and traced the contours of his cheeks as he lifted his beautiful, crow-black eyes to meet hers. A small smile twitched at the corner of his lips.

"Hello, Enchantress," he murmured in a weak voice.

"What *happened*?"

"We have to keep walking," Zeth said. "He has to rest."

Sahira went to drape his other arm around her shoulder to help Zeth with him but stopped herself. She was afraid she'd hurt him if she grasped anywhere near his missing hand.

Orin lifted his arm and draped it around her shoulders. Pulling her close, he kissed her cheek. "I can still hold you."

She choked back a sob as she slipped her arm around his waist. The guard she'd managed to evade scowled when they came closer; she hoped the man would leave them be. His kind had done enough damage for today, but she'd claw his eyes out and set his ass on fire if he tried to separate her from Orin.

Thankfully, the man didn't try to interfere. Instead, he stepped out of the way as Elsa and Pip joined them while more guards surrounded them.

Sahira and Zeth helped Orin up the stairs. His boots dragged against the ground as he slumped further against them until he was a dragging weight on Sahira's shoulders. His head remained bowed between them, and she was fairly certain he'd either passed out or was about to.

"What happened?" Sahira demanded again.

"I lost the hunt," Zeth said. "The penalty for that was to have my hand cut off. They forced Orin to do it."

Sahira didn't understand. Zeth still clearly had two hands, while Orin was missing one of his. "Then why…?"

"He took his hand instead."

Sahira gasped as her eyes flew to the man draped between them. Orin was many things—selfish, callous, stubborn, exasperating, and more than a little fucked in the head, but she'd also learned he had a big heart, was more caring than he knew, and could be selfless, smart, strong, tender, and fiercely protective of those he loved.

Despite all those good things, she never would have believed that he would choose to mutilate *himself* instead of Zeth.

Would he do it for her?

Yes, she believed he would just as he would do it for his brothers, but not *Zeth*.

They started this journey as enemies. Along the way, they'd become reluctant allies, and now she would consider them friends. They'd helped each other to survive, but while Orin stopped to rescue Zeth from the spiders, he wasn't about to *maim* himself for him. Yet, he had.

None of it made any sense.

Zeth met her eyes over the top of Orin's head. "I don't understand it either, but it's done. He's lost a lot of blood. They were too stunned and then pissed to cauterize his injury right away. I had to do it."

Sahira didn't say anything as she helped Zeth carry Orin up the stairs and into the hallway with their rooms. Before they made it to Orin's room, Desmond joined them with two dozen more guards. He ordered the men to remain outside their rooms.

"Put him in his room," he commanded Zeth, "and then leave."

Zeth's jaw clenched, and he looked at Sahira, but she didn't know what to say or do. If they tried to separate *her* from Orin, she'd fight worse than a cat about to get a bath.

Zeth helped her get Orin settled on his bed before stepping back. Orin lay with his head turned away from them and his handless arm draped across his belly.

Zeth looked helplessly from Orin to Sahira. "What can I do to help?"

"Nothing," Desmond spat. "Get out of the room, demon."

When Zeth didn't immediately obey the command, some guards slipped past Desmond and entered the room.

"It's okay," Sahira assured Zeth. The last thing they needed was a fight here when Orin couldn't defend himself. "Go on. I'll take care of him."

Zeth glanced helplessly at her again. "I'll be right across the hall."

After Zeth left the room, the door slammed shut, and a key turned in the lock. Sahira had no idea why they hadn't been taken to the dungeons, especially since all pretenses of them being welcome guests were gone, but she suspected these things had their reasons.

They'd made it clear *no* one was leaving their rooms tonight... just like no one was leaving this forsaken realm.

She turned her attention back to Orin and nearly fell off the bed when she discovered him sitting ramrod straight on it with his head up and his eyes burning with fury.

"We're getting out of here tonight," he growled.

CHAPTER FIFTY-SIX

THE BLOOD DRAINED from her face as she gawked at him. "*What?*"

"We're getting out of here tonight."

Her eyes fell on his hand... or at least what used to be his hand. He wasn't about to let the loss of his appendage hinder him.

"Cast a silencing spell," he commanded.

Shaking her head, Sahira's shoulders went back as she got over her shock at seeing him more alert than he'd pretended to be. She quickly created a spell that would conceal any noise they made.

"You looked half dead," she said when she finished.

"I'm a good actor, better than these fuckers."

"Good actor." She touched her fingers to her temple before going to her knees before him. She reached for his bandages. "I don't think you're in the condition to do *anything* tonight."

"That's what I wanted them to believe." He caressed her hands before stopping her from unraveling the bandages. "It's not pretty under there. Leave it be."

"That's not going to happen. They returned my ointment

from when we traveled through the Barren Lands. It will help you heal faster and ease the pain. I'm cleaning and treating this no matter what you say."

He didn't like the idea of her seeing what lay beneath; she was upset enough as her hands trembled. But he didn't argue with her; that ointment would come in handy right now, and they didn't have time to fight over this.

Besides, the faster it healed, the better he would feel. He'd faked being as incapacitated as he was, but he had lost a lot of blood, and his stump throbbed with every beat of his heart. Losing his hand and then having a flame held to what remained of it hadn't been the most pleasant sensation in the world.

When the last of the bandages fell away, she bit her bottom lip as tears filled her eyes. The red and blackened end of his wrist looked as bad as it felt. He swore he could see his raw flesh pulsing.

"Why did you *do* this to yourself?" she whispered.

The rage driving him since Desmond announced his new game faded when faced with her sorrow. He cupped her face with his remaining hand and rubbed her cheek with his thumb. When her tears spilled free, he wiped them away.

"Don't cry for me, Sahira. *I* made this choice."

"Why? Why would you *choose* this? What happened out there?"

"Nothing good."

She squeezed his knees. "I'm going to get something to clean this and my ointment. When I come back, you're going to tell me everything."

Before he could protest, she rose and ran into her room. He heard her rummaging through her things and doors opening and closing before she returned with a bowl, two towels over her shoulder, and a bulge in the pocket of her dress.

"Found this under the sink." She lifted the bowl a little higher as she hurried toward him. Setting the bowl on the floor, she removed the ointment from her pocket and went to her knees before him again. "Speak."

With tender care, she lifted the bowl and held it in one hand while she guided his injury into the warm water with her other hand. While she worked, he told her everything that happened on the hunt.

As he spoke, her hand trembled before she steadied it. She removed his stump from the water and gently dabbed at it with the ends of a towel. Despite her tender ministrations, he gritted his teeth against the needles firing through his veins and arm.

"If Zeth lost, then why are *you* the one without a hand?" she asked when he finished speaking.

"They said they wanted a hand and would have it... no matter what. Desmond didn't think I'd cut off my own hand, none of them did, but they *all* took bets on whether I'd cut off Zeth's or not. I gave them a hand; it just wasn't Zeth's," he said.

She lifted her head. "*You* cut off *your* hand so they would all lose a *bet?*"

"No. I cut off my hand because I'm not their pawn anymore. They can't keep me under their thumb, and now they know it."

"Have you ever heard the saying 'cutting off your nose to spite your face'?"

Orin understood why she didn't get it; he wasn't entirely sure *he* understood it, but he wouldn't change his decision even if he could.

"I lost my hand, but the look on Desmond's face when I picked it up, threw it at him, and told him to put it on his fucking mantle is a memory I will *never* lose. They assumed they knew me so well; they never had a clue."

CHAPTER FIFTY-SEVEN

SAHIRA HAD THOUGHT *she* knew him so well too, but as she gazed at the brutalized end of his wrist, she realized she'd been so wrong. Blinking away the tears blurring her vision, she dipped her fingers into her ointment and tenderly dabbed it on.

"You shouldn't have done this," she whispered.

She couldn't stand his suffering, and even if he didn't flinch from her touch, his jaw was set and sweat beaded his brow.

He clasped her chin and lifted her head. "Would you rather I'd taken the demon's hand?"

Sahira swallowed the lump in her throat as she lost herself to the beauty of his eyes. "Yes."

She was ashamed to admit it, but it was true. She'd rather see Zeth suffering than Orin. She loved him too much for that.

He tilted his head to the side while studying her. "When you first entered the Cursed Realm, you probably never thought you'd say such a thing or cry for me."

"That was before I learned you have a far kinder soul than you realize," she whispered. "I don't think you did this *just* to spite them."

A small, sad smile tugged at the corners of his mouth. "You may be the only immortal who thinks that of me."

"And now you're going to tell me I'm wrong and you're a heartless bastard."

"No. I'm going to tell you that if I have a far kinder soul than I realize, it's because *you* gave it to me. You *are* my heart. You *are* my soul."

Those words sucked the air from her lungs as his thumb stilled on her bottom lip, and his eyes held hers. Her heart raced as emotions flooded her.

That was by far one of the sweetest things she'd ever heard, and it had been uttered by *Orin*, her one-time enemy and now the man she loved. Unable to contain her emotions, she whispered, "I love you."

Her jaw dropped at what she'd revealed. Sahira didn't doubt Orin cared for her too, but the mention of *love* might make him run for the hills.

He'd *just* gotten to a point where he could admit he only wanted to be with her, and now, she'd dumped this on him. She was astonished there wasn't already an Orin-shaped hole in the wall as he bolted away from her.

Instead of fleeing, he smiled before bending to kiss her. The tenderness of his lips caused her to melt as their tongues intertwined. His good hand slid around to clasp her head as he pulled her closer.

Panting and breathless, she broke the kiss when his cock lengthened against her belly. "You *cannot* be aroused right now," she said.

He chuckled and kissed her cheek before nuzzling her ear. "I can't help it, Enchantress. I want to fuck the woman I love."

Sahira's eyes flew up to his as shock riveted her to the spot. She'd believed they were past it, but she couldn't help questioning if this was a game for him. Orin didn't *do* love.

"It's not a game," he said as if reading her mind. "After this place, I'm done playing games. And I would *never* say those words without meaning them. I never have before, and I never will again."

He traced her bottom lip with his thumb as his eyes bored into hers. He wasn't lying to her; this wasn't a game for him.

"I love you," he said again.

Sahira grinned at him. "I know."

He chuckled before resting his forehead against hers. "I'm going out there tonight, Sahira. And while I'm going to survive this place and make them *all* pay for what they've done, I don't know when I'll be back."

"You're not in any condition to go anywhere."

He brushed loose hair away from her face and tucked it behind her ear before kissing her nose. "We can't sit back and wait to see what's going to happen anymore. We already know what they plan for us, and it will only get worse."

"Then I'm going with you."

"No. I can't be worried about you while I'm out there; it will only slow me down and make it more dangerous for both of us."

"Orin—"

Before she could protest further, he reclaimed her mouth in another kiss. Despite her determination to resist him, her fingers encircled his wrist, and she leaned into him.

She loved him, he loved her, and this could be their last night together. She couldn't turn away from his kiss when she needed to feel this joining between them as badly as him.

He'd just lost his hand, was weakened, and should rest, but the stubborn man would leave tonight and not take her with him. Trying to fight him on it would be a lost cause, and she was so tired of fighting.

She tried to resist when his fingers skimmed her breast before finding the buttons running up the back of her dress. He slipped them free and broke the kiss to lean away so he could pull the dress forward.

"I'll cast a protective spell over both of us," she said as the front of her dress fell to her waist. "That way, you won't have to be concerned about me, and you'll have someone to watch your back."

He smiled at her, but she saw the truth in his eyes; she wasn't making a dent in his determination to leave her behind.

"You don't have to do this alone," she said angrily.

"I'm not doing it alone." He pulled her bra free and licked his lips. "You'll be with me in spirit."

"You're an asshole."

"I know."

A shiver ran up her spine when he bent and kissed her neck. "But you have to stay behind so they can see you, Enchantress. You'll open the balcony doors and let me out, but the guards have to see you off and on throughout the night so I can get back in. They think I'm too weak to do anything, so they shouldn't get suspicious."

As he pushed her dress lower, he purposely tried to distract her from their argument by doing things with his mouth and teeth that made her legs weak, but she refused to be distracted.

CHAPTER FIFTY-EIGHT

"THAT'S NOT A GOOD REASON, and you know it. I can leave the doors open for *both* of us to return. And you should be resting instead of molesting me."

He chuckled against her neck as his finger found her clit and stroked it. "Does it feel like I should rest?"

Sahira had to grip his shoulders to keep from falling into him. "Zeth said you lost a lot of blood."

"True, but the best thing you can do to strengthen a dark fae is fuck them."

"Orin—"

His teeth nibbling at her bottom lip cut off her words. "You strengthen me, Sahira. I *need* that."

He did need that, especially if he was going to follow through with this crazy plan of his, but damn it…. "You should rest and not go running around out there."

"And tomorrow, they might come to cut something else from one of us. I might be able to stop that."

She couldn't protest that, as it was true. They probably would arrive tomorrow with some new game; as pissed as the Elite all looked tonight, it would be vicious. And there was no doubt it would involve turning them against each other.

Sahira's fingers dug into his shoulders when his finger started teasing her clit. For a second, the passion he evoked so easily consumed her as her head fell back and his mouth found her breast.

Then she recalled their argument and dragged herself from the depths of sensuality to pant, "A protective spell will keep us both safe."

"Even with a protective spell, I can't move as fast if you're with me, and speed is of the essence. If the dagadon discover I'm gone, you'll all pay for it," he said.

"More of a reason you should take me with you."

"The others will need you here to help protect them if shit goes down. They don't know I'm leaving. It will be like we're throwing them to the wolves."

He was right about that, but the idea of him going out there alone was enough to drive her mad. "We were separated most of the day, and look what happened."

He silenced her again with a kiss, and somehow, before she knew how it happened, his pants were off. He had five fewer fingers, yet it seemed like he had eight more hands as he drew her off her knees.

When she rose, he slid her dress the rest of the way down. It pooled around her feet as he tore her underwear off and tossed it aside.

He guided her onto the bed, and Sahira wrapped her legs around his waist. He remained sitting up as she slid onto his cock.

He bit her bottom lip as a rumble of pleasure vibrated his back beneath her hands. She couldn't get enough of how his muscles rippled against her palms and his strength even after everything he'd endured today.

Joined together, she leisurely rode him as she felt the gentle tug of him feasting on the energy they created with their bodies. She rose until he was nearly out of her before drawing his thick, rigid length into her again.

His fingers dug into her back as his mouth found her nipple and his tongue caressed it. Sahira threaded her fingers through his thick hair and clasped him to her breast before rubbing the tip of a pointed ear.

He shuddered against her, and the tug of his feeding grew stronger as he strengthened himself on *her*. Her fangs tingled and lengthened in response to his hunger, but she wouldn't bite him. He'd lost enough blood today.

Her head tipped back as their joining became more frenzied until she was crying out his name while coming apart in his arms. As he groaned, deep within her, she felt the pulse of his shaft when he came too.

CHAPTER FIFTY-NINE

THEY DIDN'T SPEND as much time holding each other as he would have liked. Instead, they parted and dressed in black pants and fae tunics they uncovered from their closets before returning to his room.

Sahira's face scrunched in concentration as she cleaned his wound again. It was a clean cut; he'd made sure of that when he brought the hatchet down.

When they were free of this place, he could get a prosthetic. He'd seen some impressive ones out there, especially if they were made with fae metal and spelled by witches or warlocks. It would almost be like having his missing hand back again.

As she worked, Orin instinctively flexed the fingers of his missing hand. They were no longer there, but he felt them working to clench and unclench in his mind.

At least feeding from her had gotten his strength back to where it was before all the blood loss. He hadn't been anywhere near as weak as he'd pretended to be when the dagadon were around, but he hadn't faked all of it either, which was something Sahira would never learn.

"You should have fed," he said.

She glanced up at him from under the thick fringe of her lashes. "You lost enough blood without me taking more from you."

"I fed from you."

"I know."

"You need to stay strong too."

She focused her attention back on his injury. "I am strong."

"I felt your fangs when we kissed; you're hungry."

"I fed plenty from you yesterday, and while I craved your blood earlier, it wasn't because I'm hungry; it's because I love that connection with you."

He caressed her cheek again before bending to kiss her forehead. "We're going to get out of here."

"I know."

"I have to go alone tonight."

"No, you don't." She dabbed some ointment onto his wound. It instantly helped ease the throbbing and soothed the burn. "But you're not going to stop being ridiculously stubborn about that either."

Orin tilted his head to the side as he studied her. She had no idea how close he was to caving to her demands.

She would pay for it if something happened out there and he didn't return in time for the dagadon not to learn he was gone. At least, if she was with him, he'd know she was safe.

But she'd also slow him down. He'd be too worried about her and making sure she was in the shadows, not to make any sound or to move as freely as necessary.

Still, he didn't like the idea of leaving her behind.

Maybe I can take her....

When his gaze traveled to the balcony doors, he decided against it again. She wasn't safe anywhere in this place, but she was safer here than she would be out there.

He could do something to ensure she was safer. "I can cloak

you in shadows and take you out to the garden where you can hide or run if necessary."

"What about the others?"

He wouldn't leave the others behind; they'd earned that much loyalty from him, but he'd be happier if she ran. "I'll make sure they get out, but you could run to the forest and hide there. These things can't hunt; they'll never find you. I will."

She recapped her ointment and rested her hands on his knees. "And we both know I can't do that. I'm not leaving you or them. You wouldn't do it, and neither will I."

"You should."

"And you should take me with you."

Their gazes clashed before she lifted a set of clean bandages she'd made by tearing up a shirt from his closet. She gently bandaged his wound and tied the rags into place.

"I'll be back before morning," he promised. "They'll never know I'm gone."

"What do you plan to do out there?"

"Gather some weapons, learn more about this castle, and kill some of them."

"If you kill any of them, they'll know you left here."

"You always put a damper on my fun."

Her smile was small and fleeting. "But you're going to do it anyway."

"If I get the opportunity, especially with Sheree and Desmond. Taking out their Lords will send them into chaos; we can use that to our advantage. And if I bring back weapons, we'll have a better chance against them.

"We know more about this place now. If we can get out through the gardens and make it to the woods, we can hide and survive by hunting, and there's water out there. It's not much of a life, but at least it's something and gets us out of their cage.

"We'll have a better chance of coming up with a plan if we're not constantly questioning what they'll do to us next. We require weapons, and these assholes to be distracted so we can get out of here."

"At least you have a plan."

"I do." He stroked her silken cheek. "I have to go. It's getting late, and I have to be back before daylight. They've been coming late in the morning for us, but I'm sure that will change. They're determined to keep us on our toes."

Sahira closed her eyes and took a deep breath before squeezing his knees and rising. "I wish you'd change your mind and take me with you."

So do I, but he kept that to himself.

"I should have done this sooner, but they moved faster than I expected with their crazy shit. I thought they'd at least keep pretending for the first week, stringing us along and telling us we'd be able to leave soon. I underestimated them and paid for it; I won't let you pay because of that too."

"No one could have seen this coming."

"I should have. I'm the one who likes to play games, after all, and I let them outmaneuver me."

He'd beat himself up about that and have a missing hand as a reminder for the rest of his days.

"You're being too hard on yourself. *None* of us saw this coming or have ever experienced anything like it. Even with as dark and twisted as you can be, you've never been this warped or cruel."

"There are some who would disagree with you."

"Then they should come here for a bit."

Orin smiled before rising. She was probably right, but it didn't make him feel better. He cupped her face and kissed her forehead. "I'll be back soon."

"I'll be here."

He hoped so because there'd be hell to pay if she wasn't. "Lead the way."

Sahira turned and walked across his room to the balcony

doors. As he followed, Orin drew the shadows around himself and vanished.

When she opened the doors, the light spilling from the room and across the balcony illuminated the structure. Night had settled in, but thankfully, the moon had risen to shed its glow across the land and create shadows.

Ahead of him, Sahira's steps faltered before she crossed to grip the railing. Orin frowned, but as he stopped beside her, he saw what had unnerved her.

A row of guards stood outside. They no longer worked in shifts to patrol the land as they stood shoulder to shoulder at the garden's edge.

Well over fifty of them spread across the land in front of her balcony, his, the one to the brownies' room, and all the other rooms that followed. For as far as he could see, they stood in a line outside the castle.

They were all staring at Sahira as she lifted her chin and focused on the moon. Orin glanced from the guards to the trellis between his and Sahira's room and back again.

It would have been difficult to climb down with only one hand anyway, but he'd still planned to do so in between the guard's patrols. That had been blown out of the water. There was no way he wouldn't make any noise while climbing down.

He'd have to jump and find another way back into the room. He was sure just as many guards lined the hall outside their rooms, so trying to sneak past them would be difficult, but he could follow the servants down the hall and try to slip inside with them.

Those were his only options, as he couldn't stay here anymore.

Leaning over the rail a little, he looked at the nearly thirty-foot fall. He could slide over the side and, holding onto a railing, drop from there.

Without a word, he climbed over the balcony, gripped one of

the rails, and slid down it until he stopped. He dangled for only a second before releasing it.

His knees bent to take most of the impact, and his ankles protested the abrupt stop, but all his bones remained intact. If he stirred the grass, none of the guards noticed as they remained focused on Sahira.

Keeping himself cloaked in shadows, he ran around the side of the castle as he sought to find a way inside.

CHAPTER SIXTY

SAHIRA STOOD on the balcony for another ten minutes before retreating inside. Leaving Orin's room behind, she strolled into hers and sank onto her bed. She bowed her head as she tried to control the riotous beat of her heart.

He was gone; she hadn't seen or heard him leave but felt his absence. He'd vanished into the night, and while she knew he would do everything he could to get back to her, there were no guarantees.

And now, she was alone, with nothing but her apprehension to occupy her. Rising, Sahira paced back and forth to release some nervous energy while she sought to calm herself.

It didn't do any good.

There had to be something more she could do than sit here and wait for him to return. *If he returns.*

Don't think like that!

But the doubt and the terror it aroused niggled incessantly at it. She went to bite her nails before remembering nothing remained of them.

She was never going to sleep tonight. Even before Orin left, sleep would have been impossible for her. She probably wouldn't sit for the rest of the night, either.

So instead, she paced while pondering everything she knew about the dagadon. As far as she could tell, they didn't have any weaknesses.

She also didn't know the full extent of their powers, but manipulating time to this extent, even with the stones, was a magnificent, vicious thing. They could communicate with beasts and had some magical abilities as they'd used the symbols to spy on them.

But while she didn't know everything about them, there were things she had learned for sure. Her fingers itched for some paper and a pen so she could write it down and look at it, but there wasn't anything like that in her room.

She hadn't searched Orin's and didn't think he'd mind if she went through it. It's not like there was anything personal in them; they'd arrived here with little.

The search of his room would be simple, but she still made sure her silencing spell was in place around both rooms to keep any sounds from carrying beyond this room. She was supposed to be tending to a half-dead Orin; she wasn't about to give them any reason to suspect anything different.

Returning to his room, Sahira glanced at the open balcony doors before starting her search. While searching, she kept a list of the things she knew about the dagadon running through her head so she wouldn't forget something.

She went through all the drawers and closet but came up empty. Frustrated, she almost slammed the door to the closet closed but stopped herself as she stared at the back wall.

There was absolutely nothing eye-catching about it, and the assortment of men's and women's clothes were similar to those in her room. The dagadon hadn't known which rooms they would choose, so they'd filled them with various garments.

The articles of clothing hanging in the closet didn't conceal much, but that wasn't what caught her attention. It was the list of things running through her head that gave her pause.

The *number* one thing she'd learned about the dagadon since coming here, and probably their biggest weakness, was how much they enjoyed betting against each other. But more than that, these cruel, manipulative creatures *loved* to play games.

Their lives revolve around games.

Those five words ran on a loop through her mind as she stared into the closet. They'd set up the Cursed Realm for their entertainment. They'd made it a tournament, laughed about it, and bet on who would make it and who wouldn't.

And when they set up the original towns, *every* original building had a hidden door inside it. That trapdoor didn't reveal anything in those first three towns, but those doors would lead them to this place in the fourth and final one.

There was no way they could have known that as they made their way through the other towns. And although the brownies, Elsa, and Zeth had spent more time in the Cursed Realm than she and Orin, they hadn't known about those hidden rooms.

For centuries, Belda had spent every day in her pub, and she'd never known about the trapdoor hidden in Sahira's room until Radagast tried to kill Sahira. Someone else could have found one of the doors and kept it to themselves, but almost all the immortals in the Cursed Realm had no knowledge of the hidden rooms.

Aurora and Alda believed they knew this castle too well not to have found a hidden door, but Belda had known her pub inside and out and had never known.

Then she recalled what Alda had said about why they were given rooms in the castle… *"That was Sheree's idea. That's why she stayed back when everyone else went to greet you. She kept a handful of servants with her to ready the rooms, and I was one of them. She thought it would be fun."*

At the time, Sahira took that to mean treating them so luxuriously when they planned to kill them was nothing more than another game, but what if it was something more? What if these rooms were Sheree's personal game? Her secret little fuck you to them and every dagadon in the realm?

Sheree was the only one who knew the location of the stones. Sahira doubted that after killing off all those who originally knew where they were hid—and she was convinced that's exactly what Sheree did—she'd told anyone else their location.

They were *hers.* This realm was hers, and no one would take it from her, but that didn't mean the overconfident, arrogant *bitch* still didn't like playing games with them. She did that every single day by keeping all the dagadon trapped here.

Orin had gone out to get weapons and answers, but what if the answers were beneath their feet the whole time?

Sahira released the closet doors and stepped back as her gaze fell to the floor. She'd done a cursory search for trapdoors while looking for the symbols in her room, but she never had the time to do a more intensive search and doubted Orin had either.

In the other towns, they'd designed the trapdoor in the pub so perfectly that it was almost impossible to see without knowing what to look for. Anything inside this castle would be the same.

And how Sheree would laugh and think it was so much fun to put them in these rooms, all while knowing they were so close to the key that could break them free of this gilded prison.

That was probably why they weren't in the dungeon... yet. Sheree would get more entertainment out of knowing they were stuck in these rooms with freedom at their fingertips.

Sahira rushed into the closet and shoved the clothes aside to carefully feel over the back wall. She didn't care how many hours it took; she'd search every *inch* of her and Orin's rooms for a way out. If she failed to find anything, she'd go for the brownies' room next.

She'd worry about Zeth and Elsa's rooms later. For now, she

had to focus on this as excitement hammered through her and she made her way lower down the wall.

CHAPTER SIXTY-ONE

It took Orin longer than he would have liked to find a way into the castle as guards spread around the perimeter. After what happened on the hunt, Desmond and Sheree weren't taking any chances when it came to him and his friends.

He'd fooled them into thinking he was too weak to try anything tonight. He wouldn't succeed in doing so again, which meant he had to make this count.

He didn't have much time to accomplish what he planned to. He had to return to Sahira before the servants went to wake them, which could be at any time.

Desmond and Sheree would change the game again tomorrow because he'd changed it on them. He wouldn't be surprised if they decided to wake them all in an hour or two.

That possibility caused his throat to constrict while fear niggled along his nape, but no matter what, he couldn't turn back.

He glanced behind him, but Sahira's balcony had vanished from view a while ago. Not being able to see it caused anxiety to claw at his insides. For a man who, up until recently, wasn't familiar with emotions like anxiety or jealousy, he'd sure experienced them a lot since Sahira entered the Cursed Realm.

He still wasn't entirely familiar with the new emotions or good at handling them, and right now, he needed to keep them buried. He loved Sahira, but the mostly emotionless man he'd been for centuries was the only way he'd get through this.

With steely determination, he shut down all his concerns for her. If he didn't, he'd never get through this.

Ahead of him, a door swung open as a servant walked out to hang a rug over a wooden post. She beat the dust from it with a paddle before lifting it and heading back into the castle.

Before the door closed, Orin slid into the building behind her. He paused to take in his surroundings as the servant hurried away.

In the sconces surrounding him, magical light flickered from the torches lining the walls. The murmur of voices came from ahead, but he wasn't concerned about them, as the lights provided plenty of shadows to keep himself concealed.

Moving swiftly down the hall, he rounded a corner and spotted two servants pushing a cart of silver trays. Orin remained hidden in the shadows as they took a right and left before stopping in front of a door.

One opened the door before helping the other gather some of the trays. Curious about whether the food might be going to some of the Elite, Orin slipped past them while they were still preoccupied trying to balance as many trays as possible between them.

Almost immediately, he knew he'd been wrong as the twisting stairs descended past dimly lit torches that barely pierced the darkness ahead. There weren't as many shadows here, but he could still keep himself cloaked in them.

He couldn't turn back as the trays clicked and clattered from the servants descending behind him. Orin stepped off the last stair and into the dungeon.

The foul aromas of shit, piss, and body odor permeated the air. Groans of misery and whimpers of despair came from behind the metal doors with a single slot in the middle.

Orin edged away from the stairs so the servants wouldn't accidentally hit him when they entered the room but didn't go further into the castle's bowels. The doors stretched on until they disappeared, and he didn't doubt that unfortunate souls filled every room.

Having heard the clatter of the trays, hands poked through the slots. In the first cell, at least five or six hands emerged, and judging by the hands poking through some of the other cells, there were about the same number in each of those too. The food the servants brought to the top of the stairs was nowhere near enough to feed all these immortals.

When the two women entered the dungeon and headed to the first cell, Orin ascended the steps and left the foul-smelling place behind. At the top of the stairs, he turned left and continued through the hallways.

He had to locate the main dining room. After meals there, Desmond and Sheree left out the back door; if he could find the room, he could track them from there.

Orin left Sahira behind so he could find at least one of them. He'd prefer Sheree, as he sought information on those stones, but he would settle for Desmond.

When he did find them, he'd slice little pieces of them away until they did what he asked... and he'd start with their hands.

He moved like a wraith through the castle, passing by others without them knowing he was there. Finally, he found the main dining hall.

Voices drifted from within as silverware clattered against plates. Since leaving Sahira, time felt like it was rushing past and screaming toward a bad ending, but if dinner was still in full swing, less time had passed than he feared.

He'd forgotten that he hadn't eaten since this morning until the smell of food wafted to him. His stomach rumbled as he stepped into the dining hall, and his eyes landed on Desmond and Sheree, sitting at the head of the table.

As Orin stared at them, he recalled the servants bringing food to the prisoners. It hadn't occurred to him before because it felt far later than it was, and he'd assumed the Elite had already eaten, but what if they were also bringing dinner to his friends?

CHAPTER SIXTY-TWO

SAHIRA INCHED FORWARD on her hands and knees as she kept her face centimeters from the ground. Her fingers crept across the wooden floor as she searched for any difference in the grooves or a notch that might indicate a panel she could pull free.

She'd already searched all the walls and was about halfway through the floor. Maybe she should have started with the floors considering that's where the hidden room was in the pub, but she seriously doubted the dagadon had created the same kind of secret room everywhere.

Or maybe she was wrong and part of the fun for these assholes was making others think things might be different when they weren't. Either way, she'd already set her course and wouldn't change it.

Her back ached from her hunched-over position, and her knees *hated* her, but she was determined to explore every centimeter of this floor. Keeping her nose close to the ground, she inched forward as a knock sounded on the door.

Sahira froze before her head slowly rose. She stared at the door like it was a dragon ready to devour her and held her breath while she waited for whoever it was to go away. Instead of doing so, they knocked again.

Reluctantly, Sahira released her silencing spell with a flutter of her fingers. "What is it?"

"Your dinner," a sweet voice called back.

A sinking sense of dread caused the hair on her arms to rise as her gaze shot around the room. Then, she bolted to her feet.

"I'll be right there!" she called.

Not like it mattered, they were the ones with the keys and could enter at any time, which meant she had to move fast.

Sahira raced into the bathroom and turned on the water in the tub before twisting the knob on the wall to engage the large, handheld shower nozzle. Water pounded into the claw-foot tub as steam started to rise.

Retreating from the bathroom, she closed the door noiselessly behind her and straightened her shoulders before striding over to the door. She was almost there when a key turned in the lock and the door swung open. Aurora and two guards stood on the other side.

Sahira came to an abrupt halt, but she kept her shoulders back and her face impassive as she struggled to hide her panic.

"Where's the dark fae?" one of the guards demanded.

Sahira planted her hands on her hips. "He's in the shower. After everything he's endured today, he needed it."

She was glad the haughtiness of her words hid the terror twisting her intestines into knots as the guards exchanged a look. They leaned further into the room to hear the running water before moving back again.

Before they could say anything more, Sahira took the tray from Aurora. "I'll make sure he gets this."

Aurora's eyes were questioning as they held Sahira's, but she turned and lifted another tray from the cart. "This is yours," she said.

Sahira set Orin's tray on the small stand a few feet away

before returning to the door. She took the tray from Aurora's hands. "Thank you."

Please go. Please go, she inwardly pleaded.

If they decided to go into the bathroom, not only would they rip her out of this room and away from her newfound mission, but they'd also sound the alarm, and the whole castle would be searching for Orin.

They'd take all her friends from their rooms and parade them through these halls to face whatever horrible fate awaited them. It couldn't happen. Not now. Not when she felt like she might be onto something, and Orin was seeking a way out.

Finally, the guards leaned back from the doorway, and Aurora edged back. One of the guards pulled the door closed, and the key turned in the lock again.

Sahira's shoulders slumped in relief, and she almost crumpled to the ground with the tray in hand. Instead, she carried it over to the bed and set it on the mattress before going to turn off the water.

She shouldn't waste time eating, but she hadn't had anything since this morning, and the smell wafting from the platters caused her stomach to rumble. Lifting the lid from the one on the bed, she removed a piece of bread, slathered it in butter, and replaced the top.

Biting into the bread, she returned to where she thought her spot was on the floor. With no way to mark where she left off, she couldn't be sure where she stopped and couldn't risk missing anything.

With a sigh, she moved closer to the wall. Sahira was sure she'd already searched this section, but as disheartening as it was to redo what she'd already done, she recast her silencing spell, stuck the bread in her mouth, got back on her hands and knees, and started examining it again.

CHAPTER SIXTY-THREE

ORIN RETREATED from the dining hall as he once again shut down his concerns over Sahira. He wouldn't get anything done if every part of him continued to scream for him to return to her.

If they brought food to the rooms, Sahira would figure out how to outsmart them. If she didn't, he'd soon learn about it, as everyone in this castle would tear it apart in search of him.

He had to remain focused on his mission, and right now, he still had time before Desmond and Sheree left the unusually subdued dinner. Conversations swirled around the table, but they weren't as boisterous as normal, and Desmond scowled at his plate as he stabbed at a piece of meat.

Orin smirked as he realized the poor, golden twat was still in a foul mood over not only losing his bet but being one-upped. That alone was worth his hand.

When dinner was over, he could follow Desmond and Sheree to their rooms. He doubted they surrounded themselves with guards while inside their rooms. But before that could happen, he required a weapon.

Staying close to the wall, Orin avoided the servants hurrying from the kitchen to the dining hall and back again. He followed them to the kitchen; it wasn't as good as a sword, but a carving knife would work.

When the hall ended, he emerged into the sprawling kitchen with its cathedral ceiling and beams stretching from wall to wall across the room. Like almost everything else in this bland, sterile place, gold flecked the white beams.

Multiple pots boiled in the five fireplaces lining the back wall. The steam rising for them coiled up the chimneys as it drifted away. The fires beneath crackled as the cooks scampered from the stove to the fires and back again.

The place was a beehive as the workers sought to sate their queen. They had to realize they'd never satisfy the insidious bitch they served.

Orin flattened himself against the wall to avoid someone accidentally bumping into him. He crept along the wall until he spotted a carving knife on a butcher block.

He made sure nobody was nearby to bump into him when he moved and that no one was heading for the carving station before stepping away from the wall. Before he lifted the knife off the block, he rested his hand on it and enshrouded it in shadows.

Once it was hidden, he slipped the knife from the counter and left the room. Keeping to the wall, he returned to the main dining room as the night started winding down.

The servants placed trays before the Elite and removed the tops to reveal the strawberry-covered desserts beneath. The Elite's murmured conversation swirled around the room, but no one laughed, and the wine didn't flow as freely as they ate.

Orin was impatient for it all to end so he could get on with this, but the clock ticked away another hour before they removed the desserts. It was nearing ten when Desmond rose earlier than he normally did.

As he stood, he knocked over his wine goblet. A male servant scurried forward to clean up the mess; Desmond smacked the man in the back of the head, sending him spiraling onto the table.

Orin stiffened over the unnecessary abuse as a hush descended on the room. Desmond grasped the man by his nape, lifted him off the table, and threw him on the floor.

"Useless," he muttered as the room held their collective breaths. "Throw him in the dungeon."

"No!" the servant cried.

As the guards descended on him, the servant's fingers clawed at the floor as he attempted to escape. "No!" he screamed when the guards each grabbed a limb and carried him from the room.

His screams rebounded down the hallways as they dragged him away. No one in the room dared to breathe as Desmond glowered at them.

Still seated at the table, Sheree smirked into her wine before setting the goblet down and rising. Orin stroked the handle of his knife as the servant's screams faded. Now he had confirmation that most of those in the dungeon didn't belong there, but he couldn't do anything about it now.

Desmond would pay soon. He'd make sure of it.

When Sheree turned and started from the room, Desmond fell in beside her. A collective breath released throughout the space, but no one returned to eating or dared to speak.

Orin followed the two Lords and their contingent of guards from the dining hall as he hunted them from a distance. He would enjoy this hunt a lot more than his last one.

CHAPTER SIXTY-FOUR

SAHIRA REFUSED to feel disheartened after searching every centimeter of Orin's room and discovering nothing. She could still explore her room and the brownies'. She couldn't let herself think there might not be a trapdoor in either of those rooms… or it might not exist at all.

This gave her something to focus on and a small bit of hope; she wasn't giving up either of those things. She claimed another piece of bread and a couple of carrots before trudging over to the balcony.

She'd prefer to shut the doors but couldn't risk locking Orin out. Though she suspected he'd still be a while, she couldn't take the chance.

The drapes drifted inward as she pulled them apart to step onto the balcony. She should probably open them completely for Orin to return, but she couldn't take the chance someone could see in. He'd be able to slip past them when a breeze blew.

Munching on a carrot, she pushed the drapes aside and strolled onto the balcony. Resting her arms on the railing, she studied the moon while ignoring the contingent of guards watching her every move.

She was itching to return to her search but compelled herself to stand there for at least ten minutes before retreating again. If they saw her, they would think everything was still perfectly fine and she was coming out to get some fresh air after caring for Orin... or so she hoped.

Once back inside, she entered her room to continue her search. Like in Orin's, she started in the closet.

Running her fingers over every part of the wall, she examined it for something to lead her out of here. Satisfied there was nothing in the closet, she moved on from it to the walls.

She carried the chair from Orin's room and stood on it to help her search the higher spaces. Following the walls into the bathroom, she gradually made her way around every surface.

She had to bring in the chair to explore the area over the sink and above the doorway. Standing on the chair, her fingers came across something that didn't feel quite right above the doorframe.

Biting her lip, she explored the surface to the right of the door. It was so far up it nearly touched the ceiling. While no cobwebs would dare to mar the pristine wood, someone dusting this area wouldn't feel the difference.

Just brushing the wall didn't do anything, and she couldn't see any change in the surface, but when she felt around it again, she definitely detected a small bubble there.

Biting her bottom lip, Sahira pushed her thumb into whatever was there. It depressed until something clicked.

Sahira almost fell backward off the chair as shock caused her to sway a little. *Did I really find it?*

Her pulse thundered in her ears as she leaned back to examine the spot she'd discovered. The tiniest hint of an indent could be seen in the wall, and she'd heard a click.

With excitement screaming through her, Sahira carefully climbed off the chair and forced herself to remain calm as she looked around the bathroom. She didn't see anything different, and nothing opened under her hands when she pushed on the walls.

Confused, she wandered into her room, but everything looked the same. She walked around as she searched for any sign of something different. No matter where she looked or what she pressed on, she didn't detect anything.

Returning to the bathroom, she climbed back on the chair. From a few inches away, she couldn't see any difference between the wall and the small button she pushed, but when she stood on her tiptoes and looked closer, she saw a small bubble.

With a small click, the button popped out again. Sahira strained to hear anything, but no sound followed.

"Damn it."

She pressed it again, and the click followed. She hoped whatever this was, it wasn't hooked up to an alarm of some sort, but if that was the case, the guards would probably already be in her room.

Climbing down from the chair, Sahira returned to the bathroom doorway. Deciding it was time to make another appearance for the guards, she opened the doors to her balcony.

Trying to act casual, she strolled around it while running her fingers over the railing and trying to step on as many places as possible. A trapdoor out here wouldn't make any sense, but nothing about these monsters did, and she wouldn't leave any stone unturned.

When she finished, she rested her arms on the railing again and studied the moon before retreating. She hoped the guards assumed she was anxious because of what happened with Orin, but she had no way of knowing what those assholes thought. If they weren't storming the rooms, she didn't care.

Sahira returned to the bathroom and waited for the button to pop out again. It didn't take long before it did, and she pressed it before returning to her room.

She was beginning to feel like a rat in a maze as she

continued feeling over the walls and floorboards, but she was determined to find out what the button did. After a few minutes, she returned to the button, waited for it to pop, and hit it again.

Time stretched on, and she had to keep returning to the button, but eventually, she finished in her room and crossed into Orin's. She stared helplessly around as everything in here looked the same too.

She ran her hands over the walls before returning to ensure the button hadn't popped out again. When she pressed it once more, she ran back to Orin's room to continue her search.

Running low on patience and fighting against hopelessness, she pulled open his closet doors and froze when she spotted a small crack in the back wall. *That wasn't there before.*

Her mouth parted on a breath, and unexpected tears of triumph filled her eyes. While she gazed at the small sliver of light, the door swung silently closed again.

CHAPTER SIXTY-FIVE

LIKE A TIGER ON THE PROWL, Orin stalked his prey through the hallways. Desmond and Sheree didn't talk or touch as they strolled ahead of their guards.

He smiled as he realized these fuckers had no idea how close they were to death. If he couldn't convince Sheree to tell him where the stones were, he'd still ensure they never saw another sunrise.

Maybe it wouldn't send the rest of the Elites into the chaos he hoped it would, but even if it didn't, it was time to start taking out the enemy. He couldn't wait to get started.

Desmond stopped outside a closed door. "Good night, Sheree. Sleep well."

"You also, Desmond," Sheree replied.

Orin carefully maneuvered toward the wall when the guards shifted, and half of them broke away to remain standing outside Desmond's door. They lined the wall with their shoulders back and chins high.

Orin almost followed Desmond but decided against it. Sheree was the real evil here and the only one who knew the location of the stones; *she* was the one he wanted.

Slipping around the guards, he managed to get within a foot of Sheree when she stopped outside the next closed door. One of the guards opened it for her, and when it finished swinging inward, she strode inside.

Orin slid around the corner and, keeping his back to the wall, inched along as he entered her room. She had no idea he was there when the guard shut the door behind her, but she would soon.

Orin kept himself against the wall as she clasped her hands before her while walking further into the room. Dim lights burned from the sconces on the walls, and from the lamps beside the sprawling, white sofa in the sunken sitting area twenty feet away. Two steps descended into the space.

Lamps of various sizes and colors were scattered around the main room. Most were floor lamps, but a few sat on the white tables. They all had multihued shades or stained glass that reflected a rainbow around the room.

They provided the most color he'd seen in this castle since arriving here. It was momentarily disorienting, as were the dozens of paintings on the walls.

The paintings covered almost every inch of the available wall space. They were all assorted sizes but bore the same subject... a young girl.

In each painting, she was doing different things like playing in a garden, holding a puppy, smiling on Sheree's lap, or shaking a rattle. The ages varied, but it was easy to see the similarities between the baby and the child.

There was no rhyme or reason as to how she'd organized the paintings. They didn't go from oldest to youngest or vice versa, but none aged the child past six or seven.

Sheree walked down the steps to the sunken living room and crossed to the balcony doors. When she opened them and walked outside, Orin descended into the living room and waited for her to return.

According to the grandfather clock in the corner, nearly ten minutes passed before she returned, closed the door, and started toward the doorway on the other side of the room. Orin had no intention of letting her go any further.

Slipping up behind her, he wrapped his handless arm around her throat and yanked back. Pulled off her feet, Sheree released a startled gasp before he choked off her air supply.

He resisted the impulse to drive his blade repeatedly through her heart as he carved away small slices of her and shoved them down her throat. He'd never been a bloodthirsty man; he killed because it was necessary, not because he enjoyed it.

But he was going to relish *every second* of this bitch's death.

CHAPTER SIXTY-SIX

"WHERE ARE THE AUGMENTATION STONES?" he demanded.

When she stiffened a little, he knew he'd struck a nerve. She hadn't expected him to know about the stones.

Her fingers shredded the flesh of his arm, but it was nothing compared to the pain of losing a hand or everything else they'd endured throughout this shithole of a realm. He chuckled at her weak attempt to free herself.

"Now, it's time to play *my* game," he whispered in her ear. "*Where* are the stones?"

This time, he loosened his arm enough for her to speak. When he did, the room suddenly blurred, and a strange whomping sound reverberated in his ears as the room tilted.

Orin tightened his hold on her again, but the strange sound and disorienting effect didn't stop. The dagadon had control over time, and he knew she was using her power to disorient him by making it blur, speed up, or something else.

He struggled to maintain control and not to fall over as waves of vertigo cascaded over him, and his stomach lurched. The worst part was he couldn't tell if he was holding her or not, until he felt a tug on his arm as she tried to pull it away.

She'd run to the guards if she got free, and it would all be over. He lifted her off the ground as he tried to choke the power from her, but the whomping sound only increased.

Her feet kicked against his shins as he staggered to the side and nearly went down. Bracing his legs apart, he swayed as his stomach lurched. He was glad he hadn't eaten, or she'd be wearing it.

Unable to stand it anymore and desperate to make it stop before she could escape, Orin plunged the knife down. It sank into something as warmth spread across his hand, but the whomping sound increased as inwardly, he felt like he was lurching from side to side.

He had no way of knowing what the knife was sinking into. He didn't feel any pain, but the noise grew louder as the room listed to the side like a ship taking on too much water.

Pulling the knife free, he thrust it down again and twisted. Sheree's heels bruised his shins, and her nails raked his skin as tiny, choked cries issued from her.

Orin staggered to the side and nearly went to his knees as he yanked the knife upward, slicing through something until the blade caught on something. When it did, the noise eased, and the room settled a little, though it still felt like he was walking sideways.

Yanking the knife free, he swung it down repeatedly, seeking to break her ability's hold over him. He still couldn't see and could barely think beyond ending this insanity before he was discovered.

He stabbed again and again until the noise finally stopped, and the room slowly righted itself. Blinking, Orin tried to bring everything into focus as his vision remained blurred.

Closing his eyes, he kept them shut for ten seconds before opening them. A hazy cloud remained at the edges of his vision, but it was clearing. When he closed his eyes and opened them again, the room came into clear focus.

Looking down, he discovered his hand covered in blood and bits of flesh. Blood dripped from him to stain the pristine white floor beneath them.

Sheree slumped in his other arm. Her head hung forward, and her shoulders were still as her insides spilled onto the floor.

Disgusted by the feel of her, Orin released her, and she hit the floor with a thud. Kneeling beside her, he turned her over to examine the vast damage he'd inflicted.

Despite having sliced her from the navel to the sternum and countless stab wounds, she was still alive as her eyes rolled before focusing on him. She was too weak to cast her ability over him again as her breath rattled in and out of her chest.

Leaning over her, he pressed the blade tip under her chin. "I'm not going to let you live; we both know that, and we also know you're not going to give me what I need. But you're going to watch me chop off your head."

Her eyes widened on him before he went to work. Gurgled sounds issued from her, and her fingers twitched on the ground as Orin took his sweet time working the blade through her throat.

He worked leisurely, but it wasn't long before he finished severing her head. With a bitter grin, he lifted it by her hair and carried it over to the mantle.

He set it on the ground as he removed a snow-white clock from its position in the center and plopped her bloody head in its place. Stepping back, he smiled at the agonized expression on his prize's features.

It was *lovely*.

There was no more hiding that he'd been out here tonight, and he had nothing to use against the other dagadon since he'd killed his hostage. He smiled as he poked Sheree's nose.

It was disappointing that her death hadn't lasted longer and been a lot more painful, but he hadn't expected the devastating effects of her ability. Besides, it was still fun.

Turning away from the mantle, he spied a shadow ducking

back from the room's doorway beyond. Orin sprinted across the room, grabbed his knife from where he'd left it on the ground, leapt over the couch, and chased after whoever hid there.

CHAPTER SIXTY-SEVEN

"How did you find this?" Loth asked.

"I tried thinking like Sheree. What more fun would it be than to place us in the rooms that could provide us freedom?" Sahira asked.

When she first discovered it, she hadn't gone in to examine the inside of the hidden room before knocking on the brownies' door. They'd answered almost immediately, and she'd ushered them into the room before closing their door and locking it again. The brownies could unlock it again, but this lock might buy them the few extra seconds needed to survive.

Once they were all in Orin's room and under her silencing spell, she let them in on what happened with Orin and where he'd gone. She assumed he was still safe; if they'd discovered him, the guards would have come in to round up the rest of them.

Pip surveyed the cracked door at the back of the closet. "Do you think it provides freedom?"

"I think I have to go in and find out. Did you tell Loth and Fath what I revealed to you in the garden?"

"I did."

"The stones could be in there."

"So could a flesh-eating monster, knowing the dagadon," Loth retorted.

As was his way, Fath didn't speak; his head tilted back and forth while he examined the closet.

"So could a flesh-eating monster," Sahira agreed. "But I have to go, and we all know it."

"Then I'm coming with you," Pip said.

"You have to stay here for when Orin returns. He has to know where I went and what's back there. We could try propping the door open, but I'm not sure that will keep it open, and if it doesn't, someone has to stay here to let me out again."

She didn't think about the fact she might not be able to make it back this way. That she could become trapped in there or eaten by something. She had to go, and they all knew it.

"We can't all go, but one of us can, and the other two can stay as lookouts," Pip said.

"Or we can escape into this place if the guards decide to storm our rooms," Loth said.

"It's always good to have options," Fath murmured sarcastically. "I will go too."

"No. It's best if two stay here to keep watch; I'm going," Pip insisted as the closet door closed again.

While the brownies fought over who would join her, Sahira returned to the bathroom and pushed the button again. She'd already shown the brownies where to locate it, and the nimble creatures scrambled up the doorframe and across the top to press the button.

They could open the door for her again if necessary. She hit the button once more before removing the chair from the bathroom.

The brownies didn't require it, and she couldn't have it there if the guards decided to storm the room. There weren't many in this castle who knew about that button; she wouldn't let them in on the secret. Orin could always bring the chair back later.

She carried the chair back to Orin's room and returned it to the corner before bending to set her hand on the ground. When Pip scrambled onto it, she learned who had won the fight as the brownie settled onto her shoulder near her ear.

"I'd feel a lot better if we had weapons," Pip said.

"I'll cast another protective spell over us like I did with the spiders," Sahira assured her. "It will at least keep things off us until we can either retreat or move forward."

When the brownie gave a brisk nod, the tips of her whiskers tickled Sahira's face. "Are you sure about this?" Sahira asked.

"Of course I am. Brownies never shy away from a fight."

A smile tugged at Sahira's lips, but it would devastate her if she were the cause of the death of this small creature with a giant's heart. She wouldn't argue with Pip either. She was a six-inch-tall grown woman who knew exactly what she did and didn't want to do.

"Let's go then," Sahira said.

She pushed the door open and didn't hesitate before stepping into the dim hall beyond. She and Pip entered a hallway that stretched about twenty feet before vanishing into the shadows cloaking it.

Sahira inched past the small lights flickering on the white walls. These lights weren't in any sconces but were a part of the walls as they glowed from inside tiny holes.

The hall ended in stone stairs that spiraled downward toward a yellowish glow. Sahira wove her fingers in front of her as she cast a protective spell around them. When she finished, she and Pip glanced back at where Loth and Fath stood with their heads poked around the door.

They both gave a little wave before Sahira started down the steps. She kept her hand on the thin metal rail as the stairs twisted round and round while going lower and lower.

CHAPTER SIXTY-EIGHT

HER SOFT LEATHER boots were silent on the steps, and while she felt a little naked without a weapon, the protective air bubble would keep them safe from an immediate attack. Hopefully, they could retreat quickly if necessary.

At the bottom of the steps, the hallway stretched onward. Here, small golden sconces lined the hall; they were far enough apart that their circles of light barely touched each other.

The humidity and dampness enshrouding the place made the air thick and her clothes stick to her. Instead of the boring white she'd grown accustomed to, dark stone walls surrounded them.

The stairs had taken them below the earth. She had no idea how far down they were, but she guessed it was at least two or three hundred feet after the long descent.

As she crept forward, she felt the oppressive weight of all that dirt, stone, and castle above their heads bearing down on them. Straining to hear anything beyond these thick walls, she tipped her head to the side, but the silence was absolute.

When they turned the corner, a thick metal door came into view. Pip's whiskers tickled her cheek when the brownie's head turned toward her, but Sahira focused ahead.

If something was about to burst out of the door to eat them, she'd run out of this place as fast as she could. She wasn't going to be a meal for anything in this realm.

When she stopped in front of the door, she examined its flat surface as she tried to figure out how to open it. There was no knob, no handle, or anything to help them enter whatever lay beyond.

Sahira frowned at the door as she resisted kicking and beating on it. Maybe they were supposed to knock and someone would answer, but she was sure that someone would probably chop off their heads, so she decided against that option.

However, she refused to be dissuaded. She hadn't discovered the hidden entrance and come this far only to be thwarted by a *door*.

Stepping back, Sahira examined the walls beside the door. They were mostly smooth gray stone, but a set of rocks to the right stuck out more.

Until now, the dagadon had been meticulous about how carefully they concealed their hidden chambers and how to enter them. *Why would they make something so obvious now?*

Still, she couldn't pretend those rocks weren't there. Running her fingers over the stones, she discovered she could pull them apart a little.

"Careful," Pip cautioned.

Sahira didn't have to be told twice as she gently prodded them apart. Set on hinges, the rocks swung outward to reveal a flat stone beneath. That stone was at least a foot high and a foot wide. Inside were dozens of moveable pieces on tracks.

"What are those?" Pip asked.

Sahira was wondering the same thing as she examined the small pieces. "I think it's a puzzle."

"Oh, that can't be good."

No, it couldn't, especially since Sahira had no idea what picture it was supposed to form. It would make sense for the dagadon to do this though. Yes, it would take them time to complete the puzzle and enter this room, but what did they care when it could stop others from getting inside and possibly to the prize they sought?

Sahira looked from the pieces, to the door, and back again. Then, her gaze fell to the floor, and her heart sank.

She hadn't noticed it when they first approached the door, but a crack ran along the floor on all sides of them. Lifting her foot, she stomped down on the floor. Not only did it thwack off the solid stone, but a hollow thud also accompanied the noise.

With a lump in her throat, she pointed out the cracks to Pip. "If we get this wrong, we're dead."

"Or we'll wish we were."

"Do you want to go back?"

"Do you?"

"No."

"Neither do I. Let's hope they give us a few wrong guesses before throwing us to the wolves."

Sahira didn't know how likely that was, but she hoped for the same thing as she studied the dozens of puzzle pieces. There was nothing to do but start, and the best way to go was to try matching all the similar colors together and hope the rest fell into place.

With a tremulous hand, she clasped a dark brown piece. She steadied the tremor before sliding the puzzle piece up its track and into a new position at the top, where there was a hint of a dark mark.

When the floor didn't immediately fall out from beneath them, she released a small breath before gripping the next one.

.

CHAPTER SIXTY-NINE

ORIN CAUGHT the woman as she fled toward another doorway leading off the spacious bedroom he'd entered. She squeaked as he gripped her arm and spun her around before snaking his arm around her neck.

"I'm Alda!" she blurted before he could cut off her air supply. "I met with Sahira in the garden!"

Her words kept him from choking her, and though he still pulled her back against his chest, he didn't completely cut off her air supply. She went to her toes a little to keep from being strangled as she leaned against him.

"What are you doing here?" he demanded.

"I'm Sheree's night maid on the weekends," Alda whispered. "I help her get ready for bed... or I did, anyway."

"You're one of the servants who told Sahira about the stones."

"Yes."

"Were you telling her the truth?"

"Yes. The stones exist... somewhere. None of us know where they are, and we've all lived in this realm for centuries; some of us have been here for millennia."

He wasn't sure if he believed her, but her answer would do… for now.

"I can get you out of this room," she whispered as if she were reading his mind. "You can't do it alone without alerting the guards. Many of the servants are on your side, especially *me*. These monsters fed my brother, my last living relative, to the dogs for entertainment. They'd already killed my parents and my sister, and they'll turn on me one day too. *No one* wants them dead more than me."

The fire in her words and the vehemence of her voice led him to believe she was telling the truth, but he still didn't trust any of these things.

"I doubt that," Orin growled.

She rested her hand over the claw marks Sheree had inflicted on his arm. "The servants are on your side. We want out of this realm too."

He couldn't deny they probably were as eager to break free of this place as him and his friends. "How do you plan to get me out of this room?"

"How did *you* plan to get out of here?"

He hadn't thought that far ahead when he followed Sheree into the room; he'd been too determined to get at her to think about the consequences of it. He'd assumed her quarters wouldn't be as monitored as theirs, but he'd been wrong, as the guards had taken a position in the hall and would notice if he opened the door cloaked in shadows.

"They have guards stationed everywhere tonight," Alda continued. "They're all along the garden outside of this room too. I can walk out of here and into Desmond's rooms. That's where I'm supposed to go next."

"Why?"

Her head bowed a little, and a small tremor ran through her. "Because that's what's expected of me after leaving here."

"So you're his lover?"

"NO!"

When she shouted the word, he bore down on her throat, cutting her off. He held her completely still as he listened for the door crashing against the wall as the guards rushed in.

Her shout had sounded loud to him, but it must not have carried beyond this room as no one came to kill them. He eased his grip on her throat.

"Careful," he warned as he pressed the tip of the bloody blade under her chin. "If they come in here, I'll kill you first."

She gulped. "I didn't mean to be so loud. It's just... no, Desmond is not my lover. I hate him. I hate him so much. The things he does, that he *forces* us to do... he's... he's... a *monster*."

Orin didn't require any further details. "Sahira said you told her that Sheree was the real evil here."

"He's the monster, and she's his puppeteer. Without her, there is no him. Just because she's not with him tonight doesn't mean she's not there at other times."

"Well, she's dead, so there's that."

"And even with a knife against my flesh, I've never been happier. They expect me to leave here and go to Desmond's room; they won't question it when I do. We'll have to wait a little longer, but not much, before it's about the time I would normally leave. Sheree never liked anyone staying in her rooms with her, so she never had a maid stay the night. Probably because, and she was right, one of us would try to kill her in her sleep."

"Didn't she think you might try to kill her while she was awake?"

"She was stronger than me and would have taken me down if I tried. More than that, she always has guards nearby. All she'd have to do is scream, and they'd all be in here to save her. As much as I hate her and this realm, I don't have a death wish. I can leave this room in half an hour, and no one will think anything of it. I can take you with me when I go."

Orin pondered this before releasing her. She hadn't screamed when she discovered him decapitating Sheree. She could have alerted everyone he was here but hadn't.

He didn't trust her and would make sure she didn't try anything stupid, but she was right; he had no other way out of this room. It was her or nothing, and he hadn't come this far to have it all fall apart now.

CHAPTER SEVENTY

"IF YOU TRY ANYTHING, I'll kill you," he vowed.

"I know."

"Stay here."

He kept an eye on her as he walked around the bed and toward the drape-covered windows on the other side. When he pulled back a small sliver of the curtain, he discovered a set of balcony doors and a line of guards twenty feet beyond them.

Carefully, he settled the drape back into place and turned toward Alda. "Are they always out there in such number?"

"Yes. There are many in this realm who want all the Elites dead, but especially Sheree and Desmond. I'll help you kill every single one of them."

"They're not married, but are they a couple?"

"I'm not sure I'd call them that. They enjoy unleashing their cruelty on others and having sex with each other, but they also thoroughly enjoy watching each other torment, abuse, and rape others. They get off on it."

Orin couldn't imagine watching another man with Sahira; the idea made him so furious he had to shut it off before he completely lost control during a time when emotions were his worst enemy.

"They don't love each other," he said.

She scoffed. "I'm pretty sure they hate each other, but they like that too."

They didn't speak as Orin studied the room and the countless paintings of the same young girl lining the walls here.

"You love the witch," Alda stated.

Orin's eyes narrowed as he crossed his arms over his chest. His stump was starting to throb, but he paid it little attention as he studied the woman across from him.

"You don't have to admit it," she said. "I see it in the way you look at her."

"You're awfully watchful."

"It's what they've trained us to do here. We watch, wait, and rush in whenever we're needed. If we don't, we pay the price."

Orin didn't say anything as he glanced from her to the clock and back again. He wasn't going to confirm her assessment of his relationship with Sahira, but he wouldn't deny it either.

He waved his finger at the wall. "What's with all the paintings of the girl?"

Alda glanced around as if she were seeing them for the first time. "That's Sheree's daughter."

"Where is she?"

"Dead. She died at six, or, I should say, she was murdered at six. They say that's why Sheree convinced the other Elites to create the spell that kept us here. It's said a warlock murdered her daughter while searching for the gold the dagadon possess."

"Do you believe it?"

"It's one of the few things I do believe about her. Whether or not it was for her gold, I don't know, but her daughter was murdered. On more than one occasion, I found her weeping as she knelt before a painting. I never let her know I was there; she would have beaten, imprisoned, or killed me if she had known, but her anguish was real."

Orin felt a tug of sympathy for the beautiful child in the portraits. She had a mischievous smile, and the twinkle in her eyes radiated playfulness and innocence.

He felt no sympathy for her bitch of a mother. He didn't have children and had never expected to have them, but he'd like to one day have them with Sahira.

If someone murdered one of those children, it would break his heart, and he'd hunt the offender to the ends of the realms to destroy them. But he wouldn't use his sorrow and rage as an excuse to lock others away and turn them into playthings.

Sheree had gotten everything she deserved; her child hadn't.

Alda waved a hand at the blood he'd left on her arm. "I should clean up."

"So should I."

He followed her into the bathroom, and they both washed the blood from them before turning off the water. Orin grinned as he used the stark white towels to wipe away the rest of Sheree's blood. When he finished removing as much of the blood as he could, he tossed the towels on the floor and smiled. He'd bet dirty towels were a big no-no for Sheree.

Alda left the bathroom first and went to stand near the bedroom doorway, but he kept an eye on her before emerging.

"We can go now," Alda said.

Orin wrapped the shadows around him again and glided soundlessly across the floor to her. "If you do anything to reveal I'm with you, I'll kill you first."

She jumped a little when his words came from beside her; she hadn't known he'd moved so close, and that was how he liked it. If she was afraid for her life and aware he could be anywhere, she'd be less likely to turn against him.

"I'll get you safely out of here," she vowed.

With that, she led the way out of the bedroom, across the

blood-soaked sitting area, and onto the main door. When her hand fell on the knob, he knew this would go one of two ways... she'd get them out of here and into Desmond's suite, or she'd reveal he was with her, and he'd kill her before they captured him.

Orin braced himself for either option as she opened the door.

CHAPTER SEVENTY-ONE

THE FIRST TIME Sahira put one of the puzzle pieces in the wrong place, the floor creaked and cracked open. Pip released a tiny squeak, and her hands bit into Sahira's shoulders, but she didn't suggest going to wait on the other side.

The second time, she put one of the pieces in wrong, the floor cracked open further, and she had to lean forward to keep from sliding back across the rocks. She could still get off the precarious stage but refused to do so.

The third time she got one wrong, it opened enough to reveal the vicious spikes below. They stood at least three feet off the ground, and while no bones jutted from the lethal projectiles, she could easily picture hers rotting away down there.

Her protective spell couldn't keep her safe from impalement; they'd easily pierce through it. And there was no getting safely away from this place anymore. She either got the rest of the pieces right or ended up a watering can.

Gulping, she dug the fingers of her left hand into the rocks as she tried to keep her balance on the floor. It was becoming increasingly difficult to stay on the small stage they stood on.

"You should go," she said to Pip.

"No, I shouldn't."

"If I fall onto the spikes, you can get help."

"I can avoid the spikes. I'm a lot smaller than you."

That was most likely true, but Sahira would prefer it if the brownie got herself to safety now. But, like her, Pip was stubborn and not going anywhere.

With her fingers digging securely into the wall so she could hold on, Sahira studied what she'd put together and the remaining shapes. Hair, eyes, and a mouth were starting to take on the form of a face.

Examining the remaining colors and puzzle shapes, she moved another one into place. She breathed a sigh of relief when it clicked and she didn't drop onto the spikes below.

She moved through more of the pieces, but when she got another one wrong, the floor tilted at such a precarious angle, that if she hadn't been holding onto the rocks, she would have plunged onto the spikes, as nothing of the floor remained below her.

With her feet dangling beneath her, Sahira remained calm as she dug her toes into the rocks. The stones bit into her hand and dug beneath what remained of her nails.

That one should have sent her spiraling onto the spikes. Resting her forehead against the stones, she took a deep breath as she tried to control the riotous beat of her heart.

Her arms and legs protested her precarious position, but after climbing the mountains to get to this place, she was used to clinging to rocks. She could get through this.

Blinking away the sweat coating her lashes, Sahira tried to clear her blurry vision. She didn't dare take the time to wipe it off so she could see better or move in any way that wasn't necessary.

She had to do this fast, but fast might be what got her killed. With her lashes still coated in sweat, Sahira studied the puzzle as best she could. All she needed was a few more pieces to fit in, and she could fly through the rest.

When Sahira's fingers found another piece, Pip pointed to a missing section. "I think that goes there."

Since the brownie could see it better than her, Sahira didn't argue with her as she moved the piece and clicked it into place. Her heart raced, and her arms and legs ached as sweat cleaved her shirt to her.

She kept waiting for her sweaty fingers to lose their precarious grip and to plunge onto the spikes, but somehow, she held on and continued moving through the puzzle. It became easier as she moved more pieces until she and Pip flew through the rest.

When she put the last piece into place, a small creak filled the air as the floor rose and clicked securely. Sahira's legs trembled when she set her feet on the floor and sank to her knees.

"You okay?" Pip asked.

"Yeah. Just give me a minute."

Resting her hands on her legs, she took a steadying breath and shook out the cramps in her fingers before finally using her arm to wipe the sweat from her eyes. Her blurred vision cleared enough for her to see the puzzle was a picture of a pretty young girl who looked to be about five or six.

When the door started to vibrate, Sahira leapt to her feet and prepared to run from whatever might rush out the door. Nothing emerged, and once the door settled into place, the puzzle pieces fell apart and scattered along their tracks; the rocks closed over the top of them again.

"Good job," Pip said as Sahira stepped into the hallway beyond.

"You too."

Just inside the doorway, Sahira stopped to study the next hall. It was almost identical to the one they'd left and ended in a metal door. The hair on Sahira's nape rose; she had no idea what horrors or games this hall held for them.

When the door behind her rattled, Sahira turned to watch it slide across the way. She could jump through there and run back to Orin's room, but at this point, it was no safer there than it was here.

The door clicked into place with a note of finality, and Sahira saw no other way to open it or any rocks that might be hiding a game. The only way back was to go forward.

Yay, she thought sarcastically as she turned back to face the other door.

"More fun," Pip muttered.

Now that she knew what to look for, Sahira searched the door across from them for out-of-place rocks. She didn't see anything there, but they were still far enough away that it could be hidden from her.

There's some way to get through that door, and we'll find it.

When she stepped forward, her foot landed on a rock that sank beneath her boot. At first, she didn't understand what happened, but as a click sounded in the room, her instincts screamed at her to *move!*

Sahira threw herself backward as the floor beneath the stone she'd stepped on fell away. Unable to stop her backward momentum, she fell on her ass and sat with her hands on the cool rock as she panted for breath. Pip's hands twisted into her damp tunic.

When she was sure she wouldn't vomit on the floor, she leaned toward that space and looked down to discover more spikes in the ground below. The lethal points shone in the light reflecting off them.

Leaning away from the death trap, Sahira examined the hundred-foot-long hallway. It wasn't far, but the other door felt like it was miles away, and she had no idea which stones could lead to a bone-piercing, agonizing fate.

"Shit," Pip muttered.

Pushing herself back up, Sahira examined the floor around

the stone that had given way. She could easily avoid falling into it, but some of these other stones would be traps too.

The stones were four different colors: dark gray, light gray, medium gray, and another shade somewhere between them all. They were all similar enough that they blended together but distinct enough to separate them if someone was looking for it.

"They're different colors," Pip said.

"They are."

"Maybe we're not supposed to step on certain colors."

"Maybe. Did you happen to see what color I stepped on?" Sahira asked.

"No."

"Neither did I. So, we'll have to pay better attention."

And hope that her next pick in color wasn't her last.

"Should we start with light gray? It's the closest to the white that these assholes are so obsessed with," Sahira suggested.

"Light gray sounds good to me," Pip said.

Holding her breath and praying she wasn't wrong, Sahira stretched her leg far to the left and pushed down on a light gray stone. She snatched her leg back and waited for the floor to drop away, but nothing happened.

"Light gray for the win," Pip muttered.

Sahira shifted completely over to the light gray stone and perched on the surface. It was big enough for her to stand on but didn't offer much room beyond that.

With her heart on the verge of exploding and sweat beading her forehead again, she moved on to the next light gray stone and the next. It wouldn't astonish her if, at some point, the dagadon decided to change the game and make the light gray ones death traps, so she always tested first before putting her full weight on them.

She was almost a quarter of the way down the hall when she ran into a problem. The following light gray stone was too far away for her to reach.

They were going to have to try for another color, and Sahira wasn't sure her luck would hold out.

CHAPTER SEVENTY-TWO

ORIN WAITED for Alda to sound the alarm as she walked out the door and stepped far enough into the hall that he could move out behind her. After a few seconds, she turned to close the door.

With her shoulders back, she didn't acknowledge the guards or start screaming that he was here and Sheree was dead as she strode toward Desmond's door. This little dagadon kept her promises, unlike the Elite in this realm.

When she stopped outside Desmond's door, one of the guards leaned over and opened it for her. The man didn't look at her as he moved back into place and returned to his ramrod straight position.

Alda glided into the room and waited a few seconds before closing the door behind her. "Are you here?" she whispered.

"Yes," he murmured in her ear, and she shivered.

"Just remember, I'm on the chopping block now too. I'm also trusting you. Please don't leave me behind. The guards will kill me."

"I won't. Don't speak anymore."

Alda turned away from the door and strode further into Desmond's rooms. Like the rest of the castle and Sheree's rooms,

316 BRENDA K DAVIES

the walls were all white. At least paintings of a little girl didn't cover these walls.

Instead, a few paintings of bloody battle scenes decorated the stark space. Dozens of clocks hung on the walls, sat on the tables, and perched in the corners.

They only had one clock in Belda's town, but Desmond seemed obsessed with them, but then, the dagadon were beings of time. It was as much a part of them as the shadows were a part of him.

"Is that you, little bitch?" Desmond called in a singsong voice from what was most likely his bedroom. "I have some extra fun planned for us tonight."

Alda shuddered but kept her shoulders back and her chin high as she strode past the sitting room and into the bedroom beyond. Orin followed her.

When they entered the bedroom, Orin's eyebrows rose at the sight of the leather bonds hanging from the walls. A naked Aurora was already strapped into them.

Her feet dangled above the ground, and her arms were yanked over her head. She wore a ball gag and a blindfold, probably to hide her cries of distress as her joints looked about to give way.

Orin had enjoyed playing with others in many, *many* different ways over the years, but this wasn't fun for the woman; it was just cruelty. Maybe some would enjoy such a position, but if this was for fun, they'd have the opportunity to let their partner know they wanted out of it; Aurora had no way of communicating that.

She also couldn't stop Desmond from delivering another blow with the small whip he held. When it cracked against her red and swollen skin, Aurora jerked and released a sound that no one could mistake for pleasure.

Before him, Alda's step faltered a little, but she didn't stop.

He imagined things would get worse for her if she refused to participate. Desmond would probably like that more.

Orin studied the piece of shit before him as Desmond hit the woman again. The welt he'd created started to bleed, and sweat slid down her brow to drip from her chin.

Usually, another's suffering didn't bother him. Life was pain in many ways, and they all had to endure it. But if given the chance, this was what Desmond would do to Sahira; because of that, he felt sympathy for the woman.

After the events of this day, he suspected this asshole planned on doing it to her soon too. He might be practicing with these women tonight.

Orin's hand fisted as his blood pressure throbbed in his temples. *Keep it under control. Don't think about her. Focus only on what needs to be done here, or you won't make it back to her.*

CHAPTER SEVENTY-THREE

"Little bitch!" Desmond exclaimed when he turned to find Alda standing a few feet away. He was completely naked as he threw his arms in the air but did not embrace her. Instead, he swung the whip out and caught her on the cheek. "I'm sorry! My mistake."

Judging by his smile, it was anything but a mistake, as Alda refrained from touching the reddening welt on her cheek. The fact she didn't make a sound led Orin to believe this wasn't the first time Desmond had made a "mistake."

Orin *loathed* men who abused women. He'd done some pretty shitty things in his lifetime; some of those things were to the woman who'd come to mean the most to him, which he'd regret for the rest of his life, but he didn't lay his hands on women like this.

If they asked for certain things, he was more than happy to give it to them if it enhanced their pleasure, but neither of these women had asked for this. And out of all the things he'd done, he'd *never* forced himself on a woman.

He hadn't cared for almost all the women who had shared his bed, but he had standards and morals, even if most didn't think he did. He doubted most of the women Desmond bedded were willing, which was unacceptable to him.

Slipping around behind the man, Orin studied the whimpering woman hanging from the wall before shifting his attention back to his prey. As fast as he could, he slid his arm around the man's throat, jerked his head back, and drew his blade across Desmond's jugular.

Now, it was Alda's turn to smile as blood spurted from Desmond, and his hands flew to his throat as he attempted to staunch the flow. His eyes rolled as terror emanated from him.

Letting go of Desmond, Orin watched the man stagger into the wall as he released the shadows. He also smiled as he sauntered over to stand beside Alda.

He didn't worry Desmond would call out for the guards; he'd ensured that wouldn't happen by taking out his windpipe. Desmond's eyes widened on them as blood gushed between his fingers.

It wasn't a lethal wound, but he was losing blood too fast to heal himself and was too panicked or weakened to unleash his ability to disorient his enemy. With blood spilling down his arm and dripping onto the floor, Desmond lurched to the side and fell on his bed.

He tried to scream, but all that came out was a gurgling, wet sound; Alda's smile grew. After a few more seconds, Desmond lost consciousness.

"How do I keep him from using his power on me when he wakes?" Orin asked.

"Blindfold him," Alda answered. "We can't use our ability if we can't see. We have to be able to focus it on someone."

"Good to know."

Aurora jerked against her bonds and made a strangled sound against the ball in her mouth.

"Can we trust her enough to let her down?" Orin asked.

"Yes," Alda said. "There are few servants you can't trust to help you. We're tired of being their prisoners and playthings."

"Hopefully, that will change after tonight."

While he worked to untie Aurora from the wall and lowered her to the ground on her wobbly legs, Alda bound Desmond, blindfolded him, and rolled him off the bed and onto the floor. When she finished, she helped Aurora into the bathroom. A minute later, the sound of running water filled the room, and Alda returned.

"He needs to wake soon," Orin said. "I have no idea how long it will be before the guards enter my friends' rooms. I have to return before that happens."

"The guards won't do anything unless ordered to... or unless they become suspicious for some reason. As long as your friends stay quiet, and Desmond and Sheree aren't around to give that command, your friends will remain locked in their rooms."

Orin wanted to believe her, but he wasn't willing to take any chances with Sahira's life. "What time do these two assholes usually leave their rooms?"

"Not until late morning or early afternoon. It depends on what they did the night before."

"And when do *you* leave here?"

"We always leave before he goes to bed, usually around three."

"So, he has to wake before then."

"Maybe you shouldn't have slit his throat."

Orin shrugged; she was right, but it was a good way to keep Desmond from using his power against him. "I didn't know about the blindfold thing then. I wouldn't make the same choice now."

The bathroom water turned off, and Aurora emerged ten minutes later. Her white-blonde hair hung around her shoulders, and her dark brown eyes were red-rimmed but shone with fury when they landed on Desmond.

Alda nudged Desmond with her foot before stepping back. "He's healing; he'll wake soon."

Orin went to the other room to retrieve a chair before returning to the bedroom. He lifted Desmond onto the seat and held his shoulder while Alda tied him to the back of the sturdy piece of furniture. When they were finished, he strode over to sit on the white chair in the corner.

CHAPTER SEVENTY-FOUR

SAHIRA DIDN'T THINK it would be so obvious, but after some debate, she and Pip decided to try for the next lightest color gray. Going for the color closest to white worked the first time; maybe it would work again.

Stretching out with her toe, she hesitated before pushing down hard enough to trigger something. The second she did, a click sounded, and she yanked her foot back before the floor dropped out.

Except, this time, the floor didn't fall away. Instead, dozens of darts shot out from unseen holes in the walls.

If they hadn't been encircled by her protective air bubble, at least four darts would have hit them. As it was, one of them pierced through the spell and whistled past her ear. Thankfully, it shot through on the side where Pip wasn't sitting.

Rattled by how close the dart came to them, Sahira wiggled her fingers and murmured some words to repair where the flying projectiles fractured the bubble. She glimpsed one of the darts lying on the ground while she worked. A green coating covered its sharp point; she had no doubt it was poisonous and probably would have left them writhing in agony before killing them.

"I'm so small that I probably wouldn't set these things off," Pip said.

"I don't think you should test that theory. If you set them off, you'll be beyond the protective bubble."

"There's no *way* they designed these traps with my kind in mind. Everyone always underestimates us and never counts on us for anything."

Sahira couldn't argue with that. She'd heard about brownies before encountering them but never given them much thought, and she certainly wouldn't have recruited them for a war. But the tiny immortals were fierce, proud fighters who would make anyone who underestimated them pay for it.

"If I get to the other side and open the door, maybe it will disable all the traps and you can make it safely across," Pip continued. "Who knows what the next stone might unleash on us."

It could be poisonous snakes with which they'd be trapped inside this room. Sahira shuddered at the possibility.

Sahira didn't want to let the tiny creature go out there alone, but she had to. "Okay, but be careful."

"Of course."

With that, Pip slid down her arm and fell to the floor. With deft, unhesitating steps, she moved beyond the reach of Sahira's protective spell. She didn't even pretend to be careful; instead, she sprinted across the floor.

And as she'd predicted, her weight didn't set off any of the stones. When Pip made it to the door, she grasped the rocks beside it and scrambled up the wall to a set of stones.

From where she stood, Sahira couldn't see anything different about those stones, but there must be something there as Pip leaned closer. Then, she pulled one aside and hit a button.

Three clicks sounded as the locks disengaged. The ground quaked a little when the metal door slid to the side to reveal a dim glow beyond. Again, nothing rushed out to attack them.

Pip twisted on her perch to call to Sahira. "Are you coming?"

Taking a deep breath, Sahira braced herself before stepping onto a dark gray stone. She yanked her foot back and ducked, but the floor didn't give way, nothing shot out of the walls, and serpents didn't rise to destroy her.

Carefully lowering the hands she'd thrown over her head, Sahira rose and stepped fully onto the dark gray stone. Nothing happened.

She didn't know if that was because the stone had always been safe or if Pip's opening of the door had disabled the traps, but she wasn't taking any chances. Alternating between the lightest and darkest rocks, she moved in a zigzag pattern across the floor until she reached Pip's side.

She stood next to the brownie as they leaned forward to peer into the room beyond.

CHAPTER SEVENTY-FIVE

"THIS LITTLE PIGGY went to market. This little piggy went home. This little piggy had roast beef. This little piggy had none. And this little piggy went wee wee wee as it was chopped the *fuck* off."

With that, Orin used the hunting knife he'd uncovered in a weapon's room just off Desmond's bedroom to chop off what remained of the man's pinky finger. Desmond screamed against the ball gag Orin had shoved into his mouth as sweat poured down his florid face.

While hiding in the tunnels beneath Del's manner, Orin had gathered his fair share of refugees from the Lord's war; some were human. Nessie, who arrived with her four-year-old nephew, Jayden, would often do silly nursery rhymes to keep him entertained.

At the time, Orin hadn't appreciated the little piggy rhyme as much as he did now while Desmond continued to scream and blood flowed from his severed finger. The poor little pinky piggy had received the worst of it so far.

Two of Desmond's other fingers were missing their top joints, and he'd chopped all the others down to the knuckle, but the little pinky was the first to go completely. It wouldn't be the last.

Desmond had woken twenty minutes ago, but Orin had yet to ask him any questions. He'd make sure that by the time he removed the ball gag, Desmond would be ready to blather all his secrets.

As Desmond continued to thrash against his restraints, Alda grinned before coming forward to toss some of the powder that would stop the bleeding onto the appendage. Aurora had uncovered it in Desmond's bathroom, and it was such a handy thing, especially since Orin was just getting started.

He couldn't have the man passing out from blood loss again. Pain, sure; Orin could revive him pretty fast from that.

Aurora wasn't smiling, but she didn't suggest stopping and didn't look away while he worked. Desmond had ensured many of his followers considered him the enemy and wouldn't do anything to help him.

Orin was positive most of them would gladly throw Desmond to the dogs. Alda certainly would.

Orin started making his way through what remained of Desmond's fingers again. "This little piggy…."

Over the years, especially during the first war against the Lord, he'd tortured others to get the answers he sought but never relished it like he did with Desmond. He started singing when Desmond began sobbing against the ball gag.

And he'd finally reached the point he sought, although it was far sooner than he'd expected or anticipated. He was having too much fun with this, but the man was already breaking.

He'd prefer to remove the blindfold so Desmond could see him, but he supposed being in the dark made this scarier. He'd have to settle for that.

Orin finished singing the nursery rhyme before lopping off what remained of Desmond's thumb. When he finished, he sat back and set the knife down. Once he removed the ball gag,

Desmond sobbed gibberish as his tears soaked the blindfold and seeped free to slide slowly down his cheeks.

"There, there, Desi." Orin patted the man's cheek as he spoke. "It's not so bad. At least you still have *parts* of your hand. You might be able to still use it to jerk off."

Alda snickered, and a smile tugged at the corners of Aurora's mouth.

"Where's my hand, Desi? I thought you were going to put it on your mantel. I didn't see it there."

When the man opened his mouth to scream, Orin shoved the ball gag back in it. "I'm disappointed in you," he chided.

This time, it wasn't the fingers he went for as he placed the blade against Desmond's balls. The man kept sobbing, but he stiffened, and some of his noises subsided as his heart pounded so hard it vibrated his chest.

"I enjoy playing games too," Orin told him. "Which is something you know because you eavesdropped on us, which wasn't very nice of you." Desmond recoiled when Orin dug the blade a little deeper. "But games become boring, and I'm getting bored, Desi, so I'd suggest you start keeping me entertained by answering my questions. If you try to scream, I'm going to assure you that it won't matter how many fingers you lose because there won't be anything left to jerk off; do you understand me?"

With tears dripping from his chin and snot pouring from his nose, Desmond nodded enthusiastically. Orin kept the knife against Desmond's dick while he removed the ball gag again.

"Tell me, Desi, where are those Augmentation Stones I've heard so much about?" Orin inquired.

Desmond's head twisted toward where he'd last heard the girls; it was where they stood. "You bitches! Why are you telling the enemy our secrets?"

When Orin pressed the blade deep enough to draw blood, Desmond's breath sucked in as he stopped speaking.

"Not *our* enemy," Alda replied. "That would be *you*."

Desmond started to sputter but stopped when Orin placed the ball gag back in his mouth. "I think I made it clear you're only to speak to answer *my* questions."

With that, he sliced deep enough that he took off half his dick. Desmond screamed as more tears streamed down his cheeks.

When Desmond finally settled into pathetic whimpers, Orin started talking again. "Okay, I'm going to ask you one more time, where are the Augmentation Stones? When I remove the gag, all you'll do is answer my question. If I get anything more than that, I will make you a eunuch. Is that understood?"

Desmond nodded.

"Good."

With that, Orin removed the gag.

"I don't know where they are," Desmond gushed.

"That's not the answer I'm looking for, Desi," Orin told him.

"No, no, no, no, no, don't cut me again. I don't know where they are! I wasn't one of the Elite who cast the spell. The only survivor of that group was Sheree. *She's* the only one who knows the location of the stones."

Orin gritted his teeth as he recalled stabbing that bitch. She hadn't left him any other choice, and she *never* would have told him the location of those stones, but without her, they had almost no chance of finding them.

He could have cut her into tiny pieces, and she would have gone to her grave with the knowledge. That was probably why she never told Desmond their location; she knew he'd sing like a songbird as soon as he faced adversity.

She wasn't like little Desi, who was as weak as he was depraved. No amount of torment he inflicted could have compared to the loss of her child, and she would have endured it all with a smile.

"I don't believe you," Orin said, though he did.

"It's true," Desi sobbed. "For the love of all things, I *swear* it's true. She never told me where the stones were. She never wanted anyone else to know. Who do you think killed the original Elite? It was her because it was her secret, and if she died, she'd determined the secret was going with her. That's how she intended to keep us safe from the outsiders seeking to destroy us."

"Safe," Alda snorted. "You call being tied to a wall, beaten, raped, tossed to dogs, and thrown in the dungeon for the smallest offenses *safe*?"

"You *like* it," Desi snarled.

Orin didn't stop Alda when she walked over, picked up the kitchen knife Orin had left on a nearby table, and lopped off what remained of poor little Desi's dick. Orin shoved the ball gag back into the man's mouth as he screamed over losing his favorite appendage.

"I don't know why you're screaming," Alda said. "You like it."

Orin admired her style as she set the knife down and returned to stand beside Aurora, who hugged her. Aurora released her to grab the bag of powder. She tossed a handful at Desmond's crotch before retreating.

CHAPTER SEVENTY-SIX

HE CONTINUED LETTING Desi scream against the ball gag as he tapped the knife against his knee and studied the room. If they couldn't find the stones, they'd never escape this realm, but if he could get enough weapons and servants on their side, they could stage an uprising.

He'd never admit defeat and give up trying to get away from this place, but if they had control of this realm, they wouldn't have to live under the thumb of these twisted oppressors. It was a better option than anything else they faced.

Desmond's room had plenty of weapons; he just required an army to help him.

"Are there other servants who'd help us to overthrow these assholes?" he asked. "Desmond has quite the store of weapons. I can smuggle a lot of them out of here and get them into their hands. Without the stones, we can't break free of this realm, but maybe we can reclaim it and make it a safer place for all of us until we figure out the next step."

"There are plenty who will help," Alda said. "We've been plotting a rebellion for years, but it's mostly been talk, until now. All we wanted was freedom, but without weapons and the guards' training, they would easily overpower us, even though we outnumber them."

"We kept telling ourselves, one day an opportunity would arise, and we'd be able to break free without them destroying us or making our lives worse if we lost. And believe me, it seems bad now, but they could have made our lives a *lot* worse," Aurora said.

Orin recalled the dungeon and the lost souls trapped there. "I believe you."

"That time has come," Alda said. "Sheree's dead; Desmond isn't surviving this... or at least, I hope he's not."

"Oh, he's not," Orin assured her, and Desmond's sobs increased as beads of drool dangled from the corners of his swollen lips.

"Hush, hush," Orin soothed as he patted Desi's cheek again. "You should be happy to be joining your *wife* soon. It was so clear how much you both loved each other." He leaned forward as he examined the pathetic man. "I chopped off her head, Desi, and stuck it on her mantel... just as you said you would do with *my* hand. But I don't see my hand, Desi. Where is it?"

"He threw it in the fire," Aurora said. "I don't know why, but it was the first thing he did when he entered the room. He was in a *foul* mood and made *me* pay for it."

"That's because he doesn't like to lose," Orin said. "And while I may have lost my hand, he was the one who lost his bet when his game didn't play out the way he anticipated. But *no one* likes a sore loser, Desi. They're not fun to be around."

Orin sat back and started tapping the knife again as Desi's head bowed. The man wasn't stupid; he knew these were the last minutes of his life, and they'd all be far from pleasant.

"How much time do we have before you two are expected to leave here?" he asked.

"About an hour," Alda said.

"Do you believe he doesn't know where the stones are?"

Aurora's mouth twisted to the side while Alda bit her bottom lip. Then, they both shrugged.

"He's telling the truth about Sheree being the last living Elite who helped create the spell with the stones," Aurora answered. "Whether or not she told him where the stones were, I don't know, but I doubt it. She enjoyed the power she wielded over this realm and all those beneath her, which was *everyone*."

"Did she really kill the other Elite?"

"That's what everyone has always believed. While there are accidents, and the Elite *love* to kill us, we have no real threats here other than that. The original Elite are rumored to have died from a sickness. It took all of them... except Sheree."

"She poisoned them," Orin stated.

"Most likely," Alda confirmed. "She had them help her with the spell and the stones and then killed them to keep her secret and the rest of us trapped here."

Desmond lifted his head and hurled a rush of gibberish. Orin lowered his knife and put his hand against the gag. "I'll remove this, so you can say what you have to, but if you try to scream, that will be the end of you."

He lowered the gag from Desmond's mouth. He worked his jaw before his lips curved into a sneer he directed around the room. It wasn't intimidating from a dickless man tied to a chair with a blindfold on.

"She did all that to keep you *ungrateful* pieces of *shit* safe. You just said our population flourished here; do you think that would have happened without them... without *her*? She loved you all."

"She didn't love anyone, and neither do you," Alda said.

"We did all of this for *you*!" Desmond spat.

"You did it all for *you*," Aurora retorted. "You did it because you liked having the power and ability to unleash your cruelty and abuse on all those weaker than you. You got off on tormenting us, killing us, and making us play your *stupid* games. Those games are over now, and you've lost."

Desmond started speaking again, but Orin shoved the gag back in his mouth. Desi had nothing left to offer him, as Orin believed him when he said he didn't know where the stones were.

Sheree had established this land and killed off all those who helped her do it. In her sick, twisted mind, she probably believed she was helping her species survive and thrive as she protected them from the same fate as her daughter.

In doing so, she'd also ensured most of those who lived here had far worse lives than the short one her daughter lived.

Orin stood and rested his hand on Desi's head. "I'm done with him. I can kill him if you'd like, or you can both have the honor."

Alda and Aurora exchanged a look before smiling. Even before they went to pick weapons from the room where Desmond stored them, he knew their answer.

Orin was determined to kill Desmond when he set out on this mission, but the man had done far worse to these women, and it was only fitting Desi should meet his demise at the hands of those he'd claimed to "help."

Desmond screamed against the gag as Orin left the room to let the women have their fun.

CHAPTER SEVENTY-SEVEN

SAHIRA COULDN'T STOP herself from gaping as she entered the round twenty-by-twenty room. The multihued, gray stone floor ran in a circular pattern around it. She hesitated to step on it after everything they'd endured to get here, but *all* her instincts screamed at her to run for the middle.

Instead, she stood with Pip by her side as they gazed around the space. The ceiling was ten feet high and made of white bricks, as were the walls.

Their stark color emphasized the beauty of the five crystals in the middle of the room. All the crystals stood out from a base with smaller, clear stone formations rising from it, but the main five were various shades of orange and pink.

The tallest stone stood at three feet, while the smallest was barely a foot. All the others fell somewhere in between. With the base, the entire structure stood about five feet tall.

"Are those the Augmentation Stones?" Pip breathed.

"It could be another game."

Sahira didn't want to believe that was possible, but in this land of sick freaks, she couldn't deny it might be. But....

"I can feel their power." It vibrated against her skin and sent goose bumps up her arms. "If they're not the Augmentation Stones, they're definitely something magical."

"Is it safe to go to them?"

And that is the could-end-my-life question.

Sahira studied the floor again. If this room was another trap, she doubted the same stones as the hallway before would be safe to step on.

But they didn't have any other choice.

"I'm going to try crossing over to them," she said. "Are you going to run over there?"

Pip didn't respond as, with her easy grace, she raced over to the crystals and clambered onto them. Determined to ignore the terror trying to keep her in place, Sahira crept through the doorway; the second she crossed the threshold, it slid shut behind her.

Sahira gulped as she glanced back at the door, but unlike the others, this one had a simple red button beside it. She should continue to the stone and completely ignore the *red* button screaming *no* at her, but her fingers found and pushed it.

The door slid open with a small whoosh. At the other end of the hall, the other one opened too.

Too stunned to truly process what was happening, Sahira glanced at Pip, who had risen to the top of the stones. She rested one hand on them as she grinned at Sahira.

"It looks like we can get back," Pip said.

"It does."

The door slid closed again, and Sahira took a deep breath before stretching her foot out to test a stone. With care, she inched her way across the room. The closer she got, the more she wanted to sprint for them, but she restrained herself in case there was another trap.

That certainty proved futile when she reached the stones after far too many minutes of torture. As her hands fell on the beautiful structure, power vibrated through her palms, into her arms, and out to the rest of her body until her toes curled.

"They're so strong," she murmured. "It's going to be a shame to destroy them."

"Can you break whatever spell they cast with them?" Pip asked.

"I don't know what that spell was, and their magic is different than a witch's. The only way to destroy the spell is by destroying the stones... or at least I hope that works."

"It's not guaranteed the spell will end if we ruin the stones?"

"Nothing is guaranteed, but the stones amplified the power that sealed this realm away. Without them, the spell should fall. This is the best we can do."

"Then let's do it."

As much as Sahira regretted having to destroy something with so much power and beauty, in the wrong hands, these crystals were a treacherous thing. Even if there was a way to break the spell without destroying them, she'd still batter them into the ground. *No one* should ever wield this kind of power over another.

Gathering a current of air beneath her palms, she lifted them and pushed it as hard as she could into the stones. It hit them with a loud thud that reverberated off the stones and shattered three of them from the base.

From there, she and Pip set to work. Without any weapons, it went slower than she would have liked as she kicked and battered the stones apart. Pip hammered at them with her fists, creating small fractures and breaking away pieces.

When Sahira succeeded in tearing the biggest stone away from the base, she lifted it over her head and smashed it into the ground over and over again until it broke and pieces of it scattered around the room. She did the same to the smaller stones and then danced, kicked, and stomped over their remains until little more than powder and broken chunks littered the floor.

Breathless and with sweat dripping down her forehead and cleaving her clothes to her, she stepped back to survey the wreckage. Pip continued to pulverize a rock into dust by jumping up and down on it.

Small pieces of the crystals remained, but the power that had vibrated against her was gone. It had been sucked from the room as effectively as a tornado ripped trees from the earth.

Finally satisfied with her battered stone, Pip turned to Sahira. Her shoulders heaved as the burnt end of her tail swayed back and forth. "Now what?"

Now came the test. Now came the part where they got to see if the stones truly were the key to freedom or one more game to these creatures. And if they were another game, that meant *everyone* in this realm was against them.

The possibility was too daunting to ponder for long. She hadn't let dread hold her back from getting here, and she couldn't let it keep her from doing what she needed to do now.

Swallowing heavily, Sahira held her breath as she lifted her hands before her. She couldn't count the number of times she'd tried and failed to open a portal since arriving in the Cursed Realm.

But she hadn't given up yet, and no matter how much it would crush her if it failed, she had to try again. Releasing her breath, Sahira envisioned Orin's room above while weaving her fingers before her.

Unable to look, she closed her eyes as she worked, but when Pip's breath sucked in and she squealed, they flew open again. At first, the portal before her seemed too good to be true, and she couldn't fully comprehend it was *really* there.

A sob lodged in her throat, and her legs nearly gave out as she staggered forward. She had to stop to steady herself before she sprawled across the floor.

It was too good to be true; it couldn't be. After everything they'd endured and every horrible thing they'd encountered, there it was... the key to their freedom.

It couldn't be real, but even as she half believed this, she scooped up Pip and ran toward the beautiful, swirling portal. She almost expected to slam into a wall of air before she got to it, but as the familiar darkness that had proven so elusive these past months enveloped her, joy exploded through her.

Her feet moved so fast she could barely keep up with them as she resisted the scream of joy lodged in her throat. They had the key to freedom at their fingertips once more, but enemies in Epoch still surrounded them, and she had to find Orin.

They emerged across from the closet in Orin's bedroom. Loth and Fath stood at the back of the closet, staring at the open door. They were both leaning toward each other with their heads nearly touching.

"Hey, guys!" Pip cried.

They squeaked and jumped as they spun around and threw their hands up in a defensive boxer's stance. Then their jaws dropped and their arms fell.

"How?" Loth squeaked.

"We destroyed the stones," Pip said. "We're *free!*"

Loth and Fath exchanged a look before they clasped each other's hands and started dancing, singing, and kicking their legs while spinning in circles. Thankfully, her silencing spell was still in place. Pip jumped down to join them, and the three creatures squealed as they hugged and kissed before dancing some more.

"We're not free yet." Sahira hated to interrupt their excitement, but she had to. "Oh, you can leave if you want. I won't stop you, but Orin's still in the castle somewhere, and these monsters are still alive. I can't leave here without him."

They stopped dancing to stare at her, and some of their excitement faded as their faces hardened.

"Neither can we," Pip declared.

"What do we do?" Loth inquired.

"First, we get Elsa and Zeth, and then we form an army that these pricks will never see coming."

The brownies all cheered before scrambling up her leg and perching on her shoulder. They had a lot of work to do.

CHAPTER SEVENTY-EIGHT

HAVING GLIMPSED inside Elsa's room on the first day they arrived, Sahira could open a portal into it. Her friend had probably also set alarms, but Sahira could only hope that she'd only done perimeter ones because no one could open a portal into her room... until now.

Holding her breath, Sahira prayed nothing would start blaring as she stepped from the portal with the brownies. Thankfully, nothing did.

When she bent to rest a hand on her friend's shoulder, Elsa shot up on the bed and blinked as her hands flailed.

"Shh," Sahira urged. "It's me."

Elsa's hands fell to her sides. "*Sahira*? How did you get in here?"

Sahira squeezed her shoulder. "We've beat them at their game."

"What?" Elsa rubbed her eyes. "What are you talking about?"

"Come on, get out of bed. We have to get Zeth too."

The brownies remained on Sahira's shoulders as Elsa rose.

She'd fallen asleep fully dressed, probably in preparation for the guards storming their rooms and yanking them out.

"Are you going to tell me what's going on?" Elsa asked.

"Wait until after we get Zeth, and then I'll tell you everything. If you have a spell on the doors, can you release it?"

Elsa's fingers waved before her. When she finished, she nodded to Sahira.

Sahira strode over to tap on the door joining Elsa's room to the demon's. She hoped it was loud enough, but as if he were expecting an early morning wake up, Zeth answered almost immediately.

While he'd been awake and ready for almost anything, he did a double take when he saw her. "Did the guards let you leave your room?"

Sahira grinned at him. "They don't know I'm here."

Much like Elsa, he stared at her in confusion before smiling. "What's going on?"

"I'm hoping for a war."

When they were all gathered in Elsa's room and safe under the silencing spell Elsa created, Sahira filled them in on everything that happened. She'd already opened two portals and cast two spells tonight; she could feel their drain.

She had enough strength left in her to open one more portal. That one was the most important as it would take her to Orin.

When she finished speaking, Zeth sat back. "Are we really free to go?"

"I can open a portal, so I'm assuming that means you can too," Sahira said.

Zeth waved his fingers in front of him until a portal opened; Elsa sucked in a breath. Sahira had no idea where the portal went, but the yearning on the demon's face made her think his home lay on the other side. He was so close to seeing his wife and son again, so close to the life he'd craved for three decades.

Then he looked at both his hands and closed the portal. "What do we do?"

"I have a tracking spell on Orin so I can find him. That's how I ended up in the Cursed Realm; I was trying to bring him home for Cole and Lexi."

"And what if he's somewhere with a lot of guards or somewhere that, if you appear, will put him in danger?" Elsa asked.

"That's why I'll be the only one to go through to find him, but we'll have an army ready if necessary. Loth and Fath can go for the brownies while you and Zeth return to Belda's town. Everyone will have to be careful to stay out of the main buildings and draw the others out so the dagadon don't overhear any conversations, but we can recruit a lot of fighters from those places."

"Do you really think that, after years of being trapped in this realm, those immortals will choose to stay instead of returning to the homes they've missed for years?" Zeth asked.

"I'm sure some of them will leave, but I think if you tell them we've found the ones responsible for keeping them trapped here, they'll be more than happy to help us destroy them. Revenge is a powerful motivator, and the dagadon have ruined too many lives for too long. We can now take revenge on them; some will stay because of that."

"The brownies will fight," Fath said. "I have no doubt."

"Puth will get the children to safety, and probably most of their mothers, but the rest will stay," Loth agreed.

"The berserkers and lycans certainly will," Elsa said. "I'm sure there will be others too."

Sahira really hoped so. They needed as many fighters as they could get for this.

"You did it," Elsa whispered, resting her hand on Sahira's arm. "When this is over, we'll all be free."

Sahira enfolded Elsa's hand in hers. "When this ends, I hope you'll come to Dragonia to live with us." She looked at the others as she spoke. "I hope you *all* will. I know the demons have their own realm, and I'm sure the brownies have found a new one, but you're all welcome to come live in Dragonia."

Elsa squeezed her hand. "I look forward to it."

"And if not to live, we'll be there for a visit," Zeth promised.

"So will we," Pip agreed.

"Good, now let's get to work," Sahira said.

Releasing Elsa's hand, she stepped away from her friends as she waited for them to depart. She and Pip would remain here in case something went wrong.

They would have to alert the others if it wasn't safe to return to the castle. And the others would leave their portals open in case she and Pip had to retreat quickly. They all knew how to find each other again if necessary.

CHAPTER SEVENTY-NINE

WHILE HE WAITED for the women to take out their revenge, Orin sat on the couch with his arms draped over the back of it. He smiled as he listened to Desmond's muffled screams.

He'd wanted to personally cause that suffering and horror, but while he had a *lot* of reasons to hate Desmond, they had more. Besides, he'd gotten to play with both him and Sheree; it was far more fun that the servants Desmond tormented would be the ones to end him. That was a bet Desi never would have taken.

And the women were taking their time destroying the Golden One, which made him more okay with allowing them to do it. Desmond certainly didn't deserve a swift death.

Studying the embers in the fire while listening to Desmond's sounds of misery, Orin found the ruins of his hand. All that remained of his once trusted and more loved than he'd realized appendage were bones, but he could make out some of his fingers poking out through the logs.

He missed those fingers. Absently, he went to flex his lost hand, but of course, there was nothing to move.

He lowered his arm and settled the stump on his lap. He'd

made the right choice when he cut it off and didn't regret it, but he missed his hand.

Then he spotted the empty spot on top of the fireplace, between someone else's foot and a finger, and smiled. Desmond had made a place on his mantle for a hand, but Orin ruined it for him.

Good.

When the women finally finished with Desmond, the shower turned on as they cleaned themselves. From what he'd glimpsed before leaving the room, Alda took off her clothes before killing Desmond.

After they finished dressing, they entered the sitting room. Orin rose and returned to Desmond's bedroom. He checked to make sure Desmond was dead, but the women had left no doubt of that.

He smiled at the man and patted his cheek again before striding into the weapon's room. With Alda's help, he strapped as many swords as he could onto his back, gathered a bunch of daggers and knives, and holstered them to his waist.

Occasionally, he would stop and jump around to ensure everything was firmly in place, but none of the weapons made any noise when he moved.

"Are you ready?" he asked after they finished.

"Yes," Alda said as Aurora nodded.

Orin circled them as he examined them both for any sign of something unusual, but their hair had completely dried, and he didn't see any sign of what happened here. He stopped before them and leaned back on his heels. "It's time to go."

Their white dresses flowed across the ground as they approached the door, and he drew the shadows around him. He followed them and jumped a couple more times to ensure the weapons didn't rattle, but they'd secured them well.

While Alda and Aurora waited by the door, they searched the

room for him, but their eyes didn't linger on where he stood before flitting away. "Ready?" Alda whispered.

"Ready," he said from their right, and they both jumped a little.

They quickly covered their shock, and Alda's shoulders hunched forward in a posture of defeat and exhaustion. She ran her fingers through her hair, messing it up more. Aurora did the same, and they examined each other before Alda opened the door.

Alda stepped aside to let Aurora exit first. As she did so, Orin slipped into the hall.

He kept himself to the side of Aurora so they didn't accidentally touch when Alda entered the hall and shut the door behind her. Both women walked with their shoulders slouched and their heads bent as they passed the guards.

Some men snickered at the women while others curled their lips in disgust. Orin would bet that these men had been allowed to brutalize these women too, or at least been given other women to torture. Desmond and Sheree liked to keep their pets happy, after all.

Yet, here they were judging Aurora and Alda when the guards had choices, but the only ones they had were survival. It was another way for the guards and Elite to make these women feel worse; he couldn't wait to destroy these fuckers.

They had no idea what awaited them in the shadows, and he relished every second of knowing those shadows and the servants would soon turn on them.

Keeping close to the women but far enough away that if they stopped, he wouldn't walk into them, Orin trailed them. Their steps were noiseless on the wooden floor as they remained hunched in defeat.

Though he was hyperaware of his surroundings, his heart pounded out a steady beat, and a sense of calm ascended over him as they traversed the hall. They'd made it twenty feet when one of the guards stepped away from the wall behind him.

"Wait!" the guard commanded.

Orin stopped behind the women, who glanced at each other with furrowed brows. Judging by their reactions, this was something new and *not* good.

His mind spun as he tried to recall hearing a clatter from the weapons or the slightest noise, but there hadn't been anything to draw their attention.

"What is that?" the guard who stopped them demanded.

The women looked over themselves and around the hall before turning to the guard. "What is what?" Alda asked.

"That." The man pointed a finger at Aurora's dress. "What is *that*?"

Orin spotted a bead of bright red blood amongst all the white. It was so small most wouldn't have noticed it, but *he* would have.

That spot hadn't been there when he inspected them before leaving the room. So *how* had it gotten there?

Aurora leaned forward to inspect her dress. When she did, the knife Orin had stolen from the kitchen tumbled from under her skirt and hit the ground with a clatter.

Orin's teeth ground together as his eyes landed on the weapon. She'd cleaned it but must have been in such a rush to smuggle it out of the room, blood still clung to the blade above the hilt.

Judging by Alda's nearly unhinged jaw, she had no idea what her friend planned as she gawked at the knife and then Aurora.

CHAPTER EIGHTY

"IT'S NOT BLOOD!" Alda blurted. "It's strawberry juice. There were strawberries in the room. She shouldn't have taken the knife we used to cut the strawberries; it was a mistake, and you can take it, but it's—"

Before Alda could finish spewing her desperate lie, Aurora pointed a finger at her and shouted. "She's working with the dark fae! She brought him into Desmond's rooms. They've killed Desmond and Sheree! I took the knife to protect myself... from *them*!"

Alda's astonishment vanished as fury clouded her face. "You *stupid* bitch!"

At first, none of the guards moved as this litany of revelations and news of the deaths held them immobile. Then all the guards swung their heads toward Alda; she held up her hands as she backed away, but there was nowhere for her to go.

Emboldened by their attention on Alda, Aurora took the opportunity to sprint down the hall. The guards finally broke free of their paralysis and stepped into the idiot woman's way, blocking her flight.

"No!" Aurora wailed as she ran into the wall they'd formed.

Her fingers stretched toward the freedom she'd tried to grasp, but as the guards pulled her back, they tore it from her. There was nowhere for her to run as two of the guards caught her arms and dragged her back toward them.

More of the guards circled Alda. Orin looked around for an opening, but as they closed in on her, they also encircled *him.*

"*What* did you do?" one of them snarled.

Alda kept her hands up as she backed away, but when more of them fell in behind her, she planted her feet and lifted her chin. Her slumped shoulders went back while she glowered defiantly at them.

"*Fuck* you! And *fuck* them too! They got what they deserved." She thrust a thumb over her shoulder at Aurora. "I hope she does too."

Orin agreed with that sentiment, but they would probably get something, too, as they couldn't escape the circle of guards. The men and two women had created a barrier that ran three and sometimes four deep in the hall.

Orin twisted to the side to avoid contact with them when two guards seized Alda's arms and jerked her roughly forward. Another stood so close to his back that his heat caused sweat to bead on Orin's nape.

To his right, his arm nearly brushed a guard's while, to his left, the toes of a boot rested against his. If the man moved another centimeter forward, he would kick Orin.

He edged his boot back a little but couldn't go far as the guard at his back blocked his way. *Shit!*

He glanced around, but there was no opening for him to slip through, and he didn't dare try to pull a sword free in these tight confines. He'd hit someone with it or make a noise that could alert them to his location. For now, he remained trapped but still free.

"Check the rooms!" another guard commanded.

A guard reached for the knob to Sheree's room before halting. "What if the servant is lying and we walk in without permission? Our Lord *won't* like that."

"Once we explain what has happened, she'll understand."

The look on the guard's face said he doubted that, and Orin did too, but the man still turned the knob and entered the room. More guards followed while others entered Desmond's living area.

Orin remained trapped only a few feet from Alda as the guards dragged Aurora into the small circle and threw her on the ground. She held her head and sobbed as Alda sent her a scathing glare.

A guard picked up the knife she'd foolishly tried to hide and slid it into a holster on his hip. Orin's hand fell to one of the daggers at his side. A sword would be better, but he could noiselessly free the dagger.

He'd give anything for a sword now. The dagger wouldn't pierce as deeply through flesh or chop off a head as cleanly, and he had no doubt he could wield a sword as easily with one hand as he had with two.

During their many training sessions together, his father had insisted Orin and all his brothers learn to fight with one hand in case an injury disabled the other. He'd continued practicing it over the years, but right now, the dagger would have to do.

A few seconds later, a couple of guards staggered out of Sheree's room. They'd all paled visibly and had no idea what to do as a few stumbled down the hall before stopping and returning.

"It's… it's true," one of them stammered.

The other guards exchanged uneasy glances as more of their shaken brethren emerged from Desmond's rooms.

"He's dead," one of them stated.

Stunned silence followed this revelation, and all eyes swung toward Alda and Aurora. The guards had no way of knowing it, but they were looking at him too.

"Seize them!" the biggest guard shouted. "We'll take them to Renaldo. He, and the other Elites, will decide their fate."

A few of them started toward the women, but they all stopped when another guard inquired, "Where's the dark fae?"

The men all looked nervously around as they shifted their feet. Their gazes finally settled on the women. Alda and Aurora had no way of knowing where he was, but when some of the guards stepped closer to them, Aurora started blabbering.

"He followed us from Desmond's rooms and was by our sides. He must be somewhere in the hall. Or at least he was! Please... *please* have mercy on me!"

Orin closed his eyes while inwardly groaning. She didn't have to beg for mercy from these assholes; he'd kill her himself before this was over.

The guards looked frantically around the hall, and some turned in small circles while searching for him. He edged away from the one behind him but only squeezed another couple of inches out of the space between the guard and Alda.

He suspected the woman wouldn't reveal his location if he brushed against her... at least not on purpose. However, he might scare her into a reaction if he touched her when she wasn't expecting it.

"If he was close to them when they left the room, then he can't be far," one of the guards said.

Orin leaned slightly to the left to avoid the guard to his right as he stepped closer. He ducked a hand that swung at him and remained crouched while the guard fumbled around; the idiot only connected with Alda and the wall.

"It's *your* fault we're going to die," Alda hissed at Aurora. "I hope you know that."

Aurora scowled at her through her tears. Orin pondered if her take-pity-on-me act was just that... an act. She had to know it wouldn't work. The Elites were going to destroy her in the most horrible way possible.

The guards edged closer as they sought to tighten their circle in the hope he was inside it. Orin was rapidly losing the little space he'd claimed for himself.

Lowering his head to avoid the hand of the guard to his left, he didn't see the knee of the one to his right until it connected with his back. Orin didn't so much as breathe while waiting to see what the guard would do, but he didn't have much choice, as he couldn't go anywhere.

Unsure of what he hit, that guard pushed his knee forward and knocked into Orin again. "Here!"

"Keep him alive for Renaldo. He'll want to handle this!" someone commanded.

Cursing the cumbersome weapons strapped to him, Orin released the dagger and grabbed a sword. It rattled against the other blades as he pulled it free and drove it into the guard's belly. The guard grunted while his hands clawed at a weapon that was still invisible to him as he bent forward and his back bowed out; when Orin pulled the sword free, blood flowed with it.

He had to move, but they'd trapped him in the corner. All he could do was try to fight his way out until he could break free of them.

Hoping to keep them confused and create more panic, he held the shadows around him as he spilled the intestines of another guard. Their inability to see him, or the weapon, created some chaos, but they started to regroup and lunged at him.

If they all came at once, they could overpower him, and they knew it.

CHAPTER EIGHTY-ONE

SAHIRA SMILED at the crowd filling Elsa and Zeth's rooms. All the light fae had refused to join the battle, which was expected of the normally pacifist immortals, but most of the others had come.

So many of them sought revenge on the immortals who had imprisoned them here that some were still waiting in the street outside the pub. They were waiting for their chance to enter through the portal there and into Epoch.

To keep the dagadon from thinking it was abnormally quiet in the pub and the other buildings, the light fae and a few others had agreed to remain behind to create noise and act as if life was the same. They couldn't lose their element of surprise by having the dagadon learn they could open portals; it was their biggest advantage against these assholes.

The brownies were all gathered on top of Elsa's bed. The tiny creatures held their spears at the ready, and determination filled their faces. They would make a lot of dagadon bleed before this ended.

Even the witches and warlocks had come to fight, including Carmella and Blair, who *really* didn't like her. But since arriving, they hadn't stared at her like she was the worst form of life.

They mostly ignored her and Elsa, but some smiled at her. *I guess breaking the curse that kept them all trapped ingratiated me a little. Who knew that was all it took?* Sahira thought with an inwardly bitter laugh.

Not like she cared about their acceptance of her. She'd given up chasing those crazy, impossible, heartrending dreams centuries ago. They would have broken her if she hadn't.

"Hi, Toots," Fred said as he zipped forward to flutter in front of Sahira. A trail of red dust followed the pixie.

"It's good to see you, Fred," Sahira said.

"You too."

Thankfully, the pixie was far more sober than the last time she saw him.

"We were sure you were dead," Fred said.

Sahira laughed at his blunt honesty. "There were more than a few times when I believed the same."

Before this night was over, she was sure she'd think it again.

"Now what?" Belda demanded, and Gromuck the orc grunted.

"Now, I'll open a portal to Orin," Sahira said. "He needs to know the stones have been destroyed. I'll go through it alone, in case he's somewhere we have to be discreet. I'll do my best to go unnoticed, but that will be impossible if everyone comes with me."

"How are you going to do that?" a vamp asked.

"I put a tracking spell on him before we came to the Cursed Realm." It felt like years ago now, but it hadn't even been a year, or maybe it had; she'd lost all concept of time in this place.

"Can we start killing after that?" a berserker inquired.

Sahira smiled. "We can, but the servants in Epoch are as trapped as we were. I'm not sure they even know *how* to open a portal. There will be casualties, but we should avoid killing them as much as possible. They'll probably help us fight. There are plenty of Elites and guards to kill."

"Good. How will we know the difference?"

Zeth grinned. "That's easy; the Elite separated their classes by colors. Those who rule here wear all different colors, the guards are all dressed in blue, and the servants wear white. If you see someone in colored clothes with gold-flecked skin, kill them."

A sea of beaming faces surrounded her.

"Gladly," a vamp snarled.

"Go find Orin," Belda told Sahira as the lycan's second-in-command, Boris, walked over to stand beside her.

"I'll leave the portal open and return as fast as possible," Sahira assured them.

They all nodded their agreement and shifted their weapons as they prepared to fight. Taking a deep breath, Sahira gathered what remained of her strength to open another portal.

She'd suspected this might be the last time she could open one for a while, and as it formed before her, she became certain of it. This was her final portal until she could rebuild some of her magical powers.

Without her ability to open one, she was once again trapped here, but she'd survived this long without opening portals and would make it through this too. Eager to see Orin and to let him know about this new development, she had to tell herself not to rush through the portal and into something that could get them killed.

If she could still track him, he was okay, but she *needed* to see him. Her fingers ached to touch him while a murderous rage built inside her.

After what happened the last time they separated, she'd kill anyone who dared to harm him again… even if he had done it to himself last time. They'd forced him into it and would pay for that.

Gripping the spear Belda had given her, Sahira didn't run forward as she yearned to do, but she didn't go slow either. She had to get to him and learn what was happening before anyone noticed her portal and she ruined everything.

Finally, she emerged into a hallway filled with guards. They all had their backs turned to her while the grunts, thuds of flesh, and the clash of metal filled the air.

Rising onto her toes, she searched for Orin but couldn't see him in the melee. He was somewhere amongst this mess, struggling to break free; she was certain of it.

And then a cry of pain rang out, and she instantly knew it was *his*.

CHAPTER EIGHTY-TWO

ORIN DODGED the blade arcing toward him and threw himself to the side. He bounced off the wall and almost hit Alda as he slid along the brick surface to avoid the guards.

They still had no idea of his exact location, but they had a good idea. A sword whistled inches away from Alda's face and skimmed his ear before crashing into the bricks.

The blade tore out chunks of the wall as Alda threw her hands over her head and ducked. Before he could get away from the area, the hands of another guard came down on his shoulders. To avoid being trapped, Orin threw himself to the side. He slammed into the man and staggered the guard back a step.

With a brief reprieve from their attack, he sought to rid himself of the now cumbersome weapons strapped to his back and sides. Ducking, he shrugged off the swords and threw them a few feet away.

They bounced off a guard's legs and hit the ground with a clatter. The distraction allowed him to rid himself of most of the daggers, but he kept a few as the guards once again focused on his location.

Rising, Orin twisted to the side to dart away from Alda, but before he could move, another set of hands grasped his shoulders from behind. Throwing his head back, Orin caught the guard in the nose.

The coppery tang of blood filled the air as the man howled and released him. Lunging forward, Orin had nowhere to go as another guard drove his blade out.

Rotating away, Orin managed to avoid most of the blade, but some of it grazed his stomach and sliced through his flesh. A warm trickle of blood spilled down to stain the waistband of his pants.

Another guard crashed into his side, lifted him off the ground, and threw him into the wall. With a loud oomph, air burst from Orin's lungs as his feet kicked out, connecting with Alda.

The impact of his kick staggered her away from him as more hands came down on his shoulders. They yanked him away from the wall, and a guard's fingers tore at his arms and hand before falling on the sword.

When another one punched him in the nose, the first guard succeeded in ripping his blade away. Orin jerked against their hold and managed to yank his arm free as the stump slid beyond their grasp.

Spinning, he smashed his elbow into the face of another guard as a bone-crushing blow landed against his temple. Stars erupted before his eyes, and a loud ringing reverberated through his ears as his head spun.

He tried to shake away the lingering results of the devastating impact, but no matter how fast he blinked, he couldn't see straight or break free as more guards grabbed at him. His shirt tore away as their fingers shredded his skin and spilled blood.

The ringing in his ears continued, but his vision was returning as they pushed him onto the ground. He didn't know how so many guards could surround him in such a small space, but they managed to do it.

Jerking against their hold, he sank his teeth into one's calf. The man howled as Orin tore out a chunk of flesh and spat it away.

When the guard staggered back, Orin lurched forward to try scrambling into the space the man had created, but they didn't release him. The guards holding his arms bent them backward until excruciating pain screamed through his shoulders.

He ignored the pop in his arm as he freed himself from four of them. With their hold on him slipping, Orin dug his toes in to gain more traction on the ground.

He was so determined to break free, even if it meant tearing his arm off, that he didn't see the boots that suddenly came at him from both sides. The guards lifted him off the ground as their feet delivered rapid blows to his head, ribs, and stomach.

Bones gave way with a crack, and one of his ribs shifted to dig into his side. Grimacing, Orin stretched for the sword between two guards. When his fingers fell short of the metal handle, a boot planted into the small of his back and shoved him to the floor.

Gritting his teeth against the agony tearing through his body, he barely processed the shout of surprise on his left. The floor beneath him quaked, and the guards gripped him tighter as more cries filled the hall.

Orin lifted his head but couldn't see much beyond the guards' calves as they crowded before him. Sounds of pain reverberated through the hall as metal clashed against metal, fists thudded against flesh, and the sharp, coppery scent of blood filled the air.

Five guards hauled him to his feet and slammed him between them as they encircled him. Blinking away the blood and sweat trickling into his eyes, Orin's vision cleared enough to see between the guards. For a second, he swore he spotted Belda standing over some of the guards before the space filled in.

That can't be possible. Do I have a concussion? Am I hallucinating? Or maybe I have brain damage.

They'd kicked him in the head enough times it could be a possibility. And some would claim he'd always had brain damage. They'd be wrong, but they'd still say it.

Orin shook his head to clear it of his wayward contemplations and instantly regretted moving it. Not moving was the best option, but he had to know what was going on because he wasn't hallucinating the noise or the guards dragging him down the hall.

The guards dragged him back to stand near Alda and Aurora; they set him there while their brethren faced whatever was happening. Orin released the shadows since it was useless to still have them enshrouding him.

When he materialized between the guards, they leaned away from him even though they'd known he was there. His gaze met all of theirs as he bared teeth made bloody by the guard's calf and a gash in his mouth.

A scream of anguish and the increasing clash of metal drew his attention away from the guards he'd marked for death. Looking back through the crowd, Orin swore he glimpsed Sahira.

A fresh surge of adrenaline tore through him at the idea of her with these monsters. It wasn't safe for her here, but it wasn't safe for *any* of them. And how was it possible for her to be *here*?

She couldn't have broken free of those rooms and gotten past the guards there. They would have stopped her immediately, and she didn't have any weapons....

But if Belda really was in the castle, then she would have brought weapons. *Did the lycan decide to try crossing the Barren Lands again? Is that how she got here? But how did she get weapons into Epoch and arrive without the dagadon knowing?*

Orin wasn't exactly in the loop when it came to the plans of the Golden Ones, but he was sure he would have heard if Belda and some others had decided to try escaping again. Not to mention, he'd just listened to her voice in the pub earlier. There was no way she'd crossed the Barren Lands that fast.

It was impossible.

Orin didn't have an answer for what was happening, but if Sahira was here, he had to get to her. As adrenaline flooded him with fresh strength, he renewed his fight against the guards. Revitalized by whatever was happening, Alda did the same as she kicked at her captors.

One of the guards hit Alda in the head and knocked her to the ground. When one of his guards swung at him again, Orin dodged the blow and threw his weight into the man's side.

His broken ribs protested the movement, but his determination to get to Sahira kept him going. He flung himself to the other side and hit the guards with enough force to shove them back a couple of steps.

Nearly free of their grasp, he dug his toes into the ground and leaned forward as he strained to tear himself away. Before he could escape, Boris and Zeth broke through the grouping of guards ten feet away.

Orin gawked at them; he *was* seeing this. He didn't have a concussion and they *were* using weapons to destroy the dagadon.

The ground shook beneath Gromuck's feet as she barged through the crowd, shoving aside guards like they were nothing more than toddlers. She lifted one guard over her head and smashed him into the wall.

Orin had no idea how it happened, but immortals from the Cursed Realm had arrived in Epoch. And they were *pissed*.

CHAPTER EIGHTY-THREE

SAHIRA SPOTTED Orin caught between a group of guards. Their jaws dropped when Gromuck stormed onto the scene.

The orc used the guard she'd captured to beat the shit out of another one. Their bodies broke as bones snapped and blood sprayed the walls.

All around her, the immortals from the Cursed Realm continued to flow through her open portal. They grinned as they unleashed years of frustration, sadness, and rage on those who had relished in their misery.

Sahira sank her spear into the belly of a guard and twisted as she thrust the man back and pulled it free. From the corner of her eye, she spotted Blair and Carmella weaving a spell to create a burst of air that flung back the five guards charging them. They landed in the jaws of waiting, transformed lycans.

With the way to Orin cleared, Sahira lifted her spear and sprinted toward him. Elsa ran with her as the brownies rushed across the ground in a tidal wave of tiny bodies and feral screams.

They poured over the guards holding Orin, and as the guards tried to kick them away, the tiny creatures scampered up their legs. The brownies sank their teeth into the men, tore out hand-fuls of their hair, and ripped away skin.

They brutalized the screaming guards, who slapped them-selves as they tried to knock the creatures away. The brownies were too fast for them, and the guards succeeded only in beating themselves while the brownies tore them apart.

Determined to save themselves, the guards released Orin, who staggered forward and nearly went down before righting himself. Blood coated him, and his face was a bruised, lumpy mess, but when he lifted his eyes, they were clear as they focused on her.

He stepped toward her as something crashed into her side. Sahira's cry cut off when the impact knocked the air out of her.

The spear tumbled from her hand as she hit the wall. Knowing she couldn't hesitate, she spun to face whoever attacked her. The sword of a guard glinted in the light when he raised it over his head; determination etched his face as the sword arced downward.

Sahira didn't have time to cast a spell as death swung toward her, and she had no weapon to defend herself. Lurching to the side, she tried to avoid the deadly blade, but it was too late as the guard followed her movement.

The blade was nearly to her when the guard flew to the side with a loud grunt. The blade's tip skimmed her nose and drew blood that dripped off to hit the ground.

Her shoulders sagged, and her heart resumed beating as she sucked in a breath. She snatched up her spear and turned to discover Orin, on top of the guard, pummeling him with his fist. Even with only one hand, the guard's face caved beneath Orin's blows.

He'd looked so battered when she first saw him, but the abuse he'd received didn't slow him as the guard went limp beneath him. That didn't stop Orin as he punched him a few more times before pulling his arm back and smashing it into the guard's rib cage.

With a sound more animal than man, Orin tore out the guard's heart and tossed it aside. Perched on the man's chest, he turned toward her; his lips twisted into a snarl, and blood ran down his cheeks as malice blazed from his eyes.

The animalistic look left his expression as his eyes scanned her; he shoved himself to his feet and stalked toward her. "Are you okay?"

Sahira wiped the blood from her nose. "I'm fine. Are *you* okay?"

She didn't think he realized it, but he limped a little as he walked and his breath rattled. When he stopped before her, they studied each other before he opened his arms, and she stepped into them.

For a minute, she forgot about everything else as his strength enveloped her. She didn't care about the blood coating him but was mindful of his injuries, so she didn't squeeze as hard as she would have liked.

Tears of joy and relief filled her eyes, but she refused to shed them in this place where a handful of guards were still trying to break free. She shut out the sounds of the dying as she focused on the beat of his heart beneath her hand. It was one of the most beautiful things she'd ever felt.

His lips nuzzled her hair before settling near her ear. "How are you here?"

She lifted her head to meet both of his swollen eyes. Despite his battered and bloodied countenance, Sahira smiled as she told him, "Pip and I found the stones. We beat Sheree at *her* game."

His swollen lips tugged into a smile. "That's my girl."

Before she could say anything more, he rested his hand against her cheek and kissed her. Sahira lost herself to that kiss, but though only a few guards were left, their presence pulled her from Orin far quicker than she would have liked.

Lifting her head, she took in the carcasses littering the ground as the last guard fell. The immortals from the Cursed Realm gazed around the hall before moving closer to her and Orin.

A few of them approached Alda, who stood with a sword dripping blood off the blade. Her shoulders heaved as she gazed at them, but she kept her feet planted and didn't back away from them.

"Don't harm her," Orin said. "Desmond is dead because of her. The other one, though, she's fair game."

"Aurora's dead," Alda stated.

With those two words, she stepped aside to reveal the white dress and headless body of a servant. As she moved, she stabbed her blade through Aurora's head and lifted it off the ground.

Alda twisted the head before her. "Stupid bitch."

"I agree," Orin muttered.

Sahira would find out what happened later. For now, they had more pressing matters to deal with. There were still a lot of guards and Elite left in Epoch.

CHAPTER EIGHTY-FOUR

"Now what?" Puth, the leader of the brownies, inquired.

"Now, we can either leave or finish what we started," Sahira said. "We can make all those who caged us pay for it. In doing so, we can also set free the rest of the immortals they've imprisoned in this place. They've trapped the servants here so completely that I'm not sure they know *how* to open a portal."

When their attention shifted to Alda, she lowered her blade, and Aurora's head thudded off the ground. "We never had a reason to learn how, so no one taught us."

"Shit," Boris muttered.

"I'm not leaving here until *all* these fuckers are dead," Belda said. "I won't sleep until then."

"And we're not leaving you," Boris said.

Behind him, Belda's pack of lycans nodded their agreement.

"Can we really open a portal out of here?" Orin asked Sahira.

"Yes. I haven't opened one out of Epoch yet, but we can open portals again."

He closed his eyes as a rush of relief washed over him. They were free; they could *finally* leave.

Ignoring the pain in his battered body, his arms constricted around Sahira. Nothing had ever felt as good as she did, and now that he was holding her again, he wouldn't let her go.

He could get her out of this miserable place and back to the freedom and safety she deserved. They could finally start to build a real life *together*.

But as he thought it, he knew she wouldn't walk away and leave all these servants to fend for themselves. They'd destroyed their two worst oppressors, but there were many more to go.

As much as he wanted to get her away from Epoch and back to the happiness and love she deserved, he wouldn't walk away and leave them either. At one time, he would have opened a portal and never looked back, but not anymore.

He couldn't leave any Elites alive and free to spread into the world. And he wouldn't abandon the servants to a tyranny they didn't deserve. Alda had helped him, and he couldn't return the favor by leaving her now.

He was beaten and battered but he would get Sahira out of here and ensure her safety, but it would have to wait. Until then, he'd kill anyone who tried to hurt her.

"We're only going after the guards and the Elite," Sahira said. "Once they fall, we can teach the servants to open portals, and they can take care of themselves, but the Elite and guards have to die."

"I like this plan," Alda said as she kicked Aurora's head off her sword. "Most of the servants are out of the castle at this time of night, but the ones inside it will help us; we can get the others later. I can show you where the Elite sleep, and most guards are on duty tonight and easy to find. Once they're dead, I'll take you to their sleeping quarters, where we can destroy the rest."

The immortals from the Cursed Realm all grinned as they lifted their weapons.

"Lead the way," Belda said.

And Alda practically skipped as she led them through the halls. These bastards had no idea what was coming for them, but soon, they would.

CHAPTER EIGHTY-FIVE

IT TOOK OVER THREE HOURS, but eventually, the Elite and their guards fell. The onslaught of unexpected invaders was too much for them to overcome.

They never saw it coming and *never* anticipated anyone entering Epoch without their knowledge. The destruction of the Augmentation Stones changed all that and allowed Orin, Sahira, and the others to sweep through the castle with ruthless speed and *no* mercy.

Once the servants inside the castle were involved, they unleashed their fury in a wave of cruelty and vengeance Orin admired. The servants had spent millennia being abused and mistreated, and they took all that abuse out on those who inflicted it.

After the last guard fell and they totaled the losses, Orin learned that a few brownies and immortals from Belda's town had also fallen. He didn't like those losses, but they hadn't suffered the same number of casualties as those in Epoch.

By the time the battle ended, ten Elites were still alive, including Renaldo, but Orin suspected they'd soon be wishing they'd died. Alda and a tall thin man, who he'd learned was

Clive, had taken control of the servants and stood at the front of the line, smiling at the Elites cowering before them.

They'd released all those imprisoned in the dungeons. The recently freed prisoners stood behind the servants looking too thin and frail but very happy.

Some of the Elites wore sleeping gowns, while others were nude. All their hands were bound behind their backs to keep them from opening portals, but Orin doubted they knew how to. They were younger than Sheree, and she wouldn't have imparted that knowledge to them.

"Now is the time for *us* to have servants!" Alda declared.

A cheer ran through the crowd of servants gathered before the Elites; they grinned as they used their weapons to poke their specimens. One of the Elite women started crying, but no one showed her any sympathy.

"I think it's time for us to go," Sahira whispered. "They don't need our help anymore, and I'm ready to see my family."

She didn't say it, but he knew she was done watching this, even if these assholes deserved *everything* they got. Orin draped his arm around her shoulders and pulled her close to kiss her temple.

His ribs still ached like a son of a bitch, but two had already snapped back into place. The third gradually worked back into position by digging through his insides. It would soon reset too, and he would breathe a little easier again.

His stump throbbed so bad he could feel it in his teeth, but he wouldn't let her know. It would eventually heal, and he would adjust to not having a hand. Until then, he wouldn't say anything.

"Let's go home," he said.

The other immortals from the Cursed Realm were already starting to break up and leave Epoch. Many of them had departed, but some remained. Belda came up to clasp their hands.

"When you first arrived, I assumed you'd be nothing but trouble, and I was right," she said to Orin. "But I was also wrong. Thank you both for getting us out of here."

"Oh, you were right; I'm nothing but trouble," Orin assured her.

Belda smiled as she glanced between them. "Something tells me that's not as true as it used to be."

Orin squeezed Sahira a little tighter. He wasn't about to argue the truth with this woman.

"We weren't the only ones involved," Sahira said.

"I know, and I plan to thank them too."

"What will you do now?" Orin asked.

"I used to have a family, but after four hundred years, I can only hope they're still alive. Even if they're not, I have a pack." She waved to the lycans behind her. "At one time, we all belonged to another pack, but that time has passed. We're one now and will find a home."

"You're always welcome in Dragonia," Sahira said. "And if you don't come to live there, we hope you'll at least come to visit us."

"We will," Belda promised before squeezing their hands and releasing them to talk with Elsa and Zeth.

Fred fluttered by to kiss Sahira's cheek. "Goodbye, Toots. I'll see you again soon."

When Orin swatted at him, the pixie giggled before vanishing through a portal. More immortals came to say goodbye before leaving Epoch and this cursed place behind.

After most of them had left, Zeth came to stand before them. He rubbed one of his horns as he looked between them. "It's been a journey, and I *never* thought I'd say this, but I'm glad I took it with *both* of you. We're free now because of it."

When Sahira stepped forward, Orin reluctantly released her so she could hug the demon. He reminded himself that she was his and Zeth had a wife—or at least he used to have one—but he still loathed seeing her in the arms of another man.

"I hope you find your wife and son," Sahira said.

"So do I," Zeth whispered.

"You'll let us know, won't you? You'll get word to us in Dragonia?"

"I will."

"And you'll come to visit?"

He grinned at her before awkwardly patting her shoulders and stepping away. "Of course. I've always wanted to see a dragon."

"Maybe you can ride one."

Zeth laughed. "Let's not get carried away."

Orin rested his hand on Sahira's shoulder and pulled her back into his arms, where she belonged. When Zeth extended a hand to him, Orin took it; the demon clasped it in both of his extremely large ones.

"You're not so bad, dark fae. Or I should say, you're a lot better now than when we first met." Zeth's gaze flicked to Sahira before returning to Orin. "Don't fuck it up."

Orin grinned at him. "Is that all I get from you? You have both your hands because of me."

"That was *your* choice, you fool." Zeth's smile vanished as he squeezed Orin's hand. "If you ever need me, I'll be there. Just send word, and I'll come."

"Let's hope it never comes to that."

"I agree. Now, I'm going to set the stable animals free and then find my family. I wish you both well."

Orin snorted a laugh; the demon was a big old softy. Zeth released his hand, opened a portal, and vanished into it. Once he was gone, the brownies clambered around them, jumping and dancing as they hugged their legs before Puth finally ended it.

Pip scampered up to sit on Orin's shoulder. "We're going to find our family. After that, we're coming for a visit."

"We look forward to seeing you," Orin assured her.

And he meant it, which he never would have believed possible a short time ago. Pip kissed his cheek before leaning over to rest her hand on Sahira's shoulder.

"We make a great team," the brownie said.

"That we do," Sahira agreed.

Pip raced back down to join her brethren as Fath and Loth took turns hugging his and Sahira's legs. When they finished, the brownies all jumped and laughed with each other as Puth opened a portal. Without a backward glance, they all ran into it.

Elsa finished showing a group of ex-servants how to open a portal and shook some of their hands before turning to them. They'd told the servants, if they ever required help, they could come to Dragonia, but Orin hoped never to see them again.

"Do you think we can trust them to be in the realms?" Sahira whispered to Orin.

"Yes... or at least most of them, which is the same for every other species. Some of us are just inherently worse than others."

"True."

"Is it still okay if I go with you to Dragonia?" Elsa asked as she stopped before them.

Sahira beamed as she held out her hand, and Elsa took it. "Family is always welcome in Dragonia," Sahira assured her.

A sheen of tears filled Elsa's eyes before she blinked them away. "I can't wait to see my new home."

Orin opened a portal to the human realm. From there, they'd locate the open portal into Dragonia and travel on.

Like Elsa, he couldn't wait to go home.

CHAPTER EIGHTY-SIX

WHEN THEY EMERGED INTO DRAGONIA, the guards and dragons overseeing the open portals barely acknowledged their arrival. Then the realization of who they were sank in, and they all did double takes. A murmur ran through the guards and spread across the realm until the merchants stopped shouting their wares, and a hush settled over the kingdom.

Dragonia was much as he remembered it, except there was more of a chill in the air and patches of snow-covered sections of the ground. Snow blanketed the mountains in the distance, and plumes of warm air flowed from the dragons circling in the sky.

In the distance, the golden turrets of the palace glinted in the morning sun, but at least these weren't gilded turrets flecked with gold. Still, Orin's lip curled at the sight of that gold. It would take him a while not to hate the color... if he ever stopped hating it.

After the disbelief of their arrival wore off, the immortals they'd worked with to defeat the Lord rushed over to greet them and shake their hands. Some of them gawked when they noticed Orin's missing hand.

None of them stopped to talk, but they exchanged greetings

while determinedly continuing toward the palace. Orin wanted to see his family, learn if Brokk had gotten free, and get away from all the attention.

He also sought a safe place to sit and relax with Sahira. None of them had slept well in months. They were finally home, and he would bask in the security of their freedom.

He kept his arm locked around Sahira's waist as they made their way up the hill toward the palace. A trail of stunned immortals hovered around them, but some ran ahead to spread the word of their return to those inside.

They were a couple of hundred feet away from the main gate when Del ran out from beneath the portico and sprinted down the hill toward them. He moved so fast that Orin barely saw him before he skidded to a stop in front of Sahira.

His pale blond hair was tussled and sweaty as his bright blue eyes ran over Sahira. Cole had given him a red sun medallion that allowed him to walk in the day; it glistened in the sun as it hung against his chest.

"It's true!" Heedless of the blood still coating her, Del wrapped his arms around his sister and pulled her forward. "It's true."

The last two words were barely more than a whisper as Del closed his eyes and squeezed her. Sahira fell against her brother and clung to him while small sobs shook her.

"*Where* have you been?" Del asked. "We've been looking all over for you. I was…. I was…." His voice broke. "I was so worried."

"To Hell. We've been to Hell," Sahira answered. "But we're home now and not going anywhere again."

When Del's gaze shifted to him over Sahira's shoulder, Orin smiled and gave a little wave of his fingers. The vampire, who had *never* been his biggest fan, scowled at him, which only widened Orin's grin. Del was going to *hate* what was coming next.

When the siblings finally parted, they held each other's arms as they examined one another. "Are you okay?" Del inquired.

"I am now," Sahira said.

"Come, let's get you cleaned up and some food. We can talk about it all afterward."

When Del tried to pull Sahira further away from him, Orin stepped closer and slid his arm around her waist. Del frowned at him as Orin drew her against his side. "She's not going anywhere without me."

Sahira gently elbowed him in the stomach as she wrung her hands together and eyed her brother. He regretted instigating Del; she was far more nervous about this than he'd anticipated.

"It will be okay," he assured her.

When she looked at him, he hated the distress in her eyes. They were free and safe; she should be rejoicing, not scared of rejection or whatever wrath might unleash from her brother.

He turned to glower at Del. If the man did anything to upset her further, he'd tear the vamp's arm off and beat him bloody with it.

Sahira rested her hand on her brother's arm as she leaned closer to him. "We'll tell you everything, but we *really* want to relax somewhere safe. It's been so long since that was possible."

Some of Del's shock wore off, and his fingers enclosed hers. "Of course."

Her brother didn't release her hand as he fell in to walk on Sahira's other side. "Del, this is Elsa. She's going to live with us from now on. Elsa, this is my brother, Del," Sahira introduced.

Elsa glanced uneasily between Orin and Del before her gaze settled on Sahira's brother. "It's nice to meet you."

"You too," Del said, though Orin felt the vamp's eyes still boring into the side of his head.

They were almost to the drawbridge stretching over the moat when Lexi burst out from beneath the portico. Her auburn hair billowed behind her as she sprinted toward them.

Her sobs carried on the air as she held her arms open and practically knocked Sahira over when she plowed into her. Orin and Del managed to keep Sahira on her feet and righted her while she and Lexi embraced.

Not far behind his fiancée, Cole emerged onto the drawbridge with Varo. Their feet thudded across the wood as they ran toward them.

Neither of them slowed as they came at him with their arms open and grins on their faces. Orin had never been much of a hugger, but he gladly fell into the embrace of his oldest and youngest brothers.

CHAPTER EIGHTY-SEVEN

IT WAS after lunch by the time the three of them washed, dressed, and sat to eat. They gathered in a small sitting room around a table loaded with food that was just big enough for all of them. As they ate, Sahira, Orin, and Elsa told Del, Cole, Varo, Lexi, and Maverick about everything they'd endured.

Shade was curled in Sahira's lap, purring so loudly he sometimes drowned out the words of the others. The cat smiled as he held his head in the air while Sahira petted him.

As they spoke, they revealed the pieces of the story they didn't know. For the first time, Orin heard how Sahira found the stones, and she learned what happened to Desmond and Sheree. When they finished talking, the others sat stunned before their gazes fell to his and Sahira's joined hands.

Cole waved a hand at Orin's missing one. "You always went out of your way not to lose."

"Who likes to lose?" Orin asked with a laugh.

"Who likes to cut off their hand?"

The smile slid from Orin's face. "They weren't going to control me anymore."

"Crazy bastard," Varo muttered.

"This is true," Orin agreed.

"Will the remaining dagadon be a threat to us?" Lexi asked.

"No. The servants will eventually destroy the remaining Elite. They hate them too much to keep them alive for long. After that, who knows what they'll do, but without the stones, they can't trap anyone again," Sahira answered.

~

SAHIRA'S HEART was full as Lexi sat beside her and Shade kneaded her brown skirt. She'd missed her familiar while away from him and felt like a piece had been returned to her now that they were together again.

Del had tried to sit on her other side, but Orin refused to relinquish the spot. That had led to anger, but her brother eventually relented and sat across from her. Del leaned across the table to place his hand on top of hers.

Orin hadn't left her side since they returned; they'd even showered together before joining the others. Despite his profession of love, Sahira had secretly wondered if he'd take off and find some other woman as soon as they returned.

He showed no interest in doing such a thing, but things were different now. They weren't forced together anymore, and she wasn't his only source of nourishment.

He loved her; she didn't doubt that. He wouldn't have said it if it wasn't true, but he was a dark fae, and their instincts were to go forth and screw as many as possible. Yet, he remained by her side with his hand on hers and a defiant expression when the others all gaped at them.

"How long were we gone?" she asked.

"Three months," Lexi answered. "Three *very* long months."

Three months of her life she'd never get back. Three months that had changed, beaten, and nearly broken her.

Three months that had given her Orin, and because of that, she wouldn't change a thing, even if she ended up with a broken heart. It had all been worth it.

When their eyes met, he leaned over to kiss her temple. The others all gawked at them.

After an uncomfortable silence, Elsa cleared her throat. The others closed their mouths and exchanged glances before focusing on the three of them again.

"There's been no word of Kaylia and Brokk?" Sahira asked.

"No," Cole said as he stared at Orin with a furrowed brow. "Some of the rescue parties who went into Doomed Valley to search for them haven't returned either, but their bodies were all retrieved. All the dragons who entered the Valley have returned.

"There's been no sign of Kaylia, Brokk, or their party. I'd search for them, but I can't leave Dragonia. The realms still aren't completely stable, and if word got out that I was gone, some idiot might decide they could try to take over."

Lexi squeezed his arm. "And they'd be wrong."

"I've gone a couple of times," Varo said, "and found nothing."

Orin rubbed his freshly shaven chin. "After some rest, I'll go search for him."

Sahira almost protested his words. They were finally home, they'd *just* gotten free, and she so badly wanted to enjoy that freedom, but she couldn't stop him from going after his brother. She would do the same if Del was missing. So she wouldn't let Orin go alone.

"How have things been here?" Orin asked.

"Mostly quiet," Cole answered. "We've allied with the merfolk and are working on the berserkers and warlocks, but they're being stubborn. There are rumors of another growing rebellion."

"Nothing substantiated… yet," Del said.

"That's good," Orin said.

Cole's uncle, Maverick, pointed between Orin and Sahira. "And you two are…?"

Sahira was curious about who would ask first; she wasn't surprised it was Maverick. The lycan wasn't known for subtlety, but no lycans were.

She didn't answer as she waited for Orin's response. She knew what he'd said to her in Epoch, but they were free now, and things could change. He might decide he'd prefer to be single.

And even if he didn't, she had no idea what exactly they were to each other. Boyfriend and girlfriend sounded too casual after everything they'd endured, but they weren't engaged; marriage had never been mentioned, so she didn't know what to say.

Orin squeezed her hand as he stared at everyone around the table. "Are together." His gaze held a challenge when it settled on Del. "And it's going to stay that way."

Every eyebrow in the room shot up as their jaws dropped again. Relief filled Sahira as she smiled at him. *Together*, that's what they were to each other, and it was perfect.

"Holy shit," Lexi whispered.

"That sums up how we feel about it, too," Orin quipped.

The others laughed uneasily while they continued to stare incredulously between them. Eventually, they relaxed and settled into the situation, but their astonishment lingered in the room.

After a couple more hours passed in a blur of food, laughter, and love, Sahira was too exhausted to continue sitting with the others. Stifling a yawn, she lifted Shade as she rose from her chair. The promise of a big, inviting bed and sleep without fear of something trying to kill her was too alluring to resist anymore. The cat rubbed her chin before jumping from her arms.

"I need some sleep," Sahira said.

Del also rose from his chair. "I'll walk up with you."

"So will I," Orin said.

Sahira rested her hand on Orin's shoulder. She wanted some time alone with Del. "No, stay with your brothers. I'll see you soon."

CHAPTER EIGHTY-EIGHT

STILL HALF IN AND half out of his chair, Orin hesitated. He didn't like having her out of his view and was afraid Del might say something to upset her, but he nodded his agreement.

The siblings would have to be alone eventually and needed to work this out between them. Besides, he should learn as much as he could about Doomed Valley before entering it, and if Del upset her, he'd make the vamp pay for it.

He rested his hand over hers before shooting Del a look that promised death if he fucked this up. Then he kissed Sahira's hand. "I'll see you soon."

She released his shoulder and took the arm Del offered her.

"If you're ready," Lexi said to Elsa, "I can show you to your room."

"I'd like that," Elsa said.

"I should be going too." Maverick rose and stretched his back. "There's a pack meeting tonight."

Before Orin knew it, it was just him, Varo, and Cole sitting at the table. No one spoke for a while, but Cole finally broke the silence.

"We'll get you a prosthetic hand soon."

"I'm in no rush," Orin assured him. "I'm as good with one hand as I was with two."

Cole chuckled. "It's good to see the Cursed Realm didn't dim your confidence."

"Nothing could."

Cole's black eyes ran over him before he leaned forward. "Sahira—"

Before his brother could say anything more, Orin cut him off. "I love her, Cole. Believe me, it's not something I ever saw coming. It's not something I ever *wanted*, but now that I have her, I'm not letting her go."

Cole sat back again. "I would never ask you to give her up. I'm just… *shocked*."

Orin laughed as he lifted his goblet and gulped his wine. "*No one* is more shocked than me."

"Oh, I'm sure. I'm glad you're back."

"Cheers to that," Varo said as he lifted his goblet.

Orin was glad his youngest brother looked much better than the last time he saw him. He'd regained some of the weight he lost after the battle with the Lord and his mother's death. Color had returned to his cheeks, and his nearly white-blue eyes weren't so vacant.

Varo still didn't look as healthy as he did before all the fighting started and they chose to side against their father, but he didn't look like death was knocking at his door anymore, either.

"I'm glad to be back," Orin said, "and I'm *so* glad to see you both again."

Orin smiled as their goblets clicked together in the center of the table. They'd lost so much of their family, and Brokk was still missing, but he was back where he was meant to be.

And while he couldn't be completely happy without Brokk here or rest until he learned what became of his brother, he was glad to be home… even if he wouldn't be staying long.

"Tell me all you know about Doomed Valley," he said.

"I think you should stay here for a bit before going into Doomed Valley," Cole said. "You've endured enough and should rest."

"If you could leave, would you wait?"

"No, but I haven't gone through what you have these past months. Give yourself some time here with Sahira."

"And what of Brokk?"

"If he's alive, then we'll find him, but rushing out when you're not ready isn't going to do anyone any good."

"I've never been rational."

"You've never had someone else to worry about. What about Sahira if something happens to you?" Varo asked.

Orin sipped his wine as he contemplated this. "I have to go."

"I know," Cole said, "but give it some time. At least a couple of days."

"I wasn't planning on leaving tomorrow."

"Yes, you were."

Orin grinned. At one time, it would have annoyed him that Cole knew him so well; now, he enjoyed it. He'd missed this.

"Yeah, I was," he admitted, and they all laughed together.

CHAPTER EIGHTY-NINE

"So... THE DARK FAE?" Del asked as he walked with Sahira to her room. Shade trotted beside her.

She'd known it was coming, but he'd waited longer to broach the subject than she'd anticipated. "It was *not* something I planned. That realm changed us; him for the better... in some ways, but in many ways, he is still very much Orin."

She wouldn't change that about him.

"What about you? How did it change you?"

"Me...?" She shrugged as her voice trailed off. "I'm stronger. I had to be; it was so awful there."

"And you did what was necessary to survive."

"Yes, but... I enjoyed killing those dagadon. That's never happened to me before."

"It's understandable after everything they did, but are you going to be okay with it?"

She pondered this before responding. "Yes. I'm different but also happier than before I left." Sahira gulped before meeting her brother's gaze; concern shimmered in his blue eyes. "I know it's impossible to believe, and you must think I'm an idiot for falling for a dark fae, especially Orin, but I really *do* love him. Believe it or not, he *does* love me too."

Del released a loud breath. "Okay, but do you trust him?"

"At one time, I would have said it was impossible to trust Orin, and I would have been right. Now, I trust him with everything I am and *know* that's right... for *me*."

"So, I shouldn't trust him then," Del said with a laugh.

"Could you, after all the history between you?"

"Depends."

"On what."

"On how he treats you."

For a while, Orin's treatment of her hadn't been so great, but as they always did, things changed. In this instance, she was certain they'd changed for the better.

"The Cursed Realm changed him more than me. He's not the same man he once was. Don't get me wrong, he's still vicious, manipulative, and will destroy almost anyone who gets in his way, but he made *friends* and has *empathy*. He also gave his heart to me."

She wasn't sure it would be enough for him to settle down and stay that way, but time would tell. She could still end up with a broken heart, but until then, she would love him, and he would love her.

No one ever knew what the future held, and she planned to savor every minute of happiness they shared.

"I fought it so hard," she admitted in a whisper. "I've spent more time hating him than loving him. He drove me crazy, and I punched him a couple of times."

Del grunted. "Good."

Sahira leaned against his side as she smiled. "But no matter how relentlessly I fought it, I was still drawn to him. It was as frustrating as the man himself."

"Hmm," Del murmured before falling silent. After a minute, he asked, "Do you think he could be your consort?"

Sahira straightened away to frown at him in confusion. "What?"

"Your consort. Vampires have an intense mate bond too, like lycans. Or did you forget that?"

She stopped in the hall and gaped at her brother while her mind spun. He turned to face her. She knew vampires had consorts; of course, she did, but....

"I'm only half vamp," she said.

"So? You drink blood, you teleport, and you have fangs."

"Yeah, but...."

But what? She *was* half vamp, and Del was right, she had many of their characteristics; it had never occurred to her that *Orin* could be her *consort*.

What kind of sick, demented twist of fate was that? *The same kind that caused you to fall in love with the infuriating, loving, and stubborn man.*

But why had the possibility of such a thing never occurred to her? Probably because, though she had fangs, drank blood, and could teleport, she'd always identified more as a witch than a vampire. She'd also never known a vamp who found their consort, so it wasn't a part of her life.

"That would explain why it was so difficult to resist him even when I wanted to kill him," she muttered.

"Maybe."

Then she realized the simple truth of it all. "It doesn't matter if he is; either way, he has my heart."

Del patted her hand as they ascended the stairs toward her room. "If he hurts you, I'll kill him."

"I know." And it would destroy her to watch the two men she loved the most fight. "After what he did to you, this must be so difficult to understand, and you probably think I betrayed you—"

"No," he interrupted. "I don't feel betrayed. Stunned? Yes. Concerned? Completely. But not betrayed. We can't help who we love, Sahira, and if he is your consort, then you *really* can't help it. You would never hurt me on purpose, and this doesn't hurt me.

"I'm scared for you and your future with him, but I hope he proves me wrong and is the man you think he is. I can never forget what he did to me, but if he treats you right and makes you happy, I can eventually forgive."

Tears streamed down Sahira's face as they stopped outside her bedroom door. She threw her arms around her older brother, first best friend, and protector. She hadn't believed it was possible to love him any more than she already did, but he'd just proved her wrong.

"Thank you," she whispered.

"I'm so glad you're back."

"So am I. Though it sounds like I'll be heading to Doomed Valley soon."

Del groaned as he hugged her. "Not without me."

She didn't want to drag her brother into that place, but it was pointless to argue with him, and she was too tired to try.

She kissed his cheek. "I'll see you soon. I love you."

"I love you too."

CHAPTER NINETY

A FEW HOURS LATER, Orin discovered Del standing outside Sahira's room with his arms crossed over his chest while he leaned against the wall. He straightened when he spotted Orin.

Orin braced himself for a fight he was determined to win. "You're not going to chase me away."

"I'm not waiting here for that. She's made it clear how she feels about you, and I've only ever wanted her happiness. She deserves it. If you can make her happy, then I won't stand in the way, even if I think you're the biggest asshole ever to walk the realms."

Orin smiled. "Many would agree, and you'd all be right."

"I know, but as you saw in the Cursed Realm, she's taken a lot of abuse from a lot of asshole witches in her life. She deserves the best."

"I know."

"I don't think you're the best, not by a long shot, but *she* thinks you are, and because of that, I'll give you a chance to prove me wrong. But I'll tell you what I told her; if you hurt her, I *will* kill you. Do you understand?"

Orin resisted the impulse to laugh, blow Del off, and irritate the man. He'd always enjoyed turning the screws into the vamp and winding him up, but as he opened his mouth to tell the vamp he could kill Del without *any* hands, Orin's gaze went to Sahira's door and closed it again.

She went through so much in the Cursed Realm and throughout her life, she deserved peace. And if he continued fighting and instigating her brother, she wouldn't have it.

Sahira loved Del and Lexi deeply. He didn't have the best past with either of them, but he intended to make her future one of happiness and love.

"I understand," he said. "But that won't happen because I'm not going anywhere, and I won't *ever* hurt her. She's mine, and I'm hers; that's how it is."

"Good." Del started to walk by him but hesitated before resting his hand on Orin's shoulder. "I'm glad you've both returned."

Orin had *never* expected to hear those words from Del. While he still would have liked to see Del's face turn red and the vamp lose his shit, he'd made the right choice by not instigating a fight with him.

As Del released his shoulder, Orin spoke again. "She missed you and Lexi a lot."

"And we missed her."

With that, Del went down the hall and disappeared around the corner.

CHAPTER NINETY-ONE

SAHIRA HAD no idea what time it was when the mattress sank beside her and Orin crawled in to envelop her in his arms. Smiling, she nestled against his naked body as she fit perfectly against him.

When he leaned over to kiss her cheek, she turned her mouth into his, and their tongues entwined. His hand found all the best spots as it ran over her body, waking her to a world of pleasure and love as she grew wetter and opened her legs to him.

Her nails dug into his skin, and she lost herself to him until she came apart with a loud cry she muffled by sinking her fangs into his throat. Deep inside her, his shaft pulsed as he found his release too.

When she came down from the amazing high he'd created, she collapsed onto his chest and rested her hand over his heart. She lay in his arms for a while, but she couldn't pretend to shut the rest of the world out forever.

"When do we go to Doomed Valley?" she asked.

Orin had been running his fingers through her hair, but they stilled at her question. "I don't want you to go."

"It doesn't matter. I'm going."

"You just got home and are back with your loved ones."

She lifted her head and folded her hands beneath her chin to study him. "So did you, but you're still going."

"I have to see if I can find Brokk."

"I know, but you're one of my loved ones now too. I'm going, Orin, and that's final."

He smiled as he started playing with her hair again. "Okay, okay, no need to be so bossy, Enchantress. We'll probably go in a couple of days, after we get some rest and have a chance to spend more time with everyone."

She kissed his chin. "It feels good to be home."

"Nothing feels as good as you. You're mine, Sahira, forever."

She bit her lip as anxiety niggled at her insides. "Are you sure about that? When we were in Belda's town and on our way to do laundry, I asked you if anything was enough for you, and you said, '*Not yet.*'"

"What did I know then? I was an idiot, but I have no doubt you *are* and *always* will be far more than enough for me. You're my home, Sahira."

Her heart swelled with love as his black eyes held hers. "And you're mine."

"Always?"

"Always. And I think it's time to break a certain spell."

Rising a little, she lifted her hands before her and started weaving them in the air. He clasped them together in his hand and pinned them against his chest.

"What are you doing?" he asked.

"Removing the tracking spell."

"No. Leave it."

"But it's what you've been asking for ever since I put it on you."

"I know, but now I want you to find me *whenever* you need me. I won't let there be a time when you can't."

A lump formed in Sahira's throat as she stared at him. "You

just want me to get trapped with you again if you stumble into another Cursed Realm," she quipped as she tried to keep herself from crying.

He grinned at her. "I did enjoy being stuck with you. It was the best thing that ever happened to me."

Unable to stop it, a single tear fell free. He wiped it away with the pad of his thumb. "Me too." She swallowed the lump in her throat. "Then the spell will stay."

"Good."

"Okay." Looking to change the subject, she recalled her conversation with her brother. "Del asked me if I thought you might be my consort."

"What do you think?"

"I don't know. I never considered it until he mentioned it. I knew vampires had consorts, but it never crossed my mind it could be you… probably because you pissed me off so much."

He grinned. "But I turn you on more."

She rolled her eyes but couldn't stop smiling back at him. "Maybe."

"Maybe?"

He ran his hand up her back in a leisurely caress that caused her eyes to close as a shiver of pleasure ran up her spine. Lifting his head, he nibbled at her bottom lip before slipping his hand between her legs.

"This is far more than a maybe," he said against her mouth as his finger stroked her wetness.

"Maybe not," she teased.

With a growl, he hooked his leg around her and spun her to the side so he was on top, looking down. His shaft lengthened against her. Sahira had to bite her lip to keep from squirming beneath him.

"You know," he said as his eyes settled on hers, "when all this is over, Brokk's home, and Lexi and Cole are married, I'm going to ask you to marry me."

Her eyes widened at his words. "Orin—"

"You don't have to say anything now because I'm not asking yet, but you should know my intentions. After Lexi and Cole have their wedding and the time they deserve, our time will come, and once it does, I *am* going to ask you to marry me."

At first, she couldn't speak, but then she beamed at him. "And I'll say yes."

The beautiful, cocky smile that could incense as well as melt her heart lit his face. "I already knew that."

Sahira laughed as she playfully slapped his chest. "Since you intend to marry me, do I finally get to see how many ciphers you *really* have?"

He tilted his head to the side as he studied her before something in the air changed. Her skin tingled as the power surrounding him wavered before slipping away.

As if someone were taking a pen and writing on him, more ciphers materialized across his flesh. The markings had always been visible across his upper chest and both arms before ending at his wrists.

Now, they spread past his wrist to his fingertips on his remaining hand. She recalled sitting at a table with him and Belda in the Cursed Realm and seeing a flicker of black on the back of his hand. At the time, she'd questioned if it was a hidden cipher; now, she knew it was.

More ciphers etched his chest and abdomen to his waist. When he shifted so she could see his back, she noted they ran down to his waist there too.

"Oh, Hecate," she breathed as her fingers traced the marks. "They're beautiful."

She'd always suspected the dark fae hid some of their ciphers, but he'd confirmed it. And not only that but there were far more than she would have guessed.

He smiled as he settled on top of her again. "I much prefer it when you're saying *my* name… or should I say, screaming it."

With that, he claimed her mouth again. She wrapped her arms around him as she lost herself to him.

Soon, they would leave for Doomed Valley. Until then, she planned to enjoy every second of her time home with her loved ones and this wonderfully complicated, infuriating, loving man who would one day be her husband.

~

THE NEXT DAY a note arrived via hell hound, the demons' favorite way of sending missives. Sahira patted the massive, hairless beast on the head and removed the note clipped to its collar. The hound panted and sat on its ass.

Sahira opened the note as Orin and Elsa came to stand beside her. In neat, scrawled handwriting was a simple message...

I'm home where I belong with my family. My uncle would like to come to Dragonia to meet soon. Will send notice.

Kindest regards,

Zeth.

Sahira smiled as she patted the hound on the head and went in search of a pen.

EPILOGUE

Three months earlier

TRYING to sleep in Doomed Valley was like trying to sleep in the middle of the war he'd fought with the Lord. Brokk clearly recalled what it was like to lie awake at night, listening to the clash of steel, screams, the crashes of magic, and sometimes the humans' bombs as they sought to thwart the Lord's determination to take over their realm.

Here, there were no bombs, but dying things screamed in the distance. He had no idea what those things were, as the creatures here were fantastical beasts who didn't die easily.

The big creatures crashing through the dense jungle surrounding them didn't worry him the most. The smaller ones slid through the trees and didn't make a sound when they snuck into their campground last night and stole one of the dwarves.

Since then, Kaylia had established a protective bubble and a warning system around their camp. He could still sense the creatures watching and waiting for their chance to take another.

And the whispers....

As soon as he thought of them, he heard a murmur in the distance. Though the words they said were often too low for him to understand, he sometimes caught his name, or the names of the others, coming from the darkness.

The monsters sought to eat them, but the whispers unnerved him more. The beasts knew nothing about them; the whispers did.

Doomed Valley was full of mysteries and death. So far, that was all they'd encountered while searching for the crudue vine, but no one had suggested turning back.

They could open a portal and leave anytime, but they'd come here for a reason and wouldn't turn back. Soon, he would send someone back to check on things in Dragonia, but they'd only been here for two days. That could wait.

Looking across the small campsite they'd established, his eyes clashed with Kaylia's. She'd settled on a stump and looked as haggard as he felt, but determination etched her beautiful features and shone in her pewter gray eyes.

As something screamed again in the night and the others all stirred in their sleep, he watched the firelight play over Kaylia. He had no idea what awaited them in this lethal oasis, but they wouldn't turn back until they had the crudue vine.

He just hoped they didn't die before they found it.

∼

Read on for an excerpt from *Whispers of Ruin*, Book 10 in the series, or download now and continue reading: brendakdavies.com/WRwb

Stay in touch on updates, sales, and new releases by joining to the mailing list: brendakdavies.com/ESBKDNews

Visit the Erica Stevens/Brenda K. Davies Book Club on Facebook for exclusive giveaways and all things book related. Come join the fun: brendakdavies.com/ESBKDBookClub

SNEAK PEEK
WHISPERS OF RUIN, THE SHADOW REALMS
BOOK 10

KAYLIA'S HAIR stuck to her cheeks as she used her small sword to hack through the endless jungle of Doomed Valley. She'd known coming to this place of lore, where few escaped or survived, would be difficult, but she hadn't considered that she'd be constantly surrounded by dense, green foliage enveloping her like a warm blanket.

The density of the jungle also blocked her view of nearly everything more than a foot away from her... including her allies on this trip. Even worse, it prevented her from seeing the countless enemies lurking in the vegetation too.

And though she couldn't see them, she felt eyes following her every move. Somewhere in this land of green, humidity, and bugs, something was salivating over the idea of eating her, she was sure of it.

Glancing nervously at the trees overhead, she expected some beast to be crouched there, waiting to pounce, but the limbs remained barren of anything more than leaves and vines. Kaylia slapped at a bug buzzing around her ear before using her sword to cut through more vines.

Brokk, who was somewhere ahead of her, had already

slashed through this area, but the jungle had closed around him after he passed to block the way for the rest of them. Brokk's sword thwacked against the plants as he hacked at them, but though only a few feet separated them, she couldn't see him.

If something happened to him, she wouldn't know until either the noise stopped, or she encountered his remains. She shuddered at the possibility and swallowed to get some moisture into her parched throat.

She'd never suffered from claustrophobia before, but as the vegetation pressed against her, it felt like the jungle was determined to bury her in its verdant tomb... just as it had so many before her. Kaylia swatted at another bug before tugging at the collar of the green tunic that cleaved to her.

She could be walking through her graveyard right now. She tugged a little more at the collar as it seemed to constrict around her throat.

This is not the time. Get it together or you really will die here.

That was so very true and since she had no intention of dying in this place, she wasn't going to let her imagination run away with her... no matter how many monsters it conjured. In this place, there were plenty of *real* monsters to be worried about.

She would give anything for some armor, but after the first hour in this place, she'd learned that wearing even her lightweight protection, and not dropping from dehydration were two things that could never go together here. She'd peeled it off and left it behind. Packing it into her bag hadn't been an option; the last thing she needed was more weight slowing her down.

Kaylia lifted her tired arm to cut through more of the vines and leaves but froze when she spotted the symbol carved into a tree trunk at least fifteen feet in diameter. She lowered her sword and stepped closer to the tree.

Her fingers traced over the symbol of a circular snake, swallowing its tail. She recognized the ouroboros, and had seen it before entering this realm, but she'd seen it far more since entering here than she had anywhere else.

The symbol didn't feel anywhere near as innocuous in Doomed Valley as it did in other realms. Someone or something had put it here, she didn't know why, but nothing was *ever* innocent in this realm.

But it didn't matter, she couldn't stand here and stare at the thing. She had to get moving or the lycan behind her would cut her in two before realizing she was here.

~

WIPING the sweat from her brow, she lifted her sword and carved through the vines blocking her way. Every part of her ached and she was as wet as if she'd jumped into a lake with all her clothes on, but stopping wasn't an option.

As she worked her way through the jungle, she tried listening for anything hunting them, but it was impossible to hear much beyond the thwacks and beats of those surrounding her. Anything could be hunting them through the foliage, and they would never know until it pounced.

Just like they'd never known about the beast who stole the dwarf from their campsite shortly after arriving here. That creature came in and dragged the dwarf into the night before they ever saw their foe.

She hadn't even had a chance to put up a protection spell before the beast attacked. The dwarf's fingers had left deep gouges in the earth as it tried to keep from being torn away from them, but none of them had seen it happen.

The reminder caused the hair on her nape to rise, and she glanced nervously overhead again. Nothing was perched there, but it could happen so fast that she might never know a creature was there until it landed on her back and tore out her spine.

Stop it!

Her mother used to say her big imagination, with all its fantastic ideas and stories was a blessing. It felt like a curse in this place.

Kaylia absently rubbed her neck before scratching a bug bite and continuing. Not only did they have to worry about the unseen beasts at night, but that was also when the whispers came.

Those incessant mutterings had etched their way into her brain, where they haunted her days even though they only came when the sun set. She couldn't make out what the whispers said, other than their names on occasion, but deep in her soul, she knew they spelled ruin.

Kaylia wiped the endless sweat from her brow and resisted the urge to sit down as she continued through the jungle. It would be so easy to open a portal and leave this place, but they were here to find crudue vine so they could save Lexi.

They couldn't turn back without it, but they could send someone back to Dragonia to see if anyone else had found the vine. It would have to happen eventually, but no one had mentioned it yet.

Probably because leaving here and then returning to the exact spot would be difficult. Not only did everything here all look the same, but she swore the jungle changed around them.

This place was a living, breathing entity hellbent on destroying all who came here. If they left, it could prove impossible to return to the same location in this place of endless green, trees, and humidity. She hadn't seen anything to clearly differentiate one place from another.

Without a clear marker, they could open a portal and return anywhere in this place. They could end up searching land they'd already explored or starting new, which would be a colossal waste of time.

They could leave a portal open, but that could prove extremely dangerous for anyone who happened upon it. Or, worse, they could let something free into the realms that was *never* supposed to leave this one.

It was a problem they'd have to figure out when the time came. For now, she had to remain focused on getting through this coffin of green.

A rustle to her left snapped her head in that direction. Tensing, her fingers tightened on her sword as she braced for an attack.

∾

Download *Whispers of Ruin* now and continue reading: brendakdavies.com/WRwb

∾

Stay in touch on updates, sales, and new releases by joining to the mailing list: brendakdavies.com/ESBKDNews

Visit the Erica Stevens/Brenda K. Davies Book Club on Facebook for exclusive giveaways and all things book related. Come join the fun: brendakdavies.com/ESBKDBookClub

FIND THE AUTHOR

Brenda K. Davies Mailing List:
brendakdavies.com/News

Facebook: brendakdavies.com/BKDfb

Brenda K. Davies Book Club:
brendakdavies.com/BKDBooks

Instagram: brendakdavies.com/BKDInsta
Twitter: brendakdavies.com/BKDTweet
Website: www.brendakdavies.com

ALSO FROM THE AUTHOR

Books written under the pen name
Brenda K. Davies

The Vampire Awakenings Series

Awakened (Book 1)

Destined (Book 2)

Untamed (Book 3)

Enraptured (Book 4)

Undone (Book 5)

Fractured (Book 6)

Ravaged (Book 7)

Consumed (Book 8)

Unforeseen (Book 9)

Forsaken (Book 10)

Relentless (Book 11)

Legacy (Book 12)

The Alliance Series

Eternally Bound (Book 1)

Bound by Vengeance (Book 2)

Bound by Darkness (Book 3)

Bound by Passion (Book 4)

Bound by Torment (Book 5)

Bound by Danger (Book 6)

Bound by Deception (Book 7)

Bound by Fate (Book 8)

Bound by Blood (Book 9)

Bound by Love (Book 10)

The Road to Hell Series

Good Intentions (Book 1)

Carved (Book 2)

The Road (Book 3)

Into Hell (Book 4)

Hell on Earth (Book 5)

Into the Abyss (Book 6)

Kiss of Death (Book 7)

Edge of the Darkness (Book 8)

The Shadow Realms

Shadows of Fire (Book 1)

Shadows of Discovery (Book 2)

Shadows of Betrayal (Book 3)

Shadows of Fury (Book 4)

Shadows of Destiny (Book 5)

Shadows of Light (Book 6)

Wicked Curses (Book 7)

Sinful Curses (Book 8)

Gilded Curses (Book 9)

Whispers of Ruin (Book 10)

Secrets of Ruin (Book 11)

Tempest of Shadows

A Tempest of Shadows (Book 1)

A Tempest of Thieves (Book 2)

A Tempest of Revelations (Book 3)

A Tempest of Intrigue (Book 4)

A Tempest of Chaos (Book 5)

Historical Romance

A Stolen Heart

Books written under the pen name
Erica Stevens

The Coven Series

Nightmares (Book 1)

The Maze (Book 2)

Dream Walker (Book 3)

The Captive Series

Captured (Book 1)

Renegade (Book 2)

Refugee (Book 3)

Salvation (Book 4)

Redemption (Book 5)

Vengeance (Book 6)

Unbound (Book 7)

Broken (Book 8 - Prequel)

The Kindred Series

Kindred (Book 1)

Ashes (Book 2)

Kindled (Book 3)

Inferno (Book 4)

Phoenix Rising (Book 5)

The Fire & Ice Series

Frost Burn (Book 1)

Arctic Fire (Book 2)

Scorched Ice (Book 3)

The Ravening Series

The Ravening (Book 1)

Taken Over (Book 2)

Reclamation (Book 3)

The Survivor Chronicles

The Upheaval (Book 1)

The Divide (Book 2)

The Forsaken (Book 3)

The Risen (Book 4)

ABOUT THE AUTHOR

Brenda K. Davies is the USA Today Bestselling author of the Vampire Awakening Series, Alliance Series, Road to Hell Series, Hell on Earth Series, The Shadow Realms Series, A Tempest of Shadows Series, and historical romantic fiction. She also writes under the pen name, Erica Stevens. When not out with friends and family, she can be found at home with her husband, son, and pets.

9 798864 486962